~ A Disney PRINCE NOVEL ~

Prince
of Thorns
& Nightmares

~ A DISNEY PRINCE NOVEL ~

Prince
of Thorns
& Nightmares

LINSEY MILLER

DISNEY PRESS

Los Angeles • New York

For information address Disney Press, 1200 Grand Central Avenue,
Glendale, California 91201.
Printed in the United States of America

First Hardcover Edition, October 2023
10 9 8 7 6 5 4 3 2 1
FAC-004510-23222

Library of Congress Control Number: 2022951028
ISBN 978-1-368-06912-0
Designed by Scott Piehl

Visit disneybooks.com

SUSTAINABLE FORESTRY INITIATIVE
Certified Sourcing
www.forests.org
SFI-01681

Logo Applies to Text Stock Only

To everyone chasing their dreams.

~L. M.

Prologue

A ROSY DAWN spilled across the kingdom of Ald Tor. The forest encircling the castle on the hill was a tangle of pale greens and golden browns, its paths speckled with well-dressed travelers. They marched in neat little lines like ants toward the gate, and knights in freshly painted armor cantered ahead of them on horseback. Gable hoods bobbed in the crowd, gowns dotted with pearls glittered in the sunlight, and banners rippled in the morning breeze. Voices grew louder near the castle, mixing with the music drifting over the drawbridge. Each creaky opening of the throne room's towering doors cut through the comforting sounds as sharply as a blade.

Prince Phillip swallowed, shifting in the confines of his heavy silk tunic, and scratched his leg with a foot. The new hose itched. His freshly washed face felt red and tight. The gift gripped in his hands was heavier than it had been that morning.

"Bow, say hello, congratulate them, and give them the gift for Princess Aurora," Phillip whispered to himself.

"What are you muttering about, lad?" his father, King Hubert, asked, eyeing Phillip over his shoulder.

Phillip swallowed. "Nothing!"

The two of them were at the front of a long line of visitors before the doors to the great hall of the castle. They had spent the last few moments waiting to be announced to those gathered in the hall, giving Phillip plenty of time to worry. Earlier, he'd had the walk to distract him from his thoughts.

"Can't be talking to yourself when you meet Stefan," said the king. "This is the first time Stefan and Leah will have seen you since you were a baby, and you want to impress them, don't you?"

"Of course," said Phillip.

Phillip *had* to impress King Stefan and Queen Leah. The tales of his father's time as a knight with King Stefan—long days on the road with nothing but a sword and evildoers for company, best friends hunting down magical villains and their minions, and a final battle against the wicked fairy Maleficent before the human kingdoms finally won and trapped her in her mountain prison—were the most interesting things Phillip's father ever told him.

And the *only* things he talked about.

"Good lad." His father leaned down and straightened Phillip's new blue tunic and cape. "Are you ready to be a proper prince?"

Phillip sniffed, gripped the gift tighter, and nodded.

The great doors before them opened, trumpets blared again, and someone announced, "Their Royal Highnesses, King Hubert and Prince Phillip!"

"Finally," muttered King Hubert as he hustled toward the thrones at the other end of the room.

Phillip startled at the announcement and scrambled after his father, hoping the king hadn't noticed his near trip.

The thrones were nestled in an alcove at the other end of the room, green-and-blue silk brocade draped behind them like a treetop against a clear sky. The black-and-gold coat of arms of His Majesty, King Stefan of Ald Tor, hung from the high rafters. Even sitting, he was as tall and imposing as his castle, all sharp angles and stone. He smiled only when he glanced at a crib beside the thrones.

Phillip took a deep breath and ignored the fluttery feeling in his stomach. This was the first time he had been before so many people *and* the king and queen of another kingdom, and he knew his father was watching for any little mistake. He squared his shoulders the same way his father always did before court. "Hail to Aurora" became "Hail to our hero" if he thought hard enough. He was Prince Phillip!

He didn't need to be scared.

Phillip bowed to the two seated monarchs, like he had been told to, but his father didn't. King Hubert held out his arms to his old friend, and King Stefan rose. The two embraced.

One day, Phillip would be just like his father—loved and happy, invited to important parties and looked up to. The anticipation made him feel equal parts thrilled and anxious.

Phillip's father beckoned him, and Phillip bustled over, holding up the gift to King Stefan. The king smiled politely and patted Phillip on the head. Up close, the king of Ald Tor looked warmer and more welcoming. Queen Leah came forward and took Phillip to Princess Aurora. He peered over the edge of the crib.

The babe was small and pale, chubby fists clenched around the blue blanket swaddling her. Phillip hadn't seen any other babies, but his father said he had been a handsome, bellowing thing. This one sniffled and smiled.

She was like a wrinkly, toothless turnip. A turnip he

was supposed to marry. His father had told him over and over that it was his duty as a prince to wed the princess, and Phillip wanted to be a good prince. He just wasn't sure what marrying her meant, and no one would explain it to him. His father said he would tell him when they were older, but what if the princess didn't want to marry him? It wasn't like they could ask the baby.

The trumpets sounded again, and Phillip's father ushered him away. A beam of light shot down from the ceiling, and a gentle breeze rustled the many banners hanging from the high arches. Three figures appeared, small bodies glittering with magic.

"Their most honored and exalted excellencies, the three good fairies," cried the announcer. "Mistress Flora, Mistress Fauna, and Mistress Merryweather."

"Fairies," Phillip whispered, and his father laughed.

Phillip had heard stories about fairies but never met one. Now there were three fluttering right in front of him. They were powerful and reclusive, more so after Maleficent's failed takeover of the human kingdoms. They looked like the stories, fairy wings thin as glass fluttering behind them and their feet floating slightly off the ground. Phillip crept closer.

The three women flew toward the crib on stained glass wings.

"Always stay on the fairies' good sides," said King Hubert, tugging Phillip back by his collar. He patted Phillip's shoulder. "There's not a thing we can do against most of their magic, but their promises last forever. Once you make a deal with one, you can hold them to it."

He tapped the side of his nose, and Phillip nodded as though the king's counsel made sense. His father smiled.

The fairies were small, and each was clothed in a different color. The green was tinged with brown, like a leaf or moss. The red was more like holly berries than fire, and the blue had the same grayish quality as fog on a summer morning. They flitted to the crib and cooed over the princess before greeting the king and queen.

"Each of us the child may bless with a single gift. No more, no less," said the one in red. "Little princess, my gift shall be the gift of beauty."

She waved the bright yellow wand in her hand. Magic gathered and glittered like stars over Princess Aurora. It peppered down on the crib like fresh snow.

Beauty? Phillip scrunched his nose. Beauty was nice, but it wasn't a gift.

He had wanted to gift her a bear, like the one on the coat of arms for his home, Artwyne, but his father had said bears weren't appropriate gifts.

As quickly as she had approached, the fairy in red

moved away, and the one in green fluttered to Aurora. Phillip tried to move closer again. He had seen magic once or twice, when his father called in a wizard, but that had been ancient runes, bloodred potions, and boring incantations. No amount of studying runes would make a true knight, his father always said. A hero relied on themselves and nothing else.

But it was still magic, and Phillip gasped as the fairy's wand sparkled. They could gift the princess anything—cunning, stalwart companions, or even magic itself! This one had to be more exciting than *beauty*.

"Tiny princess," said the fairy, "my gift shall be the gift of song."

"Song?" Phillip asked, looking up at his father. "What good is that?"

"A lovely face and voice make for a lovelier wife," whispered King Hubert. "Something you should be thankful for."

Phillip wasn't sure what a wife was, but the golden music box he had given the princess had been pushed aside for the fairies' gifts. They would never have been able to push a bear aside.

"Why does that matter to me?" Phillip asked. "You said gifts are for the person you give them to. Those aren't for her. What if she doesn't like singing?"

"Hush." His father flicked his ear.

Next, the fairy in blue raised her wand, and a burst of wind nearly ripped it from her hands as she prepared to give the baby her final gift. The doors blew open, clanging against the walls, and people scattered across the hall. Phillip's father yanked him behind the thrones and squared himself next to King Stefan. Phillip peeked around his father's legs, hoping his shaking wasn't noticeable. The sounds had scared him, but his father's reaction scared him more. Nothing ever frightened his father.

Thunder crashed despite the clear skies, and lightning struck the ground outside the swinging doors. A sickly green fire sparked to life in the center of the room. Smokeless and shifting, the flames twisted in on themselves until they formed a lithe figure taller even than King Stefan. Her headdress rose over her, and her cloak moved like flickering shadows. She smiled, her sneering mouth a red slash across pale skin. A raven perched on the orb at the tip of her staff.

"Why!" cried the red fairy. "It's Maleficent!"

The name shot through Phillip like an arrow. Maleficent was supposed to be trapped, restricted to her mountain to reflect on her misdeeds. It had taken years for Phillip's father and his cohorts to beat her back to the Forbidden Mountain, and now she stood before them all. Phillip tried to be brave and not flinch, but when she looked at him, it was like a cook eyeing a ham hock. He shuddered.

Then he made sure no one had seen him.

"What does she want here?" asked the fairy in blue, who had been interrupted.

The green one shushed her.

"Well," drawled Maleficent. Her voice was like brambles brushing together or ice grinding in a frozen river. She was taller and sharper than the other fairies, wearing a pointed headdress like goat horns and a sweeping gown, and she carried herself with an arrogance that made Phillip shiver. "Quite a glittering assemblage, King Stefan. Royalty, nobility, the gentry." She glided toward the thrones and stared down her nose at the other fairies. "And—how quaint—even the rabble."

She scowled, and the other fairies had to hold the blue one back.

"I really felt quite distressed about not receiving an invitation." Maleficent stroked her raven and stopped at the foot of the thrones.

The blue fairy snarled, "You weren't wanted."

"Not want . . ." Maleficent gasped, dark eyes rolling up, and laughed. "Oh, dear. What an awkward situation.

I had hoped it was merely due to some oversight. Well, in that event, I'd best be on my way."

Phillip didn't understand what was happening. His father's fists were shaking by his side. He turned slightly and caught King Stefan's gaze. The pair shared a look of fear that shook Phillip's heart.

Maleficent turned as though to leave, but her raven stayed twisted to glare at all of them.

"And you're not offended, Your Excellency?" asked Queen Leah.

"Why, no, Your Majesty." Maleficent stopped, as if she had been waiting for the question, and smiled. "And to show I bear no ill will, I, too, shall bestow a gift on the child."

King Stefan and Queen Leah moved to the crib, and the trio of fairies threw themselves over it to protect the princess. Maleficent spread her arms wide. Phillip, trembling, couldn't take his eyes from her.

"Listen well, all of you," she said, and her voice echoed terribly. Unnaturally. Until it was all Phillip could hear. "The princess shall indeed grow in grace and beauty, beloved by all who know her, but before the sun sets on her sixteenth birthday, she shall prick her finger on the spindle of a spinning wheel and die."

The raven took flight, and Maleficent swirled her

fingers around her staff. Monstrous silhouettes sank from the green magic growing around it, and Queen Leah gasped. Phillip ripped his gaze from Maleficent. The queen scooped up Aurora into her arms.

And Maleficent only laughed at her fear.

"Seize that creature!" King Stefan yelled.

His guards surged forward, but Maleficent's staff glowed green again.

Laughing still, she said, "Stand back, you fools."

Lightning flashed, and she was gone, a green orb of dripping magic hanging in the air where she had been. Her raven cawed once and vanished into it. The magic faded.

Phillip started repeating to himself what had happened, pinching his thigh to make sure it was all real. It was like a nightmare, and no one had done anything to stop her. Two legendary kings in a hall full of knights, and Maleficent had cursed Princess Aurora and left like it was nothing.

It wasn't at all like the stories. His father and the king hadn't struck out to meet Maleficent with their swords drawn. Phillip's father only kept a firm grip on Phillip's arm and kept shuffling them away from where Maleficent had stood.

King Stefan and Queen Leah looked over Aurora

with frantic eyes, and the red fairy approached them slowly. The crowd crept forward at the edges of the hall, people trying to see the princess or talk to the guards. He heard someone ask how this could have happened. He wanted to know that, too. He tugged at his father's tunic and was ignored.

"Don't despair, Your Majesties," the fairy in red said. "Merryweather still has her gift to give."

"Then she can undo this fearful curse?" asked King Stefan, and Phillip was shocked to hear the king's voice waver.

"Oh, no, sire." The blue fairy, who Phillip now knew was called Merryweather, shook her head.

"Maleficent's powers are far too great," said the one in red.

"But she can help!" cried the third fairy.

"But . . ." Merryweather looked from the other fairies to the king, and the other two nudged her closer to the princess.

The one in green patted her shoulder and said, "Just do your best, dear."

Phillip crept out from behind his father's legs, the fear seeping out of him. Anticipation tinged the air like magic. A fairy's best would surely be *the* best.

"Sweet princess." Merryweather shook out her arms

and raised her wand. "If through this wicked witch's trick a spindle should your finger prick, a ray of hope there still may be in this, the gift I give to thee. Not in death but just in sleep the fateful prophecy you'll keep, and from this slumber you shall wake when True Love's Kiss the spell shall break."

King Stefan deflated with relief. Queen Leah kept Aurora clutched to her chest, smiling down at her as she thanked the fairies. King Hubert clapped Phillip on the back.

"See, lad?" his father asked. "Stay on their good sides."

Phillip didn't see at all.

"I thought Maleficent couldn't leave the mountain," said Phillip. "How could she come here?"

But no one was listening to him. The queen laid the baby down into her crib, and his father spoke with King Stefan.

" . . . no indication that she could leave," King Stefan was saying. "None! My scouts have reported nothing unusual, and the fairies clearly had no inkling of her escape."

Phillip's father huffed and rubbed his chin. "I'll ask Barny. Her power's returned faster than expected, or she burned it all in order to escape today. Barny will know."

King Stefan's hand never left the cradle. The fear was gone, but a tension had taken hold of all of them. Phillip peeked over the edge of the cradle, prodded the princess's cheek, and huffed. Beauty and song!

"I'll still get you a bear," he whispered to her. "Sounds like you'll need it."

I
Knighty Night

IN A DINGY inn dripping with rain and choked
with the scent of hunter's stew, in the middle of his
first throw for the penultimate round of darts, His Royal
Highness, Prince Phillip of Artwyne, knighted the year
before and skilled in all manner of princely things, missed
the dart board entirely.

Half the crowd groaned. A few threw copper rots
at him, the coins clattering to the floor. Phillip caught
one, kissed it, and bowed to his opponent. A miller with
suspiciously good aim and a good few years on him, she
saluted him with her dart.

"Losing isn't very knightly of you," she said, nod-
ding to his purse. "Though I hope you're chivalrous
enough to pay up."

Phillip had eschewed the usual trappings of royalty,
traveling with the nondescript crest of a lesser family on
his clothes, but everyone in the inn had seen him arrive on
horseback with his armor the day before. Only a knight

could afford a courser, and everyone had upped the bets on the games once he started playing. Fortunately, no one had connected him to Prince Phillip yet. Portraits were rare in such a rural area, and his name was ordinary enough to not rouse suspicions. Nobles were more common than royals, anyway.

People expected knights; they didn't expect errant princes.

"Have mercy," said Phillip. "I sold my chivalry to afford dinner."

Well, he *was* errant.

"Oh, don't show him mercy," said a woman behind him, her familiar voice making him wince. "He loses nightly, so he should be used to it."

Johanna, his squire for a year and friend for three, had no respect for him at all, and that was how Phillip preferred it.

"I have half a mind to leave you here," he said, and glanced at her over his shoulder.

"You have half of a mind?" She gasped and clutched her heart, full mouth in a completely believable O of shock. "I hadn't noticed."

It was better to let Johanna think she had the upper hand. Tall and well built, she could easily take him in a fight. She preferred camping, where she could write poetry aloud without anyone overhearing, but Phillip had dragged them to the small village yesternight after two weeks on the road. Her wet black hair was braided in a crown around her head, a sure sign she wasn't too angry about the detour. Not even Johanna would pass up a warm bath.

"Stop letting him stall, Maxine!" shouted a woman near the door. She had thrashed Phillip at chess the night before and was walking the coin she'd won from him across her knuckles. "Win so I can go home earlier and richer."

Maxine—Phillip really had to start learning people's names before he lost to them—blushed all the way up her ears.

"Perhaps missing was a well-calculated move," he muttered and faked a yawn. "She a friend of yours?"

"Emma's friendly enough," mumbled Maxine.

Phillip *had* missed on purpose. People had been playing darts off and on all day, hustling him out of his money. Maxine was a fine opponent, but her hands started shaking the moment she noticed people were watching. When she realized Emma had joined the crowd, Maxine had practically forgotten what a dart was.

Maybe if Maxine thought him tired, she wouldn't feel so pressured and would beat him outright.

She threw her dart, and it struck one of the middle rings carved into the wall.

"Six points," said Phillip, picking up his next dart. He could hit the board's edge and still lose. "Whatever shall I do?"

Maxine had bet five silver nobles on this game after watching him lose earlier. To Phillip, the riches were nothing—and he was well aware of how unappealing that thought was—but what was the harm in his enjoying himself and Maxine's taking home some easy money and impressing her crush?

His throw hit the edge of the board with a resounding thwack. Phillip gasped like Johanna had. He had learned how to look contrite and disappointed ages ago, but sardonic hyperbole was far more fun. Emma applauded, and Maxine blushed. Phillip hid his smile with another yawn.

"Rematch tomorrow?" he asked Maxine.

"Sure." Confusion wrinkled across her face. "But I figured all you knights had to prepare for the wedding, and that's only—"

In an instant, the comment ripped the happiness from him and replaced it with rage.

"I'm not that sort of knight," Phillip snapped, even though he didn't mean to.

The wedding was twenty-six days and eighteen

hours away, give or take some minutes, and he had no intention of arriving in the kingdom of Ald Tor for it until absolutely necessary.

Phillip picked up his last dart, wished Maxine good luck with the rest of the tournament, and bet on her on his way to Johanna. He dropped onto the stool next to her.

"Lose again?" she asked without looking. Her head was bowed over a thin book, a birthday gift from him, and her supper sat forgotten. She'd been scribbling in the book all year and refusing to let him see her latest work. Usually she read her newest poetry to him as they rode. "Did you always dream of losing a coin in every corner of your kingdom as your great rebellion against your father?"

Phillip smiled to himself. "I don't think gambling counts as rebellion, but if you're offering . . ."

He didn't care about the lost pride or money. His fate had been set since he was a child, so what did losing or winning anything matter? For the first and final time in his life, he wasn't training to save Princess Aurora or even thinking about her. That was the entire point of this journey—distraction.

"Keep your treasonous jokes away from me," said Johanna.

Phillip tapped the tip of her long nose with his stolen dart and tried to peek in the book. "Isn't this better than standing around the castle in overly decorated armor and playing skumps? How are you ever going to write the next great epic if all we do is sit in the castle performing ceremonial duties?"

"Most of those ceremonies require us to stand," she said, and angled the book away from him with a pointed look. "So long as you're in one piece when I return you to His Majesty for the wedding, I don't care what you do."

Phillip shushed her and glanced around to make sure none of the remaining patrons were listening.

"Don't talk to me about the wedding," he whispered, getting his emotions under control.

It wasn't even a real wedding—it was a way for King Hubert to join his family with his best friend's, regardless of how Prince Phillip and Princess Aurora, his betrothed, felt. Not that Phillip knew her feelings, as he had only met her once, when she was still a baby.

"No one's even heard from her or those fairies for fifteen years," Phillip said, each word drawn out from him like poison from a wound. "Maybe there won't even be a wedding."

"Not being heard from is the point of hiding," Johanna said. "Royals marry for business all the time, and you've known about your betrothal for ages. Why are you still acting shocked?"

Phillip couldn't say it was because he had believed all those stories about true love, dragons, and knights in shining armor as a child, so he slumped and said, "Bitter words for such a romantic."

"Romance and realism aren't opposing forces," Johanna said, and scratched out a word that might have been *slumber*. "Eat your food. I finished all of the celery for you."

She gestured to the stew of mostly carrots next to her, and Phillip smiled. His horse, Samson, would be so jealous.

"An act purely for my benefit, I'm sure," he said, and picked up the bowl. "Also, if you're writing about the curse again—"

The door to the inn crashed open. Three people flooded inside, blades dripping rainwater across the floor as they swung them about. A few folks screamed, some brandished jugs or stools, and Phillip set his bowl back on the table.

"Tell me this isn't a robbery," he said.

Johanna closed her book. "I'm hoping it will be more of a shakedown."

"You all do as he says, leave your money on the tables, and keep your hands in sight, and you'll live," said the tallest of the interlopers. They inclined their head to the one in the lead.

He was short and silver-headed, the vicious look in his blue eyes twisting his handsome face. He pulled a knife from a loop on his belt and raised it at Emma, who had still been standing near the front door when he had burst through.

"You don't," he said, "and she dies."

Phillip laid his stolen dart and both hands on the table, and Johanna tossed her purse next to his dart. The other two thieves collected everyone's money as the third one watched, his knife at Emma's throat. Two folks had grabbed Maxine by the arms and covered her mouth to hold her back. Phillip eyed the two thieves as they took Johanna's money and left his dart. They slowly finished their round.

Chasing after these thieves wouldn't be worth it. Neither Johanna nor he was ready for a fight. Their weapons and armor were in their room, and the night was thick with rain and fog. Phillip could replace the money lost twice over. If Johanna and he tried to take down the three here without their supplies, they probably wouldn't lose, but a bystander might get hurt.

"All right," said the oldest thief. He hemmed and hawed, looking like he'd expected more of a fight. "Well, we'll be going, and we'll be taking her for a little walk with us to ensure no one tries anything funny. Anyone follows, she dies."

They vanished out the door with Emma, and the inn's occupants started talking frantically and peering out the shuttered windows. Maxine slumped against the people who had held her back. Phillip picked up his supper.

"Absolutely not," said Johanna. "We're giving chase."

"They'll let her go, and then I can repay everyone," said Phillip.

"But what if they don't?"

Phillip shrugged.

"You want to be the man who bet another's life on thieves being honest?" Johanna asked. "Because that's the epic I'll write about you if you don't help me." She flicked the back of his hand. "And if you start throwing money at people, they'll know you're not an everyday knight."

Phillip sighed. It wasn't that he cared about what anyone else thought of him, but he cared about Johanna. And Emma had been a good sport when he arrived yesterday. He set everything down again.

23

"Fine, but I'll follow them at a distance and only intervene if they try to hurt her," he said, standing and stretching. "You go upstairs, grab our things, and follow me with Samson. Once they leave Emma, we can arrest them. If you insist."

It would be easier and safer to round them up when they didn't have a hostage.

"I do insist, but you can't go alone."

"I am a knight, even if I don't always act like one," he said. "I know what I'm doing."

Phillip plunged weaponless and armorless into the dreary dark. Fog as thick as smoke coated the street outside, and the humidity left behind by the warm spring rain was cloying. Night had stained the lush woods surrounding the town a deep indigo, and clouds dimmed the little moonlight there was. A drizzle-soaked Phillip crept along behind the thieves until he was close enough to intervene. The trees along the side of the road were the perfect hiding place.

The shortest one, straight brown hair slicked back with rain, hesitated and glanced over their shoulder. "I don't think anyone's coming."

Phillip ducked down below a small wall along the path.

"You told them not to," said Emma. "They don't want me dead."

"Bully for you," muttered the third one. They wiped their red curls from their eyes. "Sire, what do we do?"

"Keep walking," said Sire, who Phillip assumed was the leader. "We stick to my plan."

Sire kept the blade at the side of Emma's throat. He was comfortable wielding it, which was worrying. Less worrying was the redheaded thief's small crossbow, which they held like a venomous snake and had clearly never used before. The third one seemed completely baffled by the ax in their own hand.

"You can't keep me forever," Emma said. Her hands were fists at her sides. "We must be far enough now."

Sire smacked her with the flat of the knife. "You stop when I say you stop."

Phillip, not caring for Sire's nonchalance, darted off the path and looped wide to overtake them. The redheaded one must have heard him and fired off a shot. It tore harmlessly through the branches far to Phillip's right, and he sank to his knees behind a bush. He had often played town guard and protector as a knight, but these were the oddest thieves he had ever encountered.

"Why did you do that?" Sire tilted his head back and sighed. "You could have killed someone."

The thief ducked instead of answering. Phillip started to crawl toward the road, low enough to be out of sight. To his delight, Emma had shuffled out of Sire's reach. Phillip stopped two strides away from the thief with the ax.

"Do what I say," muttered Sire. "Why is that so hard?"

Lightning flashed overhead. Phillip lunged, timing his step with the thunder. He crashed through the underbrush and flung his stolen dart at Sire's face. It struck the thief's left cheek, sending him sprawling with a shriek, and the other two spun to Phillip.

Phillip tackled the one with the ax and kneed them hard in the side. They dropped the ax. He rose with it in hand. The thief with the crossbow fired off a shot with surprising accuracy, missing him by a hair. Phillip knocked the crossbow aside with a sweep of the ax, and they stumbled back. Strides away, Sire struggled to his feet, and Emma raced back toward the inn. Phillip slammed the handle of the ax into the crossbow thief's temple. They crumpled to the road.

Lightning flashed again, and Phillip lunged for Sire. With any luck, the others would surrender or scatter as soon as he—and the money—went down.

Phillip swung the ax at Sire. He moved with surprising speed, blocking the blow with his knife. The guard caught the ax's handle, and he nearly wrenched it from Phillip's grasp. Phillip twisted with the movement, his confidence flickering, and connected a kick with Sire's knees. Sire went down with a howl.

That ought to have done it, but when Phillip spun to face the other two thieves, they didn't run. One even laughed at Sire.

Maybe Phillip had misread this trio.

"It would be best if you all surrendered," he said, adjusting his grip on the ax.

One thief raised the crossbow, and the other lifted their fist.

"Optimistic of you," Phillip said to the one without a weapon and twirled the ax. Johanna should have caught up with them by now. Phillip was good, but he wasn't three-versus-one-in-the-rain good. "You know, if you took off running with the money right now and left well enough alone, I wouldn't stop you."

Phillip said it in a drawl, stifling his concern with false confidence. He shuffled backward and tried to lead Sire out of the middle of the road. Fog shrouded the inn from sight, but Phillip didn't want the thieves to see Johanna coming in case that made them panic. The trees lining the road would provide some cover. Maybe he could even find a branch to wield as a weapon.

"Run?" Sire stood, knife in hand, and stalked after Phillip. "When you're the one alone?"

A chill swept over Phillip, the odd tingling of it starting in his chest and spreading throughout his body. He flexed his fingers, and grass twisted around Sire's ankles like a hand. Sire took a step forward, shaking off the grass. Phillip shook his head. What had he seen?

Sire attacked. Phillip sidestepped, the knife tearing through his shirt. The crossbow twanged behind him, and a bolt tore past his cheek. Desperate for cover, Phillip dodged deeper into the tree line. A branch cracked above him and crashed to his feet. Phillip snatched it up. A prickle like lightning raced across his skin.

He had misjudged this. Like him, they didn't care about the money. Unlike him, they cared about *winning*.

Sire slashed at Phillip. Phillip blocked the knife with the branch and swung the ax. Another crossbow bolt tore through the air next to his hand, making him drop the ax, and Phillip stumbled. His back hit a tree.

Phillip pushed Sire aside with the branch. The third thief aimed their crossbow at Phillip again.

Hoofbeats pounded down the road. The thief turned, lowering their bow. Johanna, astride Samson and brandishing her sword, emerged from the fog and cleaved the crossbow in two. The thief dropped it and sprinted away. The second thief ran after them. Phillip relaxed.

"Took you long enough," he said. "Last-minute rescues make better poems, I assume?"

Johanna shushed him. "You're the one who took off without a weapon. The storm made it near impossible to find you. Mind of its own, I swear, but Emma made it back safely."

Before he could respond, a knife sliced into his arm. Phillip yelped, panic numbing the pain. Sire slammed into Phillip and pinned him to the tree. His knife pressed into Phillip's throat, and the fog smothered them until Phillip could see only the murderous glare of Sire's blue eyes. The odd prickling sensation Phillip had felt earlier returned to his fingers. Phillip's skin broke beneath Sire's blade.

"Get away from me!" Phillip grunted, and as he struck out with his fist, so did a branch from the tree behind him. Both hit Sire square in the chest.

The thief flew back, crashed through a sapling, and crumpled to the ground. Phillip froze. Branches and grass twisted around Sire's throat and hands, binding him to the ground as he struggled weakly against them. Johanna drew in a breath.

"What's happening?" she asked, trying to calm the panicking horse.

Phillip took a deep breath. The vines holding Sire sank back into the earth, the fog around them dissipated, and the storm died down. Distantly, thunder cracked, and Phillip shuddered.

"I'm not sure," he said, and wiped his hands on his shirt. "Perhaps the wind . . ."

"Phillip, that looked like magi—"

"Don't be ridiculous," snapped Phillip.

Phillip's memories of magic were tinged with the brimstone stench of Maleficent's green smoke and the cackling caw of her raven. Magic was rare, and he was besieged by a cursed betrothed and strange dreams as it was. This was a fluke. A trick of the light.

"We've been in odder fights before, and we have a job to finish," Phillip said, but when he turned to where Sire had landed, the thief was gone. Phillip squinted into the fog and barely made out Sire fleeing. "Never mind. If Emma's back safe, forget it. You pay everyone what was stolen from them out of my money, and I'll pack our things."

"We're leaving?" Johanna asked, eyeing Sire. "I could get him."

Samson snorted in agreement, but Phillip patted his neck.

"We need to leave as soon as possible to make it home before my father leaves for Ald Tor," he said. "I want to talk to him."

It was the only thing he could think of—his father would know of any reports of rogue magic or new magical deals—and he knew it would shut Johanna up.

"Right, because you wanting to see your father is perfectly normal," she muttered. "If you're sure."

"Since when have I been sure of anything?" he asked.

But really, he was scared. Magic wasn't supposed to just show up in strange towns. It was dangerous and unpredictable, and it shouldn't have happened. It couldn't have happened. If it had, he only hoped his father knew why.

2

An Unusual Prince

*I*T TOOK five days for Phillip and Johanna to reach the outskirts of Artwyne's main city. King Hubert's flags waved at them from atop the towers, shooing Phillip away. He hadn't spoken to Johanna any more about what happened with the thieves, but she had talked about it nonstop. She had spent the whole journey describing what she had seen and how it was definitely, no question, could only be, magic, and Phillip had spent the whole journey finding it harder and harder to rebuff her. She wanted to get to the bottom of it, but Phillip wanted nothing more than to prove her wrong.

Sure, the grass and branches behaving like that was odd, but it had been windy. They had been distracted and worried. It was simply a trick of their panicked minds. Phillip was certain that their trip to visit his father would confirm that magic wasn't involved.

King Hubert hailed from the school of What Doesn't Kill You Makes You Stronger. He had hired trainers and knights to surprise Phillip with attacks and challenges as he was growing up, and each time he had watched from the sidelines like it was some great show. A knight always had to be prepared, he said time and time again.

And then, usually, some new little test, like stopping a flung spear or picking out the non-poisoned tart from a tray, would begin.

"What's more likely, anyway?" Phillip leaned down from his seat atop Samson and whispered to him. "Magic suddenly appearing out of nowhere, or one of the hits I took rattling me so good I mistook normal winds and vines for mystical ones?"

Samson snorted. The courser had been with Phillip longer than anyone save his father and had spent years dragging Phillip to safety when he was a page. What Samson deemed safe was mostly his stall or the kitchens, but Phillip hadn't minded.

Five years after Maleficent's first and only escape from the Forbidden Mountain and Princess Aurora's going into hiding, Kings Hubert and Stefan had decided that marrying Phillip to the cursed princess wasn't enough. He was to be her protector once the curse was avoided, charged with keeping Maleficent from assassinating Princess Aurora, and Phillip's dreams of gallantry and heroism had been trampled by an endless parade of surprise tests and tournaments.

Phillip would never be in charge of his own life.

"You'll talk to Samson about what's bothering you but not me?" Johanna asked, nudging her horse, Taliesin, up alongside him. "Shall I find a stranger for you to discuss it with as well?"

They were a few minutes from the gates of the city, and the road around them was mostly empty. She nodded to a group of three merchants far down the road behind them. "Perhaps one of them will do."

"You're painfully stubborn," he mumbled.

As much as he loved her, Phillip knew Johanna wouldn't understand. She knew what she wanted to do with her life and was already practically living it. She spoke of being a knight the same way most people talked about the loves of their lives.

She was even writing whatever it was in her book. She'd been working on the same piece for months. Phillip hated how terribly envious he was of her certainty.

"Samson doesn't have any wild ideas about what happened," Phillip said. "Listen—it's much more likely my father concocted some plan to lure me home and the thieves were a part of it."

Johanna frowned and rose up in her seat to better

see the city walls ahead of them. They were near enough to the city now that the shadows of the short towers crept over them, and Phillip shivered in the shade. He had hoped not to return here until after he was ensnared by his wedding and Princess Aurora's curse.

"I know what you're not saying," Johanna said finally. "It's Maleficent. You're worried the magic might be connected to her. But what if there's a wizard out there who could help? Someone to defeat her once and for all."

Phillip bristled at the mention of Maleficent. It always came back to her. "If they wanted to help, they'd come forward themself," he said. The only good thing that had come from the curse was that it had used up so much of her power that she was trapped yet again in her mountain hideout. She hadn't left the ruins there since.

"Fine. Consider this, then: What if you're magical?" said Johanna. "If you're to be Princess Aurora's savior from a powerful, magical being, you'll need magic. Maybe it's a belated gift from the fairies."

"What?" Phillip couldn't hold back his laugh. Fairies didn't give belated gifts; they picked their favored baby and showered them with things like beauty and song. They didn't give errant princes the ability to hit thieves with wind. "Don't take this the wrong way, but that's the most fantastical, unlikely thing you have ever said, and you once called me honorable. People don't just develop magic, and fairies definitely don't go about gifting it randomly."

A part of Phillip, the little boy who had wandered into King Stefan's castle a child with the world at his feet and left with only one path he would be forced to undertake, would have leapt at magic as an explanation. There were so many great wizard-kings in his father's old stories.

Magic would have been another way to prove himself to the world and leave his mark on it so that some of the future stories passed down would be of him.

But this Phillip, older and wise enough, knew that none of it mattered.

Princess Aurora would return from wherever the fairies were hiding her, Maleficent's curse would most likely be avoided entirely through that deception, and Phillip would be forced to stay by her side in the time that followed to keep her safe from Maleficent's ire at her plans being foiled. Her true love would never even need to make an appearance, and Phillip's marriage to her would ensure he was always near to keep her safe. Finally, Kings Hubert and Stefan would be family, and they would be working together to crush Maleficent, just like in the old days. They were sure she would focus all her attention on killing the princess instead of trying to conquer the kingdoms like she had last time.

"Well, that's just rude to both of us," Johanna drawled, but he could see she was hurt. She urged Taliesin forward and cantered toward the city gates ahead of Phillip. "You're not the least bit intrigued by the idea of having magic?"

"I loathe everything, Johanna," said Phillip, and his frown wasn't entirely put on. Johanna refused to see the worst in anything, even him. She didn't deserve his ire. "When have you known anything to intrigue me?"

"When you told me about that dream girl of yours, it was the most wistful I'd ever seen you," she said, grinning at him over her shoulder.

And there it was. Phillip's secret: a girl who haunted his dreams. "I shouldn't have told her," he whispered to Samson, ignoring the odd looks from people leaving the city. Even hearing her mention the dreams made his heart race and his blood rush in his ears. "They're more like nightmares, honestly. I would give anything for one good night of dreamless, *silent* sleep."

For as long as Phillip could remember, he had dreamed the same dream nearly every night: He was in an ancient wood, from which he could never escape, and all he could hear was the daily goings-on of a girl behind a thick thorn wall. He never saw her, could never respond to her, and could never hear anything that might have helped him identify her. He was simply stuck listening to her.

It was like overhearing a group of players performing on the other side of a thick dusty curtain. Her voice carried the most, but it was still muffled and distant. Rarely, he could make out who she was talking to, usually her aunts or the animals they raised, and often he heard the mysterious girl singing to herself as she went about her day. In all the years he had been unwillingly eavesdropping on her, he had heard nothing that hinted at why he dreamed of her.

He had once considered that the dreams were magic, but his life was already tied to someone else. He didn't want to investigate and uncover that he was intricately linked not only to Princess Aurora in his waking life but to another stranger in his dreams. It was easier to think of the dreams as nothing more than flukes.

Phillip braced himself as they passed through the gates and slowed to a halt. "I think it would be best if I spoke with my father alone. Restock and prepare for us to leave again once I'm done."

He dismounted and handed the horse's reins to Johanna. She moved to talk, and Phillip shook his head.

He couldn't admit she was right, that she was one of two people who knew him so well it scared him, so he instead said, "I have twenty-one days until Princess Aurora's birthday and the sham that will be our marriage. I want to spend them away from here, even if we're only camping down the road."

"Of course," she said, and led Samson away. "This way, Your High Horseness."

Phillip sighed, slouched his shoulders, and glared up at the looming castle that was his home. It was rather like his father, an intimidating sprawl of stone that had been weathered by the world for years and never once fallen. No siege had ever broken through its stone walls, and no king who sat on its throne had ever surrendered. The great gate separating the main part of the castle from the city was easy enough to pass through undetected, with everyone focusing on work instead of on the faces of those slipping past them, and Phillip joined a group of workers returning to the castle to prepare for his father's imminent departure.

Phillip knew his father would be riding ahead to Ald Tor and arriving early to spend time with his best friend before the wedding. No doubt they would be discussing all their plans for Maleficent's inevitable return.

"A knight always has to be prepared," muttered Phillip, stopping outside of his father's study, where the king always was this time of day. "To fight, to outwit, to sacrifice."

And to marry girls they had never met.

Phillip shoved open the doors. The study was small and mostly for show, the hunting trophies on the wall revealing his father's true favorite place to be. A great bear was rearing behind the large wooden desk laden with letters and ledgers and half-drunk cups. King Hubert of Artwyne was clad in hunting clothes, rifling through papers and muttering to himself. He hadn't even heard the doors open.

"Now, the blueprints. Yes, good . . ."

Phillip cleared his throat.

"Phillip! My boy!" His father smiled, eyes crinkling, and swept around the desk to him. "There you are!"

King Hubert folded him into a rib-crushing hug.

"Here I am," Phillip mumbled into his father's shoulder.

"You know, in my day, knights answered to their lord," said his father, pulling away and wagging his finger before Phillip's face. "Told them where they were going and didn't vanish for weeks on end."

It wasn't even a mean statement, but it made Phillip wince. Each story of knights of old, each hope foisted upon Phillip, and each time his father had complete and utter confidence that he would succeed at protecting Princess Aurora from Maleficent—they ripped out the part of Phillip's heart that still thought he could be the hero. Each compliment only made him think of the selfishness he knew lived in him.

How could he be the good Prince Phillip when none of his choices felt good enough?

"Well, I guess I'm not like the knights of your day." Phillip slowly walked around his father's study and let his fingers skim the familiar objects. "Speaking of, though, Johanna and I had an encounter with some thieves. A trio robbed the inn we were staying at, but they didn't seem interested in the money."

"Oh, the sort who sees the fight as the spoils." King Hubert shadowboxed to his chair. "Give them the old one-two, did you? Show them what happens to those who cast aside justice?"

"Johanna showed them, mostly," said Phillip, dropping into one of the chairs before his father's desk. He propped his feet up on the corner.

His father punched his boots, lightly, and collapsed into his own chair with a huff. "Course she did. Always liked her."

"Anyway, I wanted to know if you had heard any reports of things happening about a five days' ride north-west of here?" asked Phillip. "Or if you had perhaps planned another one of your tests for me?"

"Can't say I have," said his father, an eye twitching toward his desk. He had already lost interest. "Hard to plan things when I don't know where you are."

So the king almost certainly hadn't been behind the oddness of the thieves' attack. If he had, he would've wanted to know everything and go over each of Phillip's mistakes. He also seemed unaware of any potential magic.

Just a normal fight in a stronger-than-normal storm.

Phillip dropped his gaze to his hands. "I figured I could be as unhelpful and self-deprecating on the road as I could be here, and on the road you don't have to deal with me."

"I'm in no position to deal with you since I'm han-dling wedding preparations," said King Hubert, all traces of cheer gone from his voice.

"Well." Phillip let his feet fall to the floor with a crack and rose. "That's my cue to leave. Fun chat. I'll see you at the party."

"Now hold on!" King Hubert huffed, beard bristling like an angry cat's back. "I've been lenient, lad. I've been patient. I've ignored your shrugging off important assignments and not stepping up to the lead when presented with the chance, but you're a step away from crossing the line. My guard and I are leaving tomorrow, and Stefan is meeting us halfway. You're coming with me, and you're getting ready for this wedding. We have to be prepared."

"Prepared?" Phillip laughed and stepped back from the desk. "It's a wedding. What could there possibly be to prepare for? Shouldn't we be more worried about Maleficent?"

"Stefan and I have got plans for Maleficent. Nothing for you to worry about." King Hubert huffed and smacked his chest, the desk rattling as he stomped a foot.

"What plans have you and King Stefan made?" Phillip asked, and crossed his arms. "You never mentioned anything to me."

"Couldn't have, could I?" asked his father. "You're off doing who knows what and avoiding your duties. No use telling you now, anyway. We've got it well in hand."

"It took armies to confine Maleficent to the Forbidden Mountain. Can you at least tell me if you still intend for me to single-handedly protect the princess from her?" Phillip asked.

King Hubert leaned over his desk and waggled a finger at Phillip. "It likely won't come to that. You're the last line of defense. We can get some more training in on the road, but believe me, Stefan and I have everything under control."

"Oh, well, so long as I'm the last line of defense, that's fine," said Phillip, a pit forming in his stomach. "I don't want anyone to depend on me."

"You only feel that way because you say nonsense like that." His father made an annoyed sound in the back of his throat and sipped from one of the half-empty cups on his desk. "You're lucky. No wars to speak of. No great battles. Oh, they'll temper you, make you a true knight and king, but they ruin too many. Wouldn't wish them on anyone."

Phillip gritted his teeth and ground out, "Any plans you *can* tell me about?"

"Leah has most of the wedding details worked out," said his father, falling back in his chair. He tapped his chin with a finger. "She's particular, you know. Didn't want to set the wedding so soon with Aurora having been gone for so long, but I talked her into seeing reason eventually. She wants to talk to you about Aurora, though, before the wedding."

Phillip had always liked Queen Leah, which only made this worse.

"Queen Leah was being reasonable," said Phillip. "Aurora and I have never spoken, and according to Maleficent's curse, she has some true love out there."

"This again?" His father rolled his eyes. "You'll get to know her. Your mother I hardly knew each other when we married, and I would've moved the moon for her, rest her soul."

Phillip had no memories of his mother; she died of fever shortly after he was born. However, he had heard story after story about his parents' initially contentious arrangement. Neither of them had been thrilled about being married—something Phillip thought should have made his father more empathetic about his situation—but then she had unseated him during a jousting tournament and crushed one of his knights in hand-to-hand. His father had been too impressed to be angry about marrying her after that, their arranged marriage quickly becoming a love match, so the story went. Phillip liked to imagine she was swinging a ghostly punch at everyone intent on making him Princess Aurora's guardian.

"You're entering into a contract, and that's better than any love—it's binding," said his father.

"Romantic." Phillip took a small step toward the door, but something stopped him. Despite his father's assurances that he hadn't orchestrated the strange fight, Phillip was still troubled by the oddness of the grass and branches moving to strangle Sire. Could it be possible that there was magic loose his father didn't know about?

"Have you heard from the fairies at all?" Phillip asked, trying to sound casual. "What about that wizard who used to visit? Blue Barnham or something?"

"Those fairies know better than to contact anyone. We can't risk Aurora's location being uncovered." His father snorted. "And magic is all well and good—gifts must be appreciated, after all—but Barny hasn't set foot here in years, and good riddance! There's nothing an old-fashioned fight can't take care of."

So Phillip had returned home for nothing but scorn. He had to get out of there.

"Well, I'll be leaving now," he said. "I will meet you the day of the wedding."

Phillip had run away enough to know the best moment to slip out. His father was far too dignified to chase after him or demand he be dragged back to the castle.

"Nonsense! This is your life we're talking about, lad. You're coming with me."

"You're right—it is my life." Phillip opened the door so that anyone nearby would be able to hear them. "I'm not absconding. I'm not abdicating."

His father flinched at the word.

"I will be at Princess Aurora's birthday," said Phillip loudly. "However, I am still a knight of this realm, and as such, I must make sure the thieves I ran into are not a part of something larger."

Lying was so easy after a lifetime of playing the part of the agreeable prince.

"Now see here!" His father cleared his throat and dropped his voice. "You are forming an alliance against the—"

"Greatest evil humanity has ever seen. I know." Phillip swallowed. "I'll be traveling with Johanna. She's earned her knighthood, by the way."

His father stared at him, one eye narrowed and mouth twisted into a scowl. He watched a servant walk past the open door.

"She'll earn it once she delivers you to Ald Tor twenty-one days from now," King Hubert said, voice even and reasonable. "You can flee to every corner of this kingdom and pretend you're some nobody with no responsibilities, but you are and will always be Prince Phillip."

Phillip did the only other thing he knew how to do—he ran *away*.

3
Into the Woods

$\mathcal{P}$HILLIP LEFT on horseback and galloped from the castle without a backward glance. Johanna refused to head north and instead led them on a roundabout journey that would eventually arrive in Ald Tor. She tried to find out more about what had happened, and Phillip said only that his father wasn't behind the thieves.

Once they had stopped and set up camp for the night, Phillip tried to stay awake as long as he could to enjoy Johanna's quiet, comforting company. He wanted no part of his dreams.

But, as always, when Phillip finally gave in and closed his eyes to rest, he was in the forest again.

His dream world *felt* old. Towering trunks brimmed with emerald leaves, their branches creaking beneath the weight of a canopy so thick it blotted out the sky. Moss blanketed the gnarled roots of blackthorns, and briars crowded the forest floor in fragrant full bloom. The breeze, steeped with damp evergreen and overripe black currant, whipped through the wood with a whistle. The trees went on as far as he could see.

They were the same trees that greeted him every night when he fell asleep.

He had tried to find his way out of the forest as a child, but the forest had grown closer and the tree leaves had twisted into impassable veils, herding him to the same place: a great thorn wall.

The wall was jagged and uneven, and Phillip couldn't exactly remember when it had appeared, but over time it had torn through trunks and rocks with thorns as long as swords. The wall split the forest so thoroughly that Phillip had never found its end, despite trying to walk around it hundreds of times. The bramble still grew, slithering deeper into the wood with every dream Phillip spent there. The forest lost ground with each restless night.

"Hello again," Phillip mumbled, patting the moss. He could never have a restful night when he needed it. "You're as ugly as ever."

The thorn wall loomed a few paces away, a wound of sickly yellow and rotting brown against the forest's lush greenery. He had tried to peek through it, climb over it, and dig beneath it, but the vines always snapped shut like a dragon's maw.

Phillip walked along the wall. At least he couldn't

hear *her* tonight. Maybe the universe was being merciful and giving him peace in his dreams for the first time in—

"No, no, no," came a girl's familiar voice.

The universe hated him.

She laughed, the high peal of it grating in his ears. "Pan, you cannot eat Ears's hat. This is supposed to be a proper garden party."

Phillip had been haunted by the sound of the girl's voice for years. Phillip didn't know her, couldn't see her through the wall, and couldn't communicate with her at all. In the end, he supposed he didn't even know if she was real or imagined.

All he could do was listen to her going on about her day-to-day life. It would have been like listening to a bedtime story if he didn't find her presence so irritating— as she cared for her animal friends, she continually told them about her various travels around the continent and all the different people she met during her wandering.

Even worse, he had eventually realized that the girl could hear his daily happenings as well. She had detailed parts of his life to her friends—though fortunately he had only ever heard her talking about him to her animal companions and not to any of the humans she described having met on her travels—and, trapped in the dream wood, he had been forced to listen to her commentary on his life. He hadn't cared for the way she described him as "some boy who dreams of me and my life" to a friendly owl one day. It made it sound like he was responsible for it. He didn't want to hear about her life any more than she wanted him to.

"Thank you all for coming. I believe we all know why we're here—there is a monster in our midst." The girl hesitated, and Phillip perked up. She had never mentioned any sort of monster living near her. "One of you ate every single one of the custard tarts I made last night, and I want to know who."

Phillip rolled his eyes and slumped again. Her little investigations had lost all their fun when he realized it was always the squirrel.

"Now, Ears can hop, but not high enough to get into the window," she said. "Pan is too loud to steal anything while I sleep."

Ears was a rabbit. Pan was a goat. Phillip was tired.

"Truly the most monstrous thing of all has occurred," Phillip whispered to himself. "Regale me with the dangerous robbery so that I may annoy that poor dream boy with the tale."

He crawled onto a low branch near the wall. A soft humming drifted through the cracks, and Phillip closed his eyes. When the dream girl wasn't talking, she was singing, but singing, at least, allowed him the respite sleeping should have.

"But what you were all unaware of was that I suspected treachery!" she said, and clapped.

That was funny, he hated to admit. But it still wasn't fair that this stranger consumed so much of his life.

She and Princess Aurora would have made great friends.

"Why wasn't I defending them? I was busy sitting through that dream boy's fighting with his father," she said, and unlike in every other dream, her voice wasn't muffled at all. Hearing her clearly was worse than when he had been forced to listen to her telling a deer about his final trial as a page.

"Do not talk about me," he muttered, and raised a hand at the wall.

"He was very rude to that Johanna of his." She huffed and waited for a response again. "I know! It is completely uncalled for."

Phillip rolled his eyes. "You're uncalled for."

"He thinks nothing matters," she said, "but he—"

"Don't pretend you know me!" Phillip yelled. A vine from the wall struck out like a serpent and slammed two thorns into his hand. Phillip cursed and stuck his hurt thumb into his mouth. "You're in a prickly mood tonight."

"I'm in a what?" shrieked the girl.

Phillip toppled out of the tree, his eyes widening. "What?"

She couldn't be responding to him. She couldn't hear him! Never in all the years they had been dreaming of each other had they been able to talk to each other. He had tried to speak with her when he was younger, and she had tried to talk to him; however, it had never worked. This was absurd.

"Don't 'what' me," the dream girl shouted. "What are you doing here? What did you do?"

At least that confirmed he wasn't imagining it. She was talking to him, and how dare she blame him!

"What am *I* doing here?" Phillip rolled to his knees, yanked a twig from his hair, and tossed it at the wall. The vines snapped it in two. "What are *you* doing here? This is my dream!"

"Your dream?" He could hear her stomp her foot against the ground, leaves crunching under the force of her heel. "I was having a perfectly nice dream without your interference for once."

"My inter . . ." Phillip held up a hand and laughed. "You're dreaming? But I'm dreaming. That's how this works. I dream of your life, you dream of mine, and thankfully, never the two shall meet. And if you *are* dreaming, who are you talking to? Yourself?"

She hissed, and he could practically hear the scowl she surely wore. "It's none of your business who I talk to—and why exactly are we in each other's dreams anyway? We don't know each other."

"I don't know. I always assumed I dreamed you up," he said. "And since you're really just a part of my imagination, you don't know, either."

"I'm not any part of you." She laughed. "I don't even know who you are."

"Exactly what a dream might say!"

The thorns rustled, as though blocking her from peeking through, and she muttered, "You're ridiculous."

All right, Phillip would never call himself ridiculous. Being able to communicate with the mystery dream girl wasn't anything like he imagined, and he didn't know what to do. She was more irritable than he thought she would be. What had changed that made them able to talk now after years of lonely assumptions?

"What's ridiculous is you practicing what you're going to say to animals who have no idea what you're saying ever," Phillip said, and took a seat with his back to the wall. Her affronted stutter made him smile.

"Seriously, how are we going to prove we're not the other's dream?"

She laughed under her breath, so different from the bubbling sound he was used to when she was alone. "I don't feel like a dream."

"Completely unhelpful." He sighed and rubbed his face. How would either of them know what a dream feels like? "All right—where do you live?"

He had never been able to hear anything remotely about where she was. Why would his mind do that?

"Oh, the . . ." The thorn wall writhed and twisted, the snapping of thorns drowning out her words. ". . . with my aunts."

Maybe his mind wasn't clever enough to come up with a location.

"I couldn't make out a word of that," he said.

"Of course you couldn't," said the girl with a scoff. "Where do you live?"

"Artwyne."

"No, your voice didn't carry," she said.

He laughed. "Funny how you made that sound like it's my fault."

"I haven't decided how at fault you are yet," she said, the rustling sound of her pacing from grass to stone changing with each step. "Let's start simpler. What's your name? I've never been able to hear that, only the names of your friends."

He snorted, delighted with her in a way he hadn't expected. "I haven't decided if I'll tell you that yet."

They stewed in silence, neither willing to break, and Phillip did admire her resolve. She was almost as stubborn as him.

"You're incorrigible," she finally said. "I'm Briar Rose."

Almost.

The name fit her—she had always been a thorn in his side.

"My name is Phillip."

"Odd name," said Briar Rose.

"Says the girl named for a bush," he laughed.

"It's a flower. It's right there in—"

"Don't ruin my joke with an explanation." Phillip kept as much bite as he could out of the comment and got as close to the wall as he dared. He could barely hear her laughing on the other side. "So, earlier, were you pretending there were animals with you, or are there animals on your side of the wall?"

"I was pretending," she said, almost sounding embarrassed. "There are never any creatures in this wood. Only us."

Phillip hadn't played pretend in a long time. Princes had no time for playing knight or sparring with shadows. But from what he had overheard throughout the years, Briar Rose had any number of tutors and friends to speak with, given the stories she had told the real animals of her travels. Why bother pretending?

"Why are we sharing a dream now? This can't be the first time we've been asleep at the same time, right?" Phillip asked.

"No, we've definitely been asleep at the same time. I don't think we've ever heard each other in real time before. No matter when we're asleep and awake, we dream of the other."

He sighed. It was the truth that he had lived most of his life.

"My main concern is, why us?" she asked with a huff. "Why are we, of all people, trapped together, and why have we always only heard specific pieces of the other's life?"

Trapped. He was surprised she felt the same.

"No idea. This place doesn't obey time, I suppose, but it always had rules. Why break them now?" he asked.

"I don't know," said Briar Rose. "I talked to you sometimes, when I was awake and alone, in case you were dreaming of me, but I don't think you ever were."

To his dismay, his heart clenched at that. He had heard some of those moments, but he couldn't stand to know if she had ever listened to him whispering to her as a kid, begging for understanding and comfort. "I mostly just thought about how much of my life you could spy on, and hated it."

"And you think I didn't feel the same?" she asked dryly. He licked his lips, thinking of something to ask that wasn't about why or how but about them and their shared lives, but before he could speak, she continued. "So what has changed recently that allows us to speak? Have you done anything that could have caused this?"

Phillip rolled his lips together, trying to think of what to say. No matter how much she annoyed him, they were in this together. "No, I've always dreamed of the wood, but I only started hearing you a few years after that. I was young, though, and I don't remember exactly when it was. I have done nothing unusual recently."

The dreams hadn't started until after Maleficent's curse, and Briar Rose had come some years later. The dreams were frustrating, but *she* terrified him—a person he didn't know who could hear everything he said so long as she was dreaming, and he could do nothing about it. He had no idea when she was listening or whom she could hear. Knowing her better would give him back some modicum of control over his life.

He opened his mouth to ask her a question, but she beat him to it.

"Do you think it's magic?" she asked.

He snorted. "Magic? No, no one would use magic to do something as useless as this."

Nothing good came from magic. Fairies might have gifted Princess Aurora beauty and song, but neither had done the girl any good. All they had given Phillip was a betrothed he never asked for and expectations. Then there was Maleficent.

Gifts and curses didn't seem so different.

But as much as he hoped his run-in with the thieves hadn't been magical, it was the only new thing to have happened in his life. They weren't connected to this, though. They couldn't be.

She clucked her tongue against her teeth. "Well, I don't have the faintest clue about magic other than what I've read. I've never told anyone—except the animals, of course—about these dreams, but I've also never read any mention of anything like this. Nothing at all has changed in my life recently. Oh! Unless you count one of my aunts going to town, but she does that sometimes. You're traveling with your friend, Johanna, aren't you? I do like her poetry."

"You would," he mumbled. "Look—neither of us seems to know anything about magic or dreams, so how about we talk about our lives, finally, or take exceptionally quiet naps? Where's your favorite place you've traveled?"

"Naps?" she asked, ignoring his other question. "In a dream?"

"Naps."

Briar Rose sighed. Phillip leaned back, hating the silence. They could finally talk to each other, and she didn't seem the least bit curious about him or interested in answering his questions.

"But this has never happened before!" Briar Rose made a sound like an angry fox. "Maybe this forest needs our help in real life."

"Then go play hero," Phillip snapped, his patience gone. "Why does it matter, anyway?"

She was quiet for a moment, and then said, "Maybe if we figure out why we're dreaming of each other, we can finally have real, restful dreams."

Oh. She wanted to be rid of him. Good. Phillip couldn't fault her for that when he had wished for the same thing.

"That's the first interesting thing you've ever said." He sat up and pushed his desire to know her out of his mind.

"Well, thankfully, we'll find out soon enough if this is a permanent change or not," Briar Rose said.

Phillip groaned. "No offense, but I'll be thankful if this is the last dream like this we ever have."

"No offense?" she asked, and laughed. "We both know you said it with all offense possible."

A hand gripped his shoulder, but when he looked, there was nothing there. His vision blurred. Her voice wavered. Someone in the real world was waking him up.

"You said it, not me. Remember that," said Phillip, closing his eyes and letting darkness wash over him. "I think this is it for me."

4
A Harsh Awakening

*P*HILLIP ROLLED away from the hand on his shoulder the moment he came to. His stiff, sore muscles tightened in protest, but his training took over; he raised his hands to defend himself and rose to his knees. Johanna and he knew better than to awaken each other like that. Something was wrong.

"Johanna?" he called out.

"We're not in danger," she said, voice coming from across the fire. "Probably."

"Reassuring," he said, frantically trying to blink the sleep from his eyes.

When they had gone to bed on opposite sides of the fire they had been utterly alone except for Samson, Taliesin, and whatever other animals were creeping about the hills. Now, three women stood before him, each wearing a different vibrant color—orange, purple, and yellow—and the image drew up something uncomfortably familiar in the back of his mind.

Phillip jumped up and rested his hand on the knife on his belt.

Johanna stood behind the trio, and she inclined her head to the one in yellow. So that was who had awakened him.

"Your caution is wise but unnecessary," she said. "My name is Eris, and my companions are Poena and Phrike. We are fairies."

Fairies—the very word made him squeeze his eyes shut, take a deep breath, and look to ensure this wasn't a bad joke. But on each of their backs, fluttering and casting colored light across the grass like stained glass, were wings. Phillip clenched his teeth. He'd only had one experience with fairies, and it was not one he wanted to relive any time soon.

"Why?" he asked. "Why are you here?"

The words tasted as bitter as they sounded to him.

"Here? It's where you are," the fairy, Eris, said. Her blond hair was braided and bundled in a golden net over her ears, and Phillip wasn't sure how she could hear anything through it. She wore a gown that looked as if it had been woven from dandelion petals instead of wool, and she raised her hand to her mouth to cover a dimpled smile. "We've been sent to help you."

"I don't want *your* help," said Phillip, cocking his head slightly.

"Now you are being rude," snapped the one named Poena. She was the tallest of the fairies, and had thick red curls beneath a veil and wimple of deep purple cloth.

"*Your Highness*," corrected Johanna. "'Now you're being rude, Your Highness.'"

Phillip grinned. He'd make sure she attained knighthood and finished whatever she was writing if it killed him. Eris cleared her throat.

"Apologies," Eris said. "Human monarchies are so brief compared to our lifetimes, and it is quite hard to keep up with who is who sometimes."

Fairies took an interest in only a few children every now and then, and Phillip hadn't been one of them. His father had asked for their favor, but they had refused without an explanation. Princess Aurora had been the first child blessed with a gift, much less three, in a decade.

The only reason fairies would seek Phillip out was if something was wrong with the hidden princess, because he knew, had been told over and over in word and deed, that he would never be as valuable as Princess Aurora.

"You used magic recently, didn't you?" said Eris.

Phillip froze. Johanna gasped behind the trio and mouthed, *I knew it.*

"No?" Phillip shook his head, ignoring his friend. "Can't say I did."

There was a difference between magic having occurred during his fight with Sire, and Phillip himself having magic. If Phillip had magic, he would have known.

Wouldn't he?

"I told you this was a waste of time," hissed Poena, her skin flushing until her freckles vanished.

The third one, Phrike, was covered from head to toe in a shade of burnt orange that reminded Phillip of autumn leaves. She reached out from under her long veil and patted Poena's arm. "Nothing's a waste till we're dead, dear."

Phillip was certain fairies didn't die naturally.

"Well said." Eris laced her fingers together and rested her hands against her stomach. "Phillip, we know for a fact that you used magic and you may make that face at me all you want, but it does not change the truth."

Phillip snorted, unsure what face he was making.

"Ever since your magic made itself known, we have been tracking it and you," the fairy continued.

Phillip shook his head. What Eris was saying made

no sense. Maybe he was hallucinating. Maybe his father had knocked him out and was dragging his unconscious body to his wedding in Ald Tor, and Briar Rose and these fairies were just figments of his imagination. But no matter how hard Phillip pinched himself, the scene before him remained the same.

It was a mistake. It had to be. If there had been magic at play during his fight with the thieves, it had to be because someone nearby had come into their power, and the fairies had incorrectly assumed it was Phillip.

"I don't have magic," he finally said.

"Really, boy?" Poena asked, staring at him through narrowed eyes. "What part of what we are saying is too abstruse for you?"

"Poena, if you have no faith in our plan, then you are more than welcome to leave and return to what you were doing before," Eris said, blue eyes cutting to her. Poena inclined her head, and Eris turned back to Phillip. "Forgive her—teaching is not her usual role, and time is of the essence."

"I told you!" Johanna slipped between the fairies, a bit more forceful with Poena than necessary, and grabbed Phillip's arm. "It was magic. This is fantastic!"

They couldn't be right, because Johanna would never let him live this down.

"Don't take this the wrong way, but can you prove that I have magic?" he asked.

Johanna rolled her eyes.

Poena inhaled and made a twirling gesture with her fingers. Each of the fairies' wings disappeared in a little puff of acrid smoke that cleared almost instantly. With another gesture, the wings reappeared.

"We're fairies," said Eris. "We don't make mistakes when it comes to magic."

Phillip swallowed. Their wings were undeniable proof of their power.

"Let's sit, shall we?" asked Eris. "And we'll explain."

Phillip and Johanna sat on his bedroll. Phrike plopped down where she stood, spreading her gown around herself. The horses were agitated, watching with their ears pricked back from their spot at the edge of camp, and Samson snorted when Eris pulled out a long wand of orange alder. She twirled it, magic raining down upon the grass. The blades grew and twisted into a small stool. Poena remained standing with her arms crossed over her chest.

"We've been sent to train you before Maleficent and her allies notice your abilities."

"Sent by who?" Phillip asked.

"The other fairies. There are very few humans

capable of using magic, and there are none allied with fairies against Maleficent," Eris said. "Frankly, your having magic provides us with an opportunity we would not otherwise have. When we sensed your magic awakening, we knew that someone must find you and train you. It was decided that the someone needed to be the three of us."

"But why now?" he asked slowly. "I've been around fairies before. Surely, they would have noticed if I had some sort of power."

"Merryweather and her ilk are quite shortsighted," said Poena.

"They would not have registered it because it was dormant in you," Eris said. "Magic can manifest for a number of reasons, and it is not fully understood why it does this in humans, since you are not inherently magical animals. We need to know what happened to determine what sort of magic you possess."

"He pushed a thief away from him using the wind," Johanna said. "Punched him, and the man went flying. Then a bunch of grass and branches tied him up."

"'Tied up' is a bit of a stretch," muttered Phillip.

Eris grinned. "So you used nature magic, calling the wind and plants to your aid? Excellent. That is a good type of magic to start with."

For the first time in a very long while, Phillip had no

sardonic deflection or desire to even use one. It was too hard to believe and too good to be true. A yawning ache bloomed in his chest, as though a hole that had always been in his heart was at last threatening to fill.

"It might have only been the wind," he said, but it sounded hollow even to him.

"It *was* the wind, but your magic is what called up such a strong gust," said Eris. She held out her hand to him, palm up. "Phillip, I promise—you have magic. If you didn't, we wouldn't have been able to find you."

Phillip took a deep breath, hope burning behind his eyes like some unwelcome grief. No matter how often he tried to steel himself against hope, the idea of possessing something separate from his father was too tempting. "How do I know you are telling the truth and aren't working for Maleficent?"

"We're born with magic, you know, but it changes as we do," Phrike said, and gestured for him to take her hand. "Intent's what matters. Only good fairies can heal. If a heart were to harden, the ability would fade."

It was true that evil fairies couldn't use healing magic. Even Phillip knew that from the stories passed down to him as a kid. It was for the same reason good fairies couldn't summon dragon fire like Maleficent could. Evil fairies weren't born. Children didn't just develop evil magic. They had to seek it out and really *mean* the magic they used. Ill magic required ill intentions, and casting it had consequences, like losing the ability to heal.

"Hopefully, this will be enough to prove our commitment to humanity," said Eris. "Phrike, go ahead."

Phrike's hands were clammy, and she ran her thumb across one of the yellowed bruises on Phillip's knuckles. A scent like wet earth or a damp cave crept over him, and she ran her thumb over the bruise a second time. It faded slowly until his skin looked as it normally did. Phillip took his hand back and prodded the spot. It still hurt.

"The pain will be gone soon," said Phrike, patting his hand. "Even with magic, healing's slow."

"So you are who you say you are," Phillip said, and Johanna stiffened next to him. She knew him too well to think he would give in so easily. "Me having magic is far more of a stretch, though."

Eris smiled. "Is there a demonstration that will make you believe in yourself?"

There wasn't, but he couldn't say that.

"You are not used to magic and are not trained," she said softly, as if she knew exactly what he was thinking. "You may not be able to use your magic effortlessly yet, so this may not work, but hold out your hand over the grass and imagine it curling around your finger."

He did. Phillip thought of a single blade twisting around his finger like a snake's tail. Briar Rose had a snake she talked to sometimes, a small thing that liked sunning itself where she washed her clothes. He pictured not his hand but hers. Flick, as she called him, often curled around her like a bracelet.

Agonizingly slowly, a single blade of grass grasped at his thumb and wrapped around it. Phillip stilled.

"Well," Eris said softly, "would you look at that?"

The strange ache deep in his chest grew, and Phillip yanked his hand back. There had to be some sort of trap here. A sword poised to fall on him if he said or did the wrong thing.

So much of his life was already set, and now he had magic, a new complication and responsibility. He would have to train again, whether he wanted to or not. He would have to reckon with what magic meant and how everyone else would want to use him for it. That was what it was—another way for him to be used. All of his hope soured into dread.

"So what if I have magic?" asked Phillip. "Why must I be trained?"

"There are only two armaments capable of countering fairy magic and killing us—the Sword of Truth and the Shield of Virtue. They were designed to be used against us centuries ago, so we fairies cannot touch them, and even summoning them requires either immense power or purely good intent. Though we have known where they are for over a decade, retrieving them has always been impossible because it would require a human with magic," Eris said, pointing at Phillip. "Magic in humans is exceedingly rare, and it is even rarer for those humans to survive long enough and learn enough magic to be considered a wizard. Given the falling out your father had with his last court wizard, you are now the only human with magic allied with Artwyne and Ald Tor. You are the only person who can retrieve the sword and shield. You are the only person who can truly defeat Maleficent once and for all."

Phillip shook his head. "If Maleficent can only be defeated using the sword and shield, why were King Stefan and my father so confident that we could save the princess without them? Isn't that the whole point of her being in hiding? If Maleficent can't find her, she can't curse her."

"The issue with humans is their shortsightedness," said Eris. "Even if the princess makes it to her birthday, she won't be safe forever. Without those arms, humans will be locked in a war with Maleficent for decades, because she'll stop at nothing to kill that girl and get her revenge. The kings are content to hold Maleficent off, but why hold her off when the opportunity to defeat her is right there?"

"Prior to this, you were to be Princess Aurora's protector, but with the sword and shield, you would be Maleficent's ruin," Poena added. "Why be a mere guard for a lifetime when you can be a hero as well?"

He preferred his odds as Aurora's guardian rather than as Maleficent's sole opponent. Hiding and protecting he knew he could do. He didn't know if he would ever be good enough at magic to defeat Maleficent.

"We would train you in how to use your magic so that you could retrieve the sword and shield, then in how to use them against Maleficent." Eris's gaze flicked from him to Johanna. "We have just twenty days to do so, but so long as you have the arms, it should be enough to defeat Maleficent."

The sapling of excitement that had been growing in his chest immediately withered. "I'm not interested," Phillip said. "We can stick to the original plan."

"What?" Poena asked.

Johanna closed her eyes and sighed. "Phillip, you could defeat Maleficent once and for all."

"Maybe I could," he said. "The thing is, I don't care."

Where had they been when he was a child? This gift they offered him now—teaching him to use magic—was purely for Princess Aurora's benefit. It wasn't a gift; it was another leash.

"But you have to learn magic." Poena loomed over him, the air around her warming. "You are a knight! Prince Phillip, Princess Aurora's protector and betrothed! You have to learn magic for her."

"Always for her and never for myself," said Phillip. "If you're trying to woo me with glory, I'm not interested."

Poena threw up her arms and walked away.

Johanna touched Phillip's arm.

"Phillip, you should reconsider this," she whispered.

"Look," said Phillip. "I will marry the princess, I will protect her, but I will not sacrifice my last days before I am eternally bound to her for something that will solely benefit her."

He knew that Maleficent was a threat to everyone. She was dangerous and hadn't hesitated to plunge the world into war last time she'd attacked, but she had been beaten back by his father's and King Stefan's armies. She could be again.

But there was no possible way that Phillip alone, magic or not, could defeat her. The chance of him even getting close to that was so astronomically low it was laughable.

Sure, it was selfish, but it was also his life. It was better he take a few weeks of freedom and the sure thing of protecting the princess for most of his life than he sacrifice these weeks for a long shot.

"Are you not a knight?" Poena rounded on him, and her wings fluttered behind her. "Where is your sense of honor and duty?"

"Forgot to pack it." Phillip shrugged.

Eris tilted her head to the side. "You're serious, aren't you?"

"It happens rarely, so treasure it," he said. He rose, brushed off his hands, and gestured for them to leave. "I'm terribly sorry you came all this way, but I must refuse. Safe travels."

Poena opened her mouth, and Eris raised a hand. Softly, she said, "The world has done quite a number on you, hasn't it?"

Phillip winced. Was it so wrong for him to want to enjoy his life instead of throwing it away? He couldn't defeat Maleficent. Why waste time trying?

"He is about to do a number on it!" Poena sniffed and sneered. "Hypocritical and selfish is what it is."

"Without heroes, there's only fear," said Phrike.

"I'm not a hero," said Phillip, avoiding Johanna's gaze. "I will not force myself into a role I will never be able to live up to."

"We've all got shoes to fill," said Phrike. "You've got to step into them."

"I would rather cut off my own feet." He ran his tongue over his teeth. It had taken hundreds of thousands of soldiers to defeat Maleficent last time. He was only one person. "We're done here. I'm sorry you're leaving disappointed."

Eris stood, and her magic withered into the grass. "No you're not, but leave we shall."

Poena and Phrike stepped away, their forms shrinking. They grew smaller and smaller until they were merely motes of light and only Eris remained, looming even though she came up only to his nose. Phillip inclined his head to her.

"I hope you master your magic before it grows too powerful." She flicked her wand, and a carnation tucked itself into the pocket of Johanna's tunic. "Good luck, Phillip."

He looked away from her downcast face, and she vanished, leaving only the faint scent of autumn air and yellow carnation.

5
So Fair and Foul a Day

*T*HERE WAS no going back to sleep after the fairies left. So Phillip tended to the horses while Johanna glared and softened some bread to eat.

"If we've always needed the sword and shield, why didn't my father or King Stefan figure out a way to get them sooner?" Phillip asked Samson, brushing him down. As much as he wanted to forget the fairies' warnings, he couldn't stop thinking about magic, Maleficent, and the armaments. "I knew Father and our old court wizard fought, but surely there's someone out there somewhere who could help."

His father had never told anyone why he'd fought with the wizard, though, and that was troubling. It was unfathomable to him that his father and King Stefan didn't know about the armaments, where they were, or how to get them, but this wasn't just about him. Maleficent was dangerous, and defeating her would save thousands of lives. It worried Phillip.

But what was it his father had said?—*Stefan and I have got plans for Maleficent. Nothing for you to worry about.*

"If that's what he wants, I won't worry," muttered Phillip under his breath. "About anything."

Samson shook Phillip off and nosed his way into Phillip's pocket, huffing when he found it empty.

"Fine, I'll worry about you," said Phillip, and he moved to prepare Taliesin for travel. "And you."

"Not necessary," Johanna said behind him. "I can do that. Come eat."

Phillip made a face at the chestnut courser and avoided turning to look at Johanna.

"Is there anything else you want to do before the princess's birthday?" asked Johanna, holding out a chunk of brown bread hollowed and stuffed with a boiled egg. It was a bribe. She always offered him food and a conversation topic he liked before bringing up the things he didn't.

Phillip took the offering but rolled his eyes. "You tell everyone I died in a magical accident, and I gallivant off to live my life?"

"Phillip," she said, and closed her eyes, but he knew she was rolling them.

"We have to head south if we're to reach Ald Tor in

time for Princess Aurora's return," he said flatly. "If we hurry, we should be able to see the lavender fields down south."

The lavender fields were one of Artwyne's prides, wild hills of pale violet that perfumed the air for leagues. Phillip had never seen them, though he had used plenty of soaps and tinctures derived from the flowers plucked there, but Briar Rose had visited them years ago. Upon returning, she had described the fields in such enticing detail to her animals that Phillip had listened through the thorn wall in rare rapture. They had sounded so free and delicate, two things he'd never been. He'd wanted to stand where she had and breathe in the fragrant air for himself ever since.

Johanna shook her head. "Are you really going to ignore everything the fairies said?"

"Yep." He gestured at their small camp. "Tell me what you're writing, and I'll consider listening to you."

"Absolutely not," she said, and flushed. "This isn't a game you can shrug off when you lose, Phillip. This is people's lives, and magic could save them."

"You think I don't know that?" asked Phillip, tone sharper than he'd ever taken with her. "I've been training my whole life to protect Princess Aurora. I know exactly what's at stake."

So Fair and Foul a Day

Dawn to dawn, Phillip had trained to be a knight. It had started the moment his father and he had returned from the princess's christening. He had been younger and smaller than every other page, but he had done it. He had thought there would be some sort of respite or praise at the end. There wasn't.

There had only ever been more training and more ways to disappoint his father.

"King Stefan and my father have been planning for Maleficent's return for over a decade. Princess Aurora is almost certainly not going to fall victim to the curse, given how carefully plotted out the next month is, and they've been watching the Forbidden Mountain since Maleficent retreated there. Maleficent's not out to conquer; she's out for vengeance against the people who stopped her all those years ago. When she realizes that Princess Aurora has avoided her curse, she'll try to kill the princess," said Phillip.

Last time, Maleficent's army of enchanted minions had taken her years to create, and King Stefan was certain she hadn't had the power or time to create another army as large. Phillip's father always said the curse would be Maleficent's final move, one last strike from her death throes. She didn't have the power or desire to go to war with the human kingdoms again. She simply wanted revenge.

"That is why I have spent my entire life training to protect Princess Aurora—to protect her from Maleficent once it's clear the curse can't claim her," he continued. "I know I'm not a match for Maleficent alone, but what can she do against me *plus* two whole kingdoms fully prepared for her assassination attempts?"

"You're missing the forest for the trees," Johanna said, throwing up her hands. "If Maleficent can get away with cursing Princess Aurora, what can she do to the rest of us if something goes wrong? Most of the world doesn't have the princess's status, magic, or money. If she can go after a royal, then she can do unspeakable things to everyone else. But if you defeat her outright, then there's still hope. If you are the only person capable of getting the sword and shield, why not try?"

"It's not that I don't want to ensure people aren't in danger, but I just want these last days of mine to be mine and mine alone, because soon my entire life will be about Princess Aurora."

Phillip took a deep breath, covering his mouth with a hand. It wasn't her fault, and as his squire, she couldn't disagree too much with him, but she had never dismissed his circumstances so casually before.

"You shouldn't think like that," said Johanna, "but you cannot ignore the fact that if the fairies are right, you alone can defeat Maleficent for good. At the very least you should be concerned about having magic. If you don't get that under control, who knows what could happen?"

It was tempting to be the hero he had dreamed of as a child, but it was too much too soon.

"One person rarely makes a difference," he muttered, "but thank you for being worried about me."

"I always worry about you. You're a disaster." She made a small noise in the back of her throat and shifted. "I didn't realize you felt so trapped."

"*Trapped* is a tame way to describe how I feel, but you are right about the magic. I have to do something about that, but not today, Johanna. Please," he said, and sighed. "Do you think I'd make a good wizard?"

"You just ranted about not wanting magic." Johanna rolled her eyes. "You are changeable like the moon, ever waxing and waning and whining."

"Stop that," Phillip said, and lunged for her. "That's my least favorite of your poems, and the moon doesn't whine."

"Then why does it run away every morning?" she asked, and darted up and away from him. "I wasn't aware you listened to my recitations."

He quite liked them.

"I suffer through them," he said. "It's better for my self-esteem than listening to your advice."

"Fate! Monstrous and empty, you whirling wheel," she cried, and raised her arms. "You are malevolent—"

"We're fighting. I'm going to throw you into the first river we find and let the fish have you," Phillip said, going to their packs and tossing her sheathed sword to her. "You know I prefer the ones where knights marry heartbreak or become trees."

But he was smiling and laughing and felt altogether far less gloomy than he had.

Black hair loose and wild in the wind, sword raised, and dark eyes bright, Johanna looked like one of the knights she always wrote about, and Phillip wished he could show her how the world saw her.

"I refuse to be the Gawain to your Parzival." Johanna beckoned for him to attack. "Stop moping and fight me."

He grabbed his sword. "I've never moped a day in my life."

Phillip always won their spars. Usually.

Fifty-fifty.

"Of course not, Your Highness," said Johanna, striking out toward his right thigh.

Phillip parried and thrust, the screech of steel

against steel ringing in his ears. They moved easily through the old dance they'd both learned as pages, and Phillip's head cleared as he focused on the steps. Block lower right, block lower left, sweep lower left, sweep lower right, parry a strike at his chest—he had been doing the same moves since he was young. The unease of the day seeped out of him.

He had been prickly today, hadn't he? It was hardly his fault; he had gotten no rest since he'd spent his sleep dealing with Briar Rose and their new situation. Even if the fairies hadn't woken him up and ruined his day, he would have been annoyed and exhausted.

So it was really all Briar Rose's fault.

Phillip had too much happening in his life to worry about her, too, and it was entirely unfair that she was this annoying when she wasn't even around.

"You're hesitating," Johanna said, and tapped her hilt with a finger. "You never hesitate."

"I'm trying not to think," he said, and lunged as fast as he could.

Johanna dragged her blade up just in time, stumbling to the side. He shouldn't have had so much trouble in the fight with the thieves, given all his training. It had been foolish to go empty-handed, but he had severely underestimated them and the storm. He'd been in tougher scrapes before, and if he was going to survive the next few years, he needed to be better. Maybe he should—

Johanna twisted her wrist, her blade scraping past Phillip's, and nicked his cheek.

Panic struck him like lightning. Phillip lunged out with his empty hand and caught nothing. He saw Johanna's mouth open as she said something, but her voice warbled in his ears and his vision blurred, as if he were suddenly underwater. He tripped and smacked into the ground hard, biting his tongue. Phillip groaned and rubbed his jaw.

"Johanna?" he asked, and looked up.

Vines, dozens upon dozens of spine-covered vines the same sickly purple shade as foxglove flowers, twisted around Johanna. She struggled to yank one from around her throat and gasped for air. Phillip leapt to his feet.

"Hang on!" He plunged his hands into the vines without thought and tried to tear them, but they grew faster than he could rip them. Spines split his skin.

"Let her go! Stop this!" he choked out.

He pulled his dagger from his belt and began cutting. But they regrew threefold. Phillip screamed, too horrified to think straight. He wedged his hands between her neck and the vines and tried to give her space to breath. Johanna gulped down the air.

"I'm sorry. I'm so sorry," he said. "I don't know what to do."

Phillip's hands were crushed against her throat. The skin around her mouth was paling to an ashy brownish-gray.

"Move!"

The shout came out of nowhere, and Phillip spun around. Eris, Poena, and Phrike descended on the wind with pinched, drawn faces.

"I didn't—I don't know what—" Phillip scrambled out of the way as Eris approached.

"Of course you don't know what to do," said Eris, and magic spilled from her wand. "You haven't been taught."

The vines engulfing Johanna began to recede. Johanna grabbed her throat and took a shuddering breath. Eris kept on muttering, magic flowing from her like rain, and each small speck of light that touched the vines made them flinch. Pain prickled across Phillip's hands, and he brought them closer to his face. His blood was flowing back into the wounds and the skin healing as if it had never been cut at all. Soon, the only evidence of the accident was Johanna's heavy breathing.

"There you go, dear," said Phrike, lifting up her veil and squinting at Johanna's throat with narrowed brown eyes. "Let me see what we're working against."

She laid her hands against Johanna's throat, and Johanna's breathing slowly steadied.

Poena glared down her nose at Phillip. "You are lucky we were still nearby."

They walked Johanna to Taliesin and let her rest against her courser. Phillip stayed where he was, too scared to get close.

"The magic wasn't at all like that before," he said. "I didn't do anything like *that*."

"You're untrained and your magic has just awakened," said Eris. "It will be unpredictable until you master it, especially nature magic. It requires great power and control."

Laughing hollowly, Poena said, "And you, Your Highness, lack both in regard to magic right now."

Phrike stood, ambling over to Phillip. She took his hands in hers and studied the repaired skin. "Good. Good."

"Thank you," he whispered, and flexed his fingers. The wounds hadn't even left scars, but the pain lingered as if they were still there.

"I am sorry, Johanna," Eris said, and bowed her

head to the girl. "And to you as well, Phillip. My warning was insufficient."

Phillip hadn't been afraid when the fairies mentioned his power getting out of control. Hurting himself wasn't as terrifying as hurting someone else, especially Johanna.

He hadn't even considered what might happen to Princess Aurora if he didn't train his magic. She'd been a concept, an abstract annoyance he hated considering, and that wasn't better than how his father saw him. The damage he could do to her hadn't felt real, but seeing the potential now was terrible. Given how much time he would soon spend with her, she would get hurt if this happened again.

She was a person, not a problem, and he could kill her.

Phillip looked at the gouges in the grass where Johanna had fought to stay on her feet. Panic rose like bile in his throat. "She'll be all right, won't she?" he asked the fairies.

"I'm fine. Stop talking around me and come here," Johanna said, voice cracking. She waited for Phillip to sit before her. "We are fine so long as you never do that again."

She flicked his nose between each word.

Phillip hugged her waist and avoided her neck. "I'm sorry."

"You tried to tear magical thorny vines away from me with your bare hands. We're fine," she muttered. "Good story, though."

He laughed and pulled away. "You're welcome for that, then."

"You're more powerful than we thought," said Eris, coming to sit with them. "If you are not trained, your magic will break free."

"I'm a danger to everyone around me, you mean," Phillip said.

He stared down at his unscarred, clean hands and closed his eyes. Johanna's desperate breaths rang in his head. Their mingling blood had been so warm on his hands.

And Eris had erased all of that fear with a wave of her wand.

As selfish as he wanted to be, he couldn't hurt anyone like that ever again. He had always been careless, but he didn't want to find out how easily he could become a monster.

"I'll train with you," he said, releasing a long and tired breath. "I'll retrieve the sword and shield. Just teach me how to ensure this never happens again."

"Excellent," Eris said with a smile, and she shushed Phrike's small whoop. "I think this is best for all of us."

Phrike quieted and said, "And to be celebrated."

"I want you to promise me that no harm will come to Johanna," Phillip said, ignoring her disgruntled look at being talked about as if she weren't there. "I can't hurt her. You can't hurt her. Samson can't hurt her. Promise me."

Fairies couldn't break promises, and Phillip could never allow this to happen again.

"Promise you? You want to make a deal with me." Eris's smile took a moment to settle into place, and she offered him her hand, magic glittering at the tips of her fingers. "You have my word. We will not hurt Johanna."

A prickle of something swept over Phillip, and he shivered as they shook hands.

"The deal is done," she said. "We'll begin immediately."

6

Hedge Witch

THE WORD *IMMEDIATELY* HAD a different meaning to fairies.

Phillip had expected a step-by-step plan for his magical training. Instead, Eris fluttered about—human sized but still gliding across the grass—muttering about his and Johanna's apparently insufficient camp setup. She pulled out a wand from the bell sleeves of her dress and swished it over her head. The nearby trees creaked and groaned, tilting over the little clearing until they formed a roof of leaves and branches. Phillip shuddered.

Why was it always plants?

Phrike stayed near Johanna and helped her move through a series of painful-looking stretches to keep the muscles of her neck from getting stiff.

"What, uh . . ." Phillip rubbed the back of his neck and looked around. "What should I be doing?"

Poena, arranging several newly formed magical stools that looked like they wouldn't hold up under anyone other than a fairy, glanced at him over her shoulder with wide eyes.

"Watch us," Eris said quickly. "Witness the ease with which we call upon our magic."

Phillip observed the fairies for a few minutes as they continued to wave their wands and make changes to the campsite. They didn't mutter any spells or do any intricate gestures other than waving their wands here and there. Magic didn't look so hard when they did it.

"You said I developed magic, but you never told me how," said Phillip.

Poena looked to Eris, and Eris said, "Your capacity for doing magic likely always existed. The source of your magic is likely the result of a forgotten gift—as in, one of your ancestors was gifted magic, not a physical gift—that was awakened by circumstance, like your fight with those thieves."

Phillip remembered the stories his father told him about his ancestors. He was sure if there had been a wizard on his father's side of the family, he would have heard about it, but maybe his mother had an old relative with magic that she had never gotten the chance to tell them about. Phillip supposed there was no way of knowing now.

"I've been in fights before," said Phillip. "Why didn't it show itself then?"

"Unfortunately, until we learn more about your magic, I can't say for sure why it made itself known that night," Eris said. "Now, do you see how we channel our magic?"

Eris twirled her wand in a graceful, flowing gesture. Her magic was a pale yellow glint in the air, flickering around the tent still packed atop Samson's back. Samson snorted and stamped, spinning in a circle to see what was happening above him, and a thick branch removed the tent from the pack. The magic encircled the wood in a pale gold glow, and the branch moved like a finger. Slowly, it set up the tent.

"Fairies focus magic through wands from trees that sprouted the same day we were born. This allows us to call up or stop our magic at will. You will be unable to do that since you are human. A wizard's power usually comes from a staff, or is tied to it in some way, but you have no such source or tie, and we do not have the time to craft one. You will have to use your magic differently if you are going to steal the Sword of Truth and Shield of Virtue." Eris gestured for Phillip to sit on one of the summoned stools. "What did you feel when your magic first appeared during your fight with those thieves?"

Phillip raised one shoulder. "Nothing. It just happened."

"Likely, he is too unfamiliar with the feeling to identify it," said Poena to Eris, summoning fire from her wand with a quick swish. The flames crackled in the pit between them, and she shooed Eris to a stool. "This was your idea, so you are in the lead. I will help Phrike with the girl and then finish making this place"—she glanced around at the clearing and drew in a shallow breath—"livable."

"How kind of you," Eris said, the right side of her mouth quirking up. "Now, Phillip—when you are in the water, do you feel every tide, small and large, or do you only notice that they were there once you've left the water?"

Poena flew away, and Phillip tried to focus on Eris.

"I notice them after, unless they're strong," he said. "So I guess I need to learn what my magic feels like and then I can master it?"

"Just so," Eris said, and smiled. She fluffed out the long skirts of her dress, the fabric spilling across the grass like honey, and adjusted herself so that they could speak without the others overhearing. "Magic is about belief and intuition. You must trust that what you are feeling is your magic and believe in yourself in order to utilize it."

Phillip groaned. "If I believe I can, I can?"

"Don't be impertinent," Eris said. "If you believe you can touch fire and not be burned, you can't. If you believe you can touch fire and your magic will stop you from being burned, you can. See the difference?"

Not really.

"I suppose," he said.

"The difference is that magic is not like a sword. It requires training, but its presence is often enough to allow for small workings, like the nature magic you used against Johanna."

Phillip nodded.

"When you imagine things, do you see them happening in your mind?" she asked.

Phillip nodded again. Daydreaming was one of the only ways he had survived his time as a squire.

"That's how magic works," said Eris. "You must imagine what you want your magic to do. This can cause issues. Do you see what those issues could be?"

"Not knowing what you want?" Phillip asked. He had wanted Sire and Johanna to get away from him both times, and his magic *had* done that, even if he hated how it had accomplished it.

"Exactly!" Eris said, and clapped once. "Which brings us back to belief—if you do not believe you can do something, how can you even imagine it? If you don't trust yourself to know what you want, then you can't imagine anything at all, can you?"

What Eris described felt distant and unobtainable. If Phillip never improved, was it because he didn't believe in himself or because something else was wrong? Sword fighting, at least, allowed you to know when you were getting better. Riding had visible results.

"Do you know what you want from life, Phillip?" Eris asked, seeming to sense his doubt.

Phillip startled. No one had ever asked him that, not once in all his years of training and talking about the future. They assumed he wanted what his father had decided for him or that he was willing to cast aside everything for what was needed. Worse, he worried they didn't even consider him a whole person with wants of his own. He couldn't even think of one goal he had solely for himself.

"I don't know," he said, trying to sort out the odd feeling the question dredged up in him.

Eris's brows pinched together. "Oh. Well, think on it. Magic needs a person to trust themselves. It requires a confidence most do not have. I am very good at magic. That is not egotism. That is fact. I am good at magic because I trust that I am good enough to do what I want and that what I want is right."

Phillip swallowed and fiddled with a long blade of grass. "Have you always known what you wanted to do with your life?"

"Oh, no. I was a little monster as a child. Bright-eyed and eager but with no conviction to do what was necessary to achieve my goals," Eris said, and laughed, a loud and unrestrained sound that couldn't have been anything other than sincere. "I had a mentor that set me straight. Unfortunately, I don't have decades to help you figure out what you want from your life."

A feeling Phillip couldn't place bloomed low in his stomach. It was light and fluttering, and it was almost hopeful. If Eris had been a monster and sorted it all out, surely he could?

"We have twenty days."

"Twenty days until Maleficent's curse, yes," said Eris. "But I want you to think about yourself. Do you trust yourself? Do you believe in yourself?"

And just like before, Phillip couldn't rightly answer.

Knights followed orders and trusted in their superiors enough to lead on their behalf, and they had to be certain of their orders so as to undertake them without thought. They served and believed in the king. Phillip might have been the prince, but he was still beholden to his father. He hadn't trusted the demands made of him in years. However, trusting no one else didn't mean he trusted himself.

Eris had known him for only half a day and had already cut to the heart of him.

"Don't tell me now," Eris said, and stood. Her hand came to rest on his shoulder. "Think about it. Think about what makes you believe someone knows what they're doing. Think about where your confidence comes from. As we move through your training, we will test you to make sure you have progressed appropriately. If your confidence falters, you will not pass."

Phillip sighed. He had done many things he hated in his life, but considering himself was the worst one. It was like looking into a mirror, but the mirror could talk back. He didn't want to think about what he wanted in case he could never have it.

All he could think about was the rustle of the leaves in the trees, the brush of the breeze gliding through his hair, and the sharp scent of the pines. The sky was a drowning blue, dusk crowning the lingering clouds with a dark violet. A yawn cracked open his jaws.

"Perhaps I was hasty," said Eris, drawing his attention. She patted his shoulder. "You have had a trying time, and you likely need your rest before we truly begin to train."

"Thank you," Phillip said. "I think my mind will be clearer tomorrow."

Maybe he would wake up and this would all have been a dream.

Phillip was looking forward to the void of sleep. To closing his eyes and opening them to the bright morning, having slept away the exhaustion without being any the wiser to it. He hoped Briar Rose might have already uncovered a way to stop their shared dreaming. He wouldn't put it past her to make demands upon their shared nightmare. Once, she had shushed a rooster while she was trying to read. Worse, the rooster had quieted.

He opened one eye. A lush green tapestry rippled above him, the smoky evening sky peeking through the cracks in the leaves. The scent of damp earth washed over Phillip, and he stretched before standing. Cracking his bare toes against a mossy log, he looked around.

This dream was different.

The dream wood had changed. Gone were the never-ending trees and towering thorn wall. Instead, there were hedges twice his height that writhed with thorny vines, and he was in a thin gap between two of them.

Before him, the path veered left and right. Behind him, it turned right. A maze, one that went on for as far as he could see.

"Really?" he asked. "Now I have things to do in my dreams?"

A soft laugh drifted over one of the maze walls. "You don't *have* to do anything, you know. Sitting where you are and doing nothing is an option. You're good at that."

Phillip flinched. Usually when he was dreaming, there was no one around to judge his comments. It was one of the rare times he knew for sure he wasn't being listened to or observed, either by Johanna, his father and tutors, or Briar Rose. Now, he didn't even have privacy in his dreams.

"Not if you're here," he said, not bothering to hide his annoyance. "I take it you're in a maze, too?"

"I think so. I haven't had a chance to look around." Briar Rose yawned. "Yes, there are three paths before me. First we could talk, now we're in a maze. Something's changed. Has anything new happened to you?"

"I couldn't say that it has," said Phillip, studying his nails. From Briar Rose's question, he assumed she hadn't overheard what had been happening to him in the real world, and he wasn't about to offer it to her. He wasn't even sure what to think about his magic yet. He didn't need her opinions on it. "Has anything in your life changed?"

She exhaled softly but did not answer. Phillip crept toward the wall he could hear her through.

"Briar Rose!" he exclaimed in mock shock. "We are trapped in this mystery together, and you're withholding information?"

"I am not!" She sniffed.

He liked to imagine what she looked like when she talked. She did it so often that he had no other choice. She gestured endlessly in his mind—twirling her hands as she explained things she had learned to her goat or rabbits, tapping her finger against her lip as she thought about what to say next.

It was almost cute.

Save for the frustratingly mysterious circumstances that kept trapping them together.

"Nothing out of the ordinary is happening with me," she said slowly. "I just . . . had a disagreement with my aunts. It's nothing."

"I can't imagine why anyone would ever disagree with you, since you are always so pleasant to be around," said Phillip. Getting her to complain would keep her from realizing he wasn't being truthful about his circumstances.

He could practically *hear* her rolling her eyes. "I don't disagree with my aunts often."

"Because they always agree with you." Phillip cracked his neck and slowly walked toward the split path ahead of him. "They once let you take a break from studying for a whole week just because you asked."

It had been the week of Phillip's first tournament, and he had wanted nothing more than to sleep for longer than four hours uninterrupted.

"Do you think we can peek through the walls?" Briar Rose asked.

"No," he said quickly. The leaves and vines making up the walls of this new maze moved continuously, like snakes twisting in a nest. "Given the nature of the old thorn wall, I don't trust them."

"Still," she said. "Nothing to lose by trying."

Phillip hated that she was right. They were dreaming, so they couldn't actually get hurt, and they needed to figure out why this was happening to them sooner rather than later. If she hadn't mentioned it, he probably would have done it, but he disliked that she had suggested it first.

"Might lose a finger," Phillip muttered, but neared the wall.

He wiped his face and brushed the dirt from his clothes, but given the wildness of the day, he wasn't sure what he looked like, even in the dream. He didn't want to look horrible the first time Briar Rose saw him, though.

The hedges were all identical enough—taller than him, dense with leaves and vines, and seemingly alive. They reminded Phillip more of the thorn wall than of the old dream forest, and he tried to peek through the one between Briar Rose and him. The vines snapped shut.

All he got was a flash of pale gold, like a sunrise reflected in a rippling pool, on the other side.

"No, don't touch the walls," he said, and prodded one of the vines. It unfurled, thorns gnashing together, toward him. "I am not in the mood tonight, prickly."

"Are you talking to the wall?" Briar Rose asked in an amused drawl.

Phillip sniffed and brushed a hand through his hair. "It's a popular pastime where I'm from, I assure you."

She laughed in response, and he found himself smiling.

"So this is definitely a maze. Do you think we're in the same one, or in mirrored mazes?" she asked.

It was almost endearing how focused she was on fixing this. She couldn't let anything rest—not the mystery of this maze or who had stolen her custard tarts. He admired—though he'd never admit it—how tenaciously she went after what she needed. There was no goal too lofty for Briar Rose. He had never been like that.

He wished he were.

"If it's mirrored, then I should be able to turn left and abandon you," he said, walking down the leftward path.

"I wish!" she said. Phillip could hear the smile in her voice.

"A pity, then, I must deny your wish." Phillip smirked, pleased when he turned left and her voice continued to come from over the wall to his right despite that defying all reason. "Here's my major question: What's at the end?"

"What do you mean?"

"Labyrinths all have ends—centers or escapes—so what's at the end of this one?" he asked, peeking around the corner before him. There was only more hedge in both directions. "What's the prize?"

"I don't think it's a labyrinth," said Briar Rose slowly. "Labyrinths are unicursal. It would be difficult for us to be in the same labyrinth and not know it. That means there's only one path, by the way."

"Oh, so one path to the outside of the labyrinth we're in. Got it."

He knew she knew that he knew what a labyrinth was and what *unicursal* meant, and he didn't care for it one bit.

"Forgive me," she said. "I've caught you skipping so many lessons in my dreams that I can't remember which ones I overheard you attending."

That squashed Phillip's growing affection for her. He stomped down his path. He had been a good student, always listening and obeying and exhausting himself in the pursuit of perfection, until about thirteen. It was an unspoken agreement among the pages—neglecting their health to be better students—and tired eyes were as much a badge of honor as making it to squire. He'd been younger than everyone, and there he'd been competing to be the best. He had to be the best, unless he wanted to be the prince who couldn't cut it as a knight.

It didn't matter that he was younger and smaller. He was to be Princess Aurora's protector, so he had to train far longer than everyone else. His life had been nothing but "not quite there" and "could always learn a bit more." And he had tried, really tried, until his first tournament.

"I hope the end of this maze rids me of you forever."

"Don't be rude," she replied.

He ground his teeth together. "Then don't pretend you know me."

Phillip took off down the left-hand path. It should have led him away from her, far out of earshot and hopefully toward whatever was at the end of this. It would have been different if he could have spoken directly to Briar Rose before, but she had possibly heard so many of his worst moments, his vulnerable moments, and his moments that should have been only for *him*. It had all been one-sided, and he didn't fully know what all she had seen. His lessons had certainly figured into her dreams, given what she had said. Had she seen only the worst of him?

Phillip stopped and took a breath.

Had he seen only the worst of her?

"Briar Rose?" he called out. "Can you still hear me?"

"I know you walked away, but it still sounds like you're right next to me," she said, and he could hear her easily despite the thick thorn wall and her quiet tone. "I moved as far as I could from the wall I thought was separating us as well."

Of course she had ignored his outburst and was still trying to solve this.

"Architecture in dreams never makes sense normally, according to Johanna, so this isn't too much of a surprise," said Phillip. It was probably his fault they were in this mess, not that he would ever admit that. "This maze is going to be a problem. It's already exhausting to go to sleep expecting rest and—"

"Suddenly having to listen to the emotional turmoil being wrought upon a stranger who you can never help, even if you know exactly what they need?" She sighed. "I'm sorry. You're just off traveling, and that's all I want right now."

Phillip froze.

"You wanted to help me?" he asked quietly.

"Of course! You sounded so sad."

Well, he hated when she put it like that, but she didn't sound like she was lying. She sounded like she cared.

Briar Rose scoffed. "Look, Phillip, we're stuck here whether we like it or not. We should, as adults, be able to set aside our differences and pasts to work together."

Phillip had been trapped in enough overly pruned hedge mazes at various noble parties to know what a hedge maze looked like. And he'd eavesdropped on Briar Rose long enough to know where she was going with this. She was as competitive as he was.

"I bet I can get there first," said Phillip, leaning

as close to the wall as he dared. "I bet I get there long before you."

"What are we betting?" Briar Rose asked, and it sounded as if she was as near the wall as he was.

Phillip glanced around and said, "Whatever's at the end. There has to be something there. Otherwise, why make the maze and drop us in it? Whoever gets there first gets it for good."

"You think our dreams have been leading up to a competition?" From the sound of it, she had started walking. "That's a bit bleak."

"Is it?" he asked, and followed her lead. "You agree?"

"Of course!" she said, laughing. "And when I get there first, I'll have the decency to tell you what I won."

"You are the soul of generosity."

She laughed again, loud and full-throated and utterly unlike the titter her aunts had taught her to do.

"Don't lose too quickly," she said. "I like a challenge."

"Not more than me." Phillip grinned. If he couldn't succeed in his waking life, he would crush the problems of his dreaming world.

7
Strangers

*P*HILLIP BLINKED while turning a corner in the maze, and when he opened his eyes, he was awake again. The stain of dawn was seeping through the deep purple night through the crack in their tent. Phillip rolled over.

He was almost disappointed—the competition with Briar Rose was a little fun.

She had sprinted off the moment they agreed to the challenge. He'd followed her laughter through the maze, half expecting to stumble into her every time he turned a corner. Each whisper of her feet on the grass filled him with an unfamiliar anticipation. He had been enjoying himself in a way he did only on the road. Briar Rose had told him everything from the latest argument between two of her aunts over what color flowers to plant around the cottage. She mentioned her failed attempts at translating a poem she was certain Johanna would love in a language she was trying to learn. She insisted he absolutely had to tell Johanna about it, and she would be listening to make sure he did.

He told her about the towns he'd stopped in last month. And it was strangely nice to share the stories with someone who hadn't been there. Briar Rose listened and laughed, and for the first time Phillip felt truly heard.

Johanna was asleep in her bedroll across from him. The trials of yesterday had been erased from her face, not a single bruise or scratch left. Phillip flexed his hands, which, despite looking pristine, still hurt as if freshly scabbed. He hoped Johanna felt better.

"Phillip, so help me, stop thinking so loudly," Johanna mumbled. "Go back to sleep."

"How did you even know I was awake?" he whispered.

"You stopped snoring," she said.

He sat up. "I do not snore."

"Then how did I know you were awake?"

Phillip glared at her, and she pulled her blanket over her head.

"I'm going to read your new work," he said, not meaning it.

Johanna patted her chest pocket, checked on her book, and rolled onto her stomach. "Good luck."

Honestly, her secrecy was becoming suspicious. She was lucky he had other stuff to deal with.

"Sleep well," he said softly, and went to find the fairies.

Eris, Poena, and Phrike were standing in the center of the clearing, whispering to one another in sharp tones. Phrike caught sight of him and touched Eris's arm. The three of them quieted. Phillip waved.

"Morning," he said, uncomfortable with the sudden silence.

"Phillip! Come." Eris beckoned him over. "We were discussing what to do with you today. How are you feeling?"

"Better. Thank you," he said as he went to them, admittedly somewhat nervous. "What is the plan?"

"Oh, you're in for a treat!" Phrike clapped. "I can't wait to watch."

The sun was barely peeking over the horizon and cast long shadows across the grass like a rippling chessboard. Eris and Phrike stood before him, pawns staring up at a knight. Phrike, uncomfortably, possessed no shadow. Poena watched from a few steps away, arms crossed over her chest. Phillip avoided her gaze.

She was less frightening with the crease on her cheek from where she'd slept, but she was still terrifying.

"To retrieve the Sword of Truth and Shield of Virtue, you will need to have a solid understanding of what your magic can do and what type of magic best suits you. Obviously, we don't have long. However, we should have enough time to pinpoint what your strengths are," said Eris. "Each of us has specialized in a different magic. I deal mainly in nature magic, Poena in fire, and Phrike with shadow magic and some healing."

Phillip nodded along. Healing would be the most useful and the most hated by his father. Using a healer was like admitting defeat to King Hubert—you should prevent yourself from being injured, and if you absolutely couldn't, there was nothing a good walk or bout couldn't fix.

It was one of the king's least appealing beliefs.

"I want to learn how to heal," Phillip said, casting a sideways glance at Johanna, who had apparently changed her mind and had risen to watch them with interest.

Phrike wrinkled her nose. She looked like the fairies who had come for Princess Aurora that day—short, stout, and inscrutable. "Healing's one of the most difficult magics to learn, and it's rare anyone's got an affinity for it. I fear healing magic's a goal for the future, not one for now."

"There is little time to waste," said Eris. "We will have to make our play for the Sword of Truth soon. I would prefer to test your grasp of nature magic and hopefully fire magic before that."

Phillip nodded, but his mind drifted back to Briar Rose and the dream. After all, she could still be there, navigating the maze without him distracting her. It was terribly unfair.

Johanna came over to them slowly, clearly listening, and asked, "What happens if we can't get the sword and shield?"

"Phillip will retrieve them," said Poena, "or he will die."

"No, thank you," Phillip said, and turned to Eris. "I know they will help defend against Maleficent, but surely we don't have to get them before Princess Aurora's birthday? Why not take more time to train me to ensure everything goes right? We should wait until after the curse has come to pass or been foiled, when I have more knowledge of magic."

Eris opened her mouth, narrowed her eyes, and tilted her head to the side, and Phillip's unease worsened instantly.

"What?" he asked.

"What do you mean 'been foiled,' boy?" asked Poena, brown eyes wide with shock for the first time since Phillip had met her.

"The normal meaning?" Phillip looked between her and Eris, and both shared the same confused look. "The chance of the curse taking hold is slim."

"What?" Eris asked, expressions wrinkling across her face so quickly he couldn't track them. "What have you been training for if not what to do after the curse happens?"

"What to do once Maleficent returns and is furious her curse was negated," he said. It had been drilled into him for years. "That's part of why I'm marrying Princess Aurora. I'm to protect her. Forever. Till death do us part."

Eris gasped. "You think the curse will fail? That it won't happen if you keep that girl safe for long enough? That you can simply remove all spindles and spare her life?"

"That's why she was hidden away. Everyone knows that," said Johanna. "Don't they?"

"Can't avoid a curse," said Phrike, dismayed. "They're not just words. They're absolute. Deals, gifts, and curses—they're the same thing. Each is a promise, and we fairies always keep our promises. They always come to pass no matter what you do."

"And when this curse comes to pass," said Eris, "Maleficent will not stop with the princess."

A chill swept over Phillip. That changed things. That changed a lot of things. He had always been reassured that every measure possible was being taken to keep the curse at bay. The curse had always been something he *might* have to deal with, but knowing that it would happen no matter what any of them did, and that Maleficent wouldn't be satisfied with that . . .

"But if all curses come to pass, why didn't her fairy godmothers say anything?" he asked.

"Fauna, Flora, and Merryweather have always been fond of hope as a first line of defense," said Poena, spreading her arms wide. "And humans do get rather morose when they realize that some things happen regardless of who they are or what they do. Curses and gifts can be altered slightly if they are vague enough, so perhaps they hope to change the curse. Regardless, they most likely have a plan and haven't shared it with anyone."

Eris laughed. "Unusually generous of you."

"They are her guardians for a reason," Poena said. "Are you comfortable, then, Your Highness, assuming they've uncovered a way to stop a curse, something no one has ever managed in the history of magic?"

"I wouldn't describe any of my current feelings as 'comfortable,' no," he said, rubbing his face. "What will Maleficent do?"

Eris turned to Phillip, expression grim. "Maleficent may not have her old army, but if you believe she will only go after Princess Aurora, you're wrong. She has not set aside her dreams of conquering the human kingdoms."

"She wouldn't win that war," said Phillip with a shake of his head. "No, my father always said that this was her end goal. She wants to ruin King Stefan's life."

"Oh, she does desire that, but killing Princess Aurora is not her end goal," Eris said. "It's her opening move."

Phillip squeezed his eyes shut and covered his face. This would change everything. His father had expected a fight, but nothing of this magnitude.

"If she doesn't have an army like she did before, what does she hope to do?" Johanna asked.

Phillip uncovered his face and nodded.

"As much damage to the kingdoms that insulted her as possible," Poena said. "With attentions split between the cursed princess, her unfound true love, and Maleficent's attacks, Maleficent's loss is not guaranteed."

Phillip glanced at Eris. "What else do I need to know?"

"Now that we have clarified what is at stake here, all that's left is your training," said Eris. "Maleficent hates what the princess represents—her initial failure to conquer Ald Tor and the rest of the human kingdoms. She wants to strike at hearts first and foremost."

"Metaphorically and literally," mumbled Johanna.

Eris nodded. "Fairies cannot physically handle the sword and shield and can rarely handle them magically.

We are certain that Maleficent is researching how to acquire them herself but is restricted by her inability to leave the Forbidden Mountain for extended periods. And without them, you will stand no chance against her. Whoever acquires them first will win the coming war."

"You're putting all of our eggs in one basket," said Phillip. "And I'm the basket."

"We are not speaking of eggs and baskets, boy," said Poena. "You must take this seriously."

"It's a human saying." Eris pinched the bridge of her nose. "Though, to use the metaphor, you're *our* basket."

Phillip held back a laugh. "And Princess Aurora is the other fairies' basket?"

"Exactly," said Eris. "Better two baskets than one."

"You are getting as inscrutable as humans," Poena said, and scowled. "Have you met the princess since she went into hiding, Phillip?"

"No one's heard from her," said Phillip. "Not even her parents know where she is or how she's doing."

"Tragic." Eris clucked her tongue. "Let's get to work."

Eris led Phillip to a little clearing near camp. She looked like a dandelion on a field of green, standing in the grassy clearing with her sweeping gown rustling in the breeze. The spot she had chosen was far away from everything and everyone at their camp, and they stood across from each other, Eris studying him.

"We have a deal, after all," she said, grinning. "Now, do not expect immediate results today. It may even all feel fruitless, but I assure you it isn't."

That was encouraging.

Her brows pinched together, but Eris shook her head. "Did you think about what you want out of life? Do you trust yourself?"

"That's a bit personal to share," he said, and swallowed.

"Fair point," said Eris. "Do you trust yourself enough to attempt to use magic later today?"

Later? Time was supposedly of the essence, so he needed to use it soon whether he trusted himself or not. He nodded.

"Good," she said, and pinched his wrist between two fingers until he winced. "Usually, you would spend months studying the basics, but we'll have to make do. First, the conduit—you."

Slowly, Eris began to pose Phillip. She squared his feet with his shoulders and twisted his body until he was standing at a slight angle, the muscles along his ribs tense. His left arm she placed at his side, raised slightly so that his elbow was cocked out, and his right arm she lifted until his hand was even with his chest.

"Palm out, fingers up," she muttered, putting each digit into the right position. "There. It's not as good as a wand, but as a human, you could never use one. So don't get any ideas." She waggled a finger at him. "You must learn how to move your magic through and out of yourself first. Then you can learn to manipulate it."

"Great," said Phillip, feeling far less confident than he had when he'd been a scrawny ten-year-old in too-big cloth armor, trying to lift a lance as his father looked on. "How do I do that?"

"Tune out the petty distractions of humanity. Allow your mind to clear completely," said Eris. "You must feel your magic. Do nothing but focus on finding it within you."

"Clear my mind. Sure." Phillip cracked his neck and tried not to stiffen up. This would be easy. He excelled at doing nothing. "For how long?"

Despite being almost a head shorter, Eris managed to stare down her nose at him. "For as long as it takes."

Five minutes became thirty and then an hour and then two. A warm, needling sensation spread up Phillip's legs and crept down his arms. An ache came and went in his heels, the muscles of his neck twitched, and the straight, square stance Eris had molded him into began to waver. His raised arm drooped first, and she flicked his hand. Sweat beaded along his forehead, dripping into his eyes. He shuddered.

"I don't feel any closer to clearing my mind and feeling my magic," Phillip said. "How do I do it? What should I feel?"

He felt many things—sweaty, bored, worried—but none of them felt magical.

Eris, who had been before him the whole time and still acted as if only a few minutes had passed, sighed and tilted her head side to side. "I fear it's one of those things where you can only know it once you feel it. My teacher once called it a brush against the soul."

"Enlightening." Phillip frowned to try to get rid of an itch on his nose. "How does this help with learning nature magic?"

"It helps with control and making sure no errant vines strangle people," said Eris, and Phillip winced. "To use magic, you must call it forth from yourself and channel it into the world. Once it is in the world, then it can be used—to bring on gales, to summon fire in your hand, or to misdirect with an illusion—but it will fight your control. If magic thinks you are using it incorrectly or that you are not fully certain of what you want it to do, it will do as it pleases."

"Like strangle Johanna to get her away from me?" he asked.

"Exactly."

"You make magic sound like a person," Phillip said.

"Not a person . . ." Eris trailed off and reconsidered. "It's more like a wild horse. You must break it and bend it to your will. Conquer it. If you do not, it will throw you into the mud and trample your corpse."

"Conquer it?" Phillip frowned, thinking of Samson when he had first learned to ride. Phillip had spent every morning before training and every evening after it in the fields with the horse. Sometimes they practiced, but mostly Phillip doted on the only creature who didn't judge him when he made a mistake. Winning or losing a bout made no difference to Samson. Skittish and lanky even for a horse, Samson had nearly been overlooked when the horse masters were selecting coursers for the pages. Phillip had liked that; underdogs made the best heroes in all of the stories. And Samson had liked how often Phillip treated him to the celery he picked out of his own food.

The more carrots he'd smuggled the horse, the fewer times he got nipped during training. Fair tradeoff.

"Perhaps you need a more physical goal," Eris said, and raised her arms. "It is easy to know when you are succeeding with nature magic."

Every plant turned toward her as if she were the sun. Magic speckled her skin, glittered in the blades of the grass, and settled around them like a warm autumn wind. She twisted her fingers, and a flower tore itself from the ground. It grew and wrapped itself around her wrist, thorns sprouting from the side not against her skin. Her magic lingered around her like a mantle.

She looked powerful and sure of herself in a way Phillip wanted.

He had pretended to be certain of who he was for so long, but feeling that way, knowing himself, didn't seem so distant now.

"I believe you have an affinity for nature magic, given the plants and wind you used to attack the thief," Eris said, stroking the flower. "The wizard who stole and harbors the Sword of Truth favors it as well, and while fire magic would be more useful in countering her defenses, I think this will be easier for you to learn first. Poena and I rarely align on anything, and even we agree that you should attempt to retrieve the sword first before trying for the shield."

Phillip had heard stories about the Shield of Virtue—it was entombed with and protected by its creator, who lingered after death to ensure no one unworthy stole it. Facing off against a wizard did sound far less frightening than facing off against an immortal warrior.

"Do people only have one kind of magic?" he asked.

"No. Most simply cannot master more than one, so they pick," said Eris. "Maleficent, however, is an expert in many. That is what makes her so powerful. We are unsure if you will be able to learn multiple types of magic, but better to try with what you'll likely master and go from there than not try at all."

If Phillip had an affinity for nature magic, he wondered if he should tell Briar Rose. He could have unknowingly caused the thorn wall to transform in their dream.

Even though he usually hated the idea of revealing anything personal to her, and he was still furious as ever that his dreams weren't his alone, talking to her in the maze hadn't been so bad.

"Try calling one of the flowers near us to your hand,"

said Eris, forcing Phillip away from his thoughts. "Bend it to your will."

Phillip narrowed his eyes at the closest pale pink primrose. He imagined its stalk growing longer and longer, winding across the ground like a snake and slithering up his leg. It didn't so much as rustle.

"Phillip," she said softly, like Briar Rose to one of her broken-legged animals. "Do you want magic? Magic is about belief, and if you do not believe that you have it and that you can use it, it will not work."

"I just . . ." He sighed and let his head fall back. It was embarrassing to admit. "I don't see the point in me having it. All I will ever be allowed to use it for is to save *her*. It's not like I'll get to be a wizard. I'll be defending her until I die, probably at Maleficent's hands."

It hurt to say the words aloud, and he hadn't wanted to admit it to Eris, but she was the first to ask him what he wanted in years. Maybe she would understand his hesitance. Maybe she would have a solution.

She was a fairy, after all.

"Oh." Eris opened her mouth a few times but shook her head. She glanced away from him. "Your unhappiness at being involved was clear from the start, but that is a much more morose opinion than I expected. Would studying magic seriously be something you wanted?"

Princes and knights didn't use magic; they battled through life with money and swords, brandishing both until they got what they wanted. Phillip was supposed to be all of that and more, and his father was always watching for Phillip to follow in his footsteps.

"I'm a prince," he said, and laughed. "My future is set in stone."

Magic wouldn't make a difference if he had to use it how his father wanted.

"Stone is not immutable, especially not to those with magic." Eris eyed him curiously, tapping a finger against her chin. "Your father is who has pressed you into this role, yes?"

Phillip shrugged. "More or less."

History and circumstance played equal parts.

"Does your father have magic?" she asked.

Phillip shook his head.

"Are wizards not respected as they once were?" asked Eris. "What in the world makes you think that he or anyone else could tell you what to do with your magic once you learn how to use it?"

His father had always had one up on him since he had done it all first, but Phillip would be the only one with magic. With the court wizard gone, he would be his father's last resort for magical help.

"I have magic," he whispered, slowly realizing for the first time the importance of the words, "and my father doesn't."

Eris smirked and dropped her hand. "True."

"I could be that powerful?" he asked quietly.

"Well," said Eris, gesturing to the primroses and then fluttering her hand to her heart, "not if you don't listen to me."

For the first time in a very long time, Phillip didn't feel trapped.

"How?" he asked, eager. "Wizards use spells sometimes. Should I learn those?"

Eris made a face. "No, those are for specific circumstances, but saying what you want your magic to do aloud can't hurt. It will strengthen your resolve. Gesture and demand it."

Phillip took a deep breath and nodded.

"Come here," he whispered, reaching out to the primrose.

The flower next to it trembled, as if thinking it over, and then stretched toward his open palm. Its leaves curled around his fingers like the talons of a falcon, and the flower perched on his hand. Phillip brushed the petals with his thumb.

Close enough.

The bright pleasure of a job well done bubbled up in him, and he held back a grin. "Like that?"

"Excellent!" Eris applauded. "Now, try to summon something else."

Phillip set the primrose on the ground. Summoning a gust of wind was harder, the air always cold and biting. He found it far too difficult to summon fog and flinched at the little burst of lightning that came from his fingers once. The vines, though they had hurt Johanna, felt the friendliest to summon and manipulate. He could weave a shield of grass and wield dagger-sized thorns.

Talking to himself and reaching out to nothing was embarrassing, but the payoff was fun enough.

"It's still not doing exactly as I imagine," Phillip said, studying the buckler he had created from bark. "I wanted a shield."

Eris said, "Perhaps specifying will help? It will take time for your mind and magic to meld perfectly, but I believe in you."

"Thank you." He ducked to hide his blush. "It's just embarrassing to shout everything."

"You're saving the world. Why should you be embarrassed?" she asked, and then shrugged when he looked at her. "Johanna! Come here for a moment, please."

Johanna, who had been teaching a scowling Poena

to use a sword, walked over with the fairy trailing behind her.

"When he was training to be a knight, did Phillip ever avoid anything because he didn't want to be embarrassed?" asked Eris, ignoring his glare.

"Oh, always." Johanna nodded and didn't even glance at him. "A fencer from another kingdom taught for a few days once, and Phillip skipped the lessons. He hates being bad at things so much that he hates practicing."

Phillip swallowed uncomfortably. "Why should I want to do something I'm not good at?"

"You have to practice to get good at things," said Johanna with an exasperated sigh. "That's why I write all the time and we spar so often. The more we fail, the better we get."

"And let everyone who can see know I'm bad at it? No, thank you," said Phillip. "Either way, I can't shout complicated commands in a fight. People will know exactly how to counter me then, and it will take too long."

"Practice some commands and gestures today, and then tonight tell me the ones you think will work best. I'll help you develop a repertoire," Eris said, and smiled. "Think of it like how we wave our wands. It's not for show, you know."

Softly, Poena said, "Well done, and with over two weeks left to go."

"Thank you," said Eris with a smirk. "Now, Phillip— are you willing to embarrass yourself a few times to master your magic? You must be certain in your resolve, and I believe you can do it. You must know what you are willing to do, though."

For most of his life, Phillip had thought Maleficent's curse could be avoided. He had trained endlessly to protect the princess and help keep her safe once the curse failed, and he had trusted his father to know what needed to be done about Maleficent. He shouldn't have; his father was wrong. The curse couldn't be stopped.

In less than a month, Princess Aurora would be asleep and defenseless save for him, Maleficent would have started another war with the human kingdoms, and Phillip would be stuck keeping the sleeping princess safe.

Unless he mastered his magic. For the first time in his life, he had something his father couldn't hold over his head. No one could take magic away from him, and he could accomplish everything with it if he played his cards right. As a wizard, he wouldn't be bound to the future his father had decreed for him. He could be far more than the princess's steadfast defender.

"Anything," he said. "I'll do anything."

8
The Curse of Gallantry and Glibness

PHILLIP PRACTICED nature magic for the next five days. He slept little, never long enough to dream of Briar Rose or the maze. Eris seemed impressed by his advancement, but all he could do consistently was create swords from thorns and shields from grass, and ruffle Johanna's hair with wind. It had been thrilling the first few times, but the small instances of magic didn't feel like much after five days, when he knew he would probably have to fight Maleficent. Still, Poena had, begrudgingly, complimented his quick thinking to blow dust in her eyes with a gust while they were sparring.

So, at midnight on the fifth day when he finally got to collapse and sleep, Phillip didn't expect to wake up in the dream wood. Yet he opened his eyes and saw the hedge maze. The walls were taller and the thorns thicker, sharp points dripping with a sickly-looking yellow sap. He rolled to his feet, holding his breath to hear if Briar Rose was there, and a soft whispering drifted over the wall. She was talking to someone, but her voice was far clearer and closer than it usually was when he eavesdropped on her waking hours. Was she rehearsing for a conversation or confrontation?

"I feel you're being rather unfair about everything," she was saying, though it was stilted and over-rehearsed. "I'm no longer a child, and I should be allowed to visit town. I know you are my aunts and that you love me, and I love each of you, but I—"

Visit town? Phillip ambled over to the thorn wall as quietly as he could. Briar Rose spoke constantly to her animal friends about the places she had been, often in those places' languages. She might have lived in a cottage in the wood with her aunts, but he had always assumed that she was well educated and well traveled. He had pegged her as a lesser noble—wealthy enough for all of that, but not important enough for Phillip to have known her.

What had perfect Briar Rose done to get banned from going to town? Her aunts so rarely denied her.

"No, no. That won't work." Briar Rose sucked in a deep breath, held it, and whistled as she exhaled. "I need to come up with an advantage to me going into town, like learning how to socialize, but not that one, because

I've tried it. So. Many. Times." The thorn wall creaked. "You're less help than Ears."

"What help is a rabbit when deciding how to word something, and why practice when we both know you never stick to it?" Phillip asked. He laughed when she shrieked. "Also, don't use such passive terms. You're the one saying the words, so if they don't know you feel that way, that's their problem."

"How long have you been here?" asked Briar Rose, voice pinched in surprise.

"Oh, ages." Phillip grinned, glad she couldn't see him, and started walking down the maze's path. He had awoken where he left the dream last time, so at least their progress through the maze seemed to be kept no matter when they next dreamed. "Aunts. Town. Ears. Hey, what did you do that they're not letting you leave? You love traveling! Must have been bad."

"You don't have room to judge my rehearsal," she said stiffly. "I overheard that little play you were in when you were eleven. You forgot half of your lines."

Phillip scowled. He had been twelve and hated the yearly reenactments of past glories—like his father's defeat of Maleficent—and he hadn't forgotten his lines so much as swapped them out for funnier ones.

He clucked his tongue and asked, "What color are your eyes?"

"What? Why?"

"I'm trying to think of what your expression looks like when you say such mean things."

"I would rather you not think of me at all," Briar Rose said, but he heard her stop walking after a few steps. "Are you coming? There's no fun in reaching the end unless I beat you, and you have to actually try for it to count."

Phillip grinned. "Lead on!"

The maze felt smaller than the first time it had appeared. The walls were taller or thicker, pressing in from each side so that Phillip had to angle his body to make a few turns he wanted to take. He was dragging his toe through the grass every few strides and leaving markers for himself in case he ever needed to double back. Briar Rose, too, sounded as if she was leaving a path in the grass. She had probably done it in the first dream even though he hadn't remembered to.

Had she dreamed the last five days and gotten to navigate the maze without him? He wouldn't ask and be the first to break the silence, though.

"You know, I haven't heard much of your life recently. I used to dream of the wood and be forced to listen to you whine at least once a week," Briar Rose said.

"But it has been days and I haven't heard anything."

Phillip pantomimed punching the wall and mouthed, "Finally!" Asking would've meant he cared.

"Oh, sorry," he said. "Did you say something?"

Briar Rose sighed. "Never mind."

"I haven't dreamed of you either, so consider us even. It's been fantastic. I've been able to focus on my training," said Phillip, cracking his neck and hesitating at a two-way path. "Have you been able to investigate without me being here?"

"No, I was stuck in the same hall of the maze as before," she said. Her voice pitched up as she continued, and he could practically hear her leaning toward him. "Training? I thought you were taking a relaxing trip around the countryside with Johanna?"

Phillip wasn't quite sure what her tone—angry and sad and prying all at once but not fully any of them—meant, but he didn't care for it.

"I am. Johanna and I . . ." He swallowed. "Spar."

"Spar?"

"It's when two people fight each other but don't land heavy blows in order to practice—"

A mossy pebble fell onto his shoulder, and Phillip leapt back.

"Did you throw a rock at me?" He found the

pebble on the ground and rolled it around in his palm.

"Oh, did that work?" She hummed and started walking again. "I was curious if our physical positions were actually near each other or if it was some sort of dream magic."

"No you weren't," he said, loving it. She, good little Briar Rose who never did anything wrong, had thrown a rock at him. "We know it's magic because I keep taking lefts and you keep taking rights, and yet we're still right next to each other."

"What?" She drew out the word. "Are you suggesting I intentionally threw a rock at you for nonscientific purposes?"

"Yes!"

"Why would I ever do such a thing?" asked Briar Rose.

"Because I . . ." He pocketed the rock and shook his head. "I couldn't say. You're a monster, obviously. No motive required."

Briar Rose laughed so hard she snorted, and Phillip chuckled. Not that he let her hear, of course.

He had never heard her laugh so hard before, not with her aunts or any of her forest friends. He liked having been the one to make her laugh.

"You have terrible aim," he said.

"No one ever taught me to throw anything, and not all of us have been training since we were children," she drawled. "I can't believe you're willingly training more and not researching these dreams."

"You and me both," he said. "What sort of research is there to even do? Do you have books on dream mazes?"

"Oh, well, I mean . . . I'm not allowed to read about magic. My aunts don't care for it."

"So you don't know anything about magic," he said, "and you can't learn anything more."

"I snuck some of the books that my aunts have never let me read, but they're mostly recent histories. At least I'm trying, which is more than you can say," said Briar Rose. "Aren't you the least bit curious about the dreams and the wood and why they changed? Do you think it's magic? Well, some new magic affecting the dream magic, I suppose."

He thought back to his nature magic and his suspicions he could be responsible. He was curious, but he was also in the midst of the most stressful thing that had ever happened in his life. As she liked to remind him, Briar Rose had already listened in on his darkest moments— his nerves before his first tournament, the first and only time Samson had thrown him, his father's furious lecturing after Phillip objected to his intensive, training-filled future—and spoken of them to her real-life friends. Surely she didn't want to suffer through more of his life. At least he had some knowledge of magic he could share without revealing too much about himself.

"I don't think so. Everyone's magic has a different sense about it. The dream changed, but it doesn't feel like there's different magic." He started walking, taking the right-hand path, and heard her turn left toward him. It was nice to finally know something she didn't. The thorn wall might have grown into a maze, but it and the dream wood still felt the same as they had. "Some people's magic leaves the air cold and sharp like a winter snap, and others' smells like a freshly oiled sword and smoke."

Poena's fire magic reminded him of skirmishes and house fires.

"Is it always scent?" she asked.

"No, it can be any sense. I've seen shadow magic that makes everything taste of brimstone," he said, recalling Maleficent's appearance at Princess Aurora's christening. "But don't take my word for it."

"As if I have ever taken you at your word," Briar Rose said. There came a sound as if she was walking back and forth across a stone. It was too soft for her to be in boots, but Phillip usually wore his day clothes in the dreams. Did she go about barefoot every day? "I used to sit on this rock and listen to your life pass you by, and I know you well enough to know when you're keeping something from me."

The accusation, and truth of it, smothered the fun he had been having.

"I hate that you know me at all," he muttered. "Don't worry about what I'm not telling you. It's not bad. It's just personal."

"Oh, thank you ever so much for permission not to worry," said Briar Rose. "My eyes are violet, by the way, and I am rolling them."

"I would expect nothing less."

"You're not the only one with personal problems, you know," she said, twisting her hands together so frantically he could hear it. "How do I know this isn't your fault? That the wood and the wall didn't change because of you?"

The fact that they probably had made the words hurt all the more. Everything was always his fault no matter what he did. He hadn't gone looking for a fight or for magic. It had simply happened to him, but he still had to deal with the consequences. She didn't even know about the magic yet and still she *knew*.

"Your monologue made it very clear that you, too, have problems," said Phillip, and he refused to let her hear any concern in his voice. She didn't need to worry, because the dream world wasn't real. There were far larger concerns in the waking world. "You talk all the time, you know, and I always thought you were bragging. You never answered my question—why are you banned from going back to town? Or did you not answer because your practiced argument tonight was a lie to earn sympathy so I'll let you win?"

"That's very hypocritical of you. I asked last time if there were any changes in your life and you said there weren't."

"What a delightful way to avoid my question again," he said.

"You're avoiding mine!"

"So your aunts baby you. What a tragedy to be so loved." Phillip swallowed. So often as a child he had been jealous of the ways Briar Rose's aunts doted on her. She talked about how they brushed her hair every night and got her a new book whenever she mastered one of her lessons. It was as far from his childhood—full of training for a curse that he now knew was right around the corner—as possible. "I don't know why you're so desperate to prove your worth by solving why we have these dreams, but I don't want you to prove anything to me, because I don't care."

"Of course you don't," she said, and the enunciation could be caused only by a sneer. "You think everyone and everything is beneath you. You had one bad day at your first tournament and one bad fight with your father after, and then you gave up trying at everything completely!"

Phillip recoiled at the unwelcome reminder of that day. He *never* thought of it. He never spoke of it. He didn't even want the memories of it.

"You have no idea what you're talking about." The frustration that had been building in him for years took control of his mouth. "You and these dreams are the least important thing in my life because I'm dealing with *real* problems in the *real* world."

"You don't know me!" she shouted. "For some people, dreams are all they have!"

"Don't be—"

A vine shot out from the wall and grabbed his ankle, yanking him to the ground. Phillip landed hard and cracked his head. He groaned.

"Phillip?" Briar Rose asked. "Don't try to trick me. It won't work."

"I'm not trying anything," he said, and sat up.

"Wake up!"

"What?" asked Phillip. The words echoed in his aching head.

"What?" She tossed a small rock over the wall, and it landed a few strides from him. "Phillip, what's wrong? Are you all right?"

"Your worry is almost believable," he said, reaching for the vine.

"Wake up!" came the voice again.

The vine tightened around him and dragged him toward the wall. The thorns opened up, revealing a hole in the vines, and Phillip clawed at the grass. He tried to slow down, but the vine only tugged harder. It pulled him into the dark of the wall. The thorns snapped down on him.

9
Temper

PHILLIP JERKED awake with a scream, throwing his hands up before his face. Poena was at the foot of his bedroll, and she had one hand on his ankle. He glanced around.

The tent. He was in the tent at the camp with Johanna and the fairies. It was still dark, the moonlight hollowing out Poena's face. Her eyes glittered in the night like a cat's.

"Oh, good. You are awake," she said, and dropped his foot. "You seem to have been having a nightmare."

Phillip took a few breaths to slow his heart and nodded. He stumbled to his feet. His ankle was unhurt, with no thorns or marks from the vine. His heart was still racing, though, and he could still hear the echo of Briar Rose's frantic shout.

"If I wasn't awake, I am now," he finally said, refocusing on Poena. "What's wrong?"

"A number of things you could not even begin to comprehend," she said, and straightened to her full height, red hair tumbling around her shoulders like flames. She looked him up and down. "Eris has decided that your knowledge of nature magic is sufficient and it is time to move on to fire magic."

"Fire magic?" he asked excitedly, and rubbed the sleep from his eyes.

Poena arched a single brow and exhaled sharply through her nose. "The branch of magic that concerns the summoning, manipulation, and extinguishing of fire."

Phillip's cheeks warmed. His father had *nothing* on Poena.

"Get dressed and meet me outside," she said. "Unlike Eris, I refuse to coddle you."

Phillip dressed faster than he ever had before and rinsed his mouth with water, still reeling from how real his expulsion from the dream had felt. He was groggy and his mind felt fuzzy, as if he were watching the waking world through a veil of fog, and a feeling of guilt was beginning to build inside of him.

He and Briar Rose truly got the worst of each other, meeting only when tired and desperate for sleep. Not knowing how much the other had heard was a peculiar sort of nightmare. They knew everything about each other.

Except they didn't—he had never known her aunts to forbid her from doing anything, but she was now trapped at their cottage. Much of what he knew about her was built on assumptions.

And what if some of those were wrong? He flinched at the sudden remorse rushing through him. She had been so quick to try to help him despite their fight. He had to stop assuming the worst when she was consistently the best of the two of them. He hoped Briar Rose wouldn't worry too much over him after his sudden departure.

He blinked. This wasn't a dream. He needed to focus. He could deal with whatever feelings he was having about his behavior toward Briar Rose later.

"Fire magic is a branch of nature magic, but rarely does one person have an affinity for both," said Poena the moment he joined her. She had lit a fire at the center of camp. "However, even if you do not master it, you must be able to defend against it."

Poena gestured toward the low fire. Phillip's panic over Maleficent's encroaching curse had abated from a constant flutter in his chest to an occasional shock. When dawn broke, he would have only fourteen days left to master magic.

"What's Maleficent's specialty?" he asked, stoking the fire and trying to ignore his nerves.

Poena eyed him. "Maleficent's abilities are beyond definition or categorization."

Of course they were.

"Great," muttered Phillip. "So what do I do first?"

"We will begin with fire manipulation," Poena said. "Watch me."

The acrid scent of smoke clogged his throat despite the bright, clean fire, and the flames leapt from the wood to Poena's palms. They curled serpentlike around her fingers and passed over her clothes without scorching them. She held out the fire to him.

"Coax it to you." Poena wiggled her fingers. "Such vocalizations helped before."

Phillip reached for the fire. "Hello, handsome. Come here, please."

The fire didn't so much as flicker. He spent hours trying to move it and didn't manage a single spark. Poena lost her patience after a while, tired of showing him how it was done and of letting him take breaks to suck on his blistering fingertips when he exhaustedly listed toward the fire. She inhaled sharply when his sleeve smoldered, and he smacked his arm against the ground. Poena left him alone to ask Eris what to do, though she hadn't admitted to any such thing. Phillip went to get a drink as an excuse to eavesdrop.

". . . do with what we have, and we only have fourteen more days," Eris was saying. "You're going easy on him. He'll think the training is a farce."

Phillip crept a bit closer and tilted his ear into the wind.

"Of course I am going easy on him! What else am I supposed to do? Have him stand in it like I used to? Any fire I summon will burn him unless you're willing to protect him magically every hour of every day," Poena hissed. "You concocted this plan, so you figure out what to do."

Phillip's disappointment tasted like ash. Poena was going easy on him even though she had claimed she wouldn't. He knew he was a beginner, but he wanted to succeed on his own merits, not because she was pulling her punches. He had been looking forward to learning fire magic, too.

Eris sighed. "Fine. Give me a moment."

Poena huffed, Phillip darted back to his seat, and the two fairies returned to the fire together. Eris sat down next to him.

"Phillip," she said, but she looked at Poena. "Could you try to manipulate the fire one last time?"

Phillip nodded, not trusting himself to speak. He reached out and wiggled his fingers at the fire. A log cracked and sent up sparks, catching his sleeve on fire. Phillip hissed and shook it out.

"Fire would be exceptionally useful against Barnaby." Eris grabbed his wrist and studied the burn mark on his clothes. "Old Barnaby is the wizard who stole the Sword of Truth from your father. She's a grouch of a person these days but a rather obsessive gardener. She specializes in nature magic, specifically plants and animation."

"Old Barnaby?" The name scratched at Phillip's brain. It brought up memories of brown eyes, blue robes with silver moons, and the scent of fresh flowers. "Oh! Barny!"

She had introduced herself as Barny when he was a kid, and the nickname had stuck.

Johanna emerged from the tent with a yawn. "Barny? What happened to her?"

Barny and Phillip's father had disagreed on so many things to do with the curse and he had been so busy training that he'd rarely interacted with her. He shouldn't have been surprised Johanna knew more about her than he did. She probably spent as much time in the library as wizards.

Temper

Sitting about a step from Phillip, Johanna watched the fire flicker and sighed before taking out her book. She balanced her inkpot on one knee and her book on the other. He caught sight of *Untold Stories from* on the first page, next to a dozen crossed-out lines.

"I thought she retired to some seaside cottage with her wife?" Johanna asked.

Phillip nodded. "She did, but I think it was a light-house."

"She didn't. It was a cover story," said Eris quickly. "She absconded with the sword after a disagreement with Phillip's father."

"How am I supposed to get the sword from her?" Phillip asked. He hadn't realized Barny would be the wizard he would have to steal from. "She's one of the best wizards this side of the world."

"Steal it, I would assume." Eris gestured for Phillip to return his attention to the fire. "Unfortunately, it appears that you don't have an affinity for fire magic at all. This means we must focus on teaching you to defend against fire magic and how to stop nature magic without it."

"Of course," said Phillip, trying to hide his disappointment. "How am I going to *steal* the sword from Barnaby, then?"

Eris shook her head. "I must admit that I am not entirely sure. Barnaby's home is well guarded against magical and mundane observation. I will go observe Barnaby and her wife, Zohra, for the next few days, and then we will know what to do."

"You're leaving?" Phillip's heart dropped to his feet. "Now?"

"You have yet to learn how to defend against fire magic, which requires Poena to teach and Phrike to heal you when she gets overzealous," Eris said. "I'm unnecessary."

Phillip nodded, a hollow ache in his chest, but he couldn't place the feeling. Eris was the only one who had acknowledged that Phillip was doing this for himself, and she was the one who never balked when he didn't grasp something immediately. She had taught him how to cheat at darts using wind magic the night before, and that would be utterly useless in the fight against Maleficent. She'd only done it because she knew he liked games. Without her, it would all be about the princess again.

"You have made amazing progress," said Eris, flexing her fingers, "but we need the sword and shield so that you will be able to stand against Maleficent."

"While you're gone, I will have my shadow scout the tomb of Amis," said Phrike.

"Excellent," Eris said. Her form shrank, and she drifted into the sky along the wind. "I'll return soon. If you know what's good for you, you'll be able to defend yourself against fire magic by then."

Poena did not let Phillip sleep the next day. They worked through the day and then the night, his exhaustion shifting to a trembling, frantic energy around dawn. She was determined to teach him how to rebuff fire magic if it killed him.

Or she just wanted to kill him. It was a toss-up.

She had started with motes of flame no bigger than her palm and lobbed them to him like normal people tossed apples. Instinct had driven Phillip to catch a few even after burning himself the first time. Next came whips of gold fire, hotter than the motes, that seared Phillip's skin even when they didn't hit, and she taught him how to predict the flicker of the fire to avoid it. Though the first hour had left his skin charred and pink like a half-cooked supper, he could dodge by the end of it.

But he could have learned to do that by her throwing any number of undeadly things at him.

During training Phillip thought of the last time he saw Briar Rose—her teasing as they struggled to find their way out of the maze, her confidence that they would solve it, and her terrible aim that Poena definitely didn't share. Thinking about her and their fight filled him with a bittersweet feeling he didn't recognize. His failures at fire magic didn't help; he wouldn't be able to solve the dream maze that way. Keeping his new magic from Briar Rose was holding them both back.

Johanna helped occasionally, though she mostly sat with Phrike and discussed what they already knew about Barnaby. The old wizard loved her garden; lived in a tower by the sea with her wife, who had no magical powers to speak of; and once, possibly, maybe, had used a thief for fertilizer after catching them breaking into her home.

But Johanna didn't understand him. She knew him well, but not as well as Briar Rose. Until recently, he hadn't wanted to talk to Briar Rose, but Poena was so merciless and his magic so fickle that his dream world and Briar Rose were the only constants he had left. She might have been prickly and overly talkative, but at least he knew to expect that from her. He didn't really want to talk to Briar Rose about his training and the upheaval of his life, but he likely needed to if he wanted to solve the mystery of the maze.

When Phillip awoke in the hedge maze after his second day of learning fire magic, he rose on unsteady feet and squinted at the wall. One of the vines waved at him and tried to snatch his ankle. Phillip kicked it aside, then wandered a ways down the path to get away from the part of the hedge that had attacked him last dream. His and Briar Rose's fight had been poorly done and unfair. To both of them.

"Briar Rose?" he called out.

She didn't answer. Phillip groaned and picked the right-hand path of the maze. Maybe she had been so furious with him and so pleased with his disappearance that she had solved the maze without him, and now he was stuck and she was alone in the silence he had always wanted.

No, she had once helped an injured owl no matter how often it pecked at her. If not too kind, she was too prideful to abandon him.

Phillip winced and kicked a stone out of the path. He hoped her pride wasn't the only reason she would talk to him. Best not to think about how poorly that conversation had gone and focus on the maze. The markers he had left were still there, but it was a dream, so he wasn't sure how much they even mattered.

He focused on listening for Briar Rose. A familiar voice echoed down the right path. She was singing, something he'd heard often enough, though it was clearer here in the maze. When he'd heard her sing in her waking life, the dream muffled and distorted her voice, but even then, her singing had been beautiful. He sighed, lying down in the middle of the maze once he was close enough. The song, something about birds and roses, was almost certainly her own creation, and as tired as he was, it was nice.

He had been horribly unfair, hadn't he, accusing her of lying as he lied to her several times over?

"You have a lovely voice," he said.

Briar Rose quieted and approached the wall separating them. "Phillip? Are you all right? What happened to you?"

"I got woken up in the real world last time we were here." He crossed his arms behind his head. "It reacted badly with the maze. One of the vines dragged me into the hedges, but when I woke up, it was just someone touching my ankle. Very fun and not scary at all. Anyway, we need to talk."

"Do we?" Briar Rose asked. There was a muttering, like she was talking to herself, and then she quieted.

He groaned. "Are you really not going to talk to me?"

As annoyed as he had been, he didn't want to go back to their old way of dreaming. He liked talking to her.

"I just think we don't . . ." She huffed and trailed off, like he had caught her talking to him when it was against the rules.

"Don't have an outlet for our anger in real life and have been taking it out on each other?" he asked.

She exhaled loudly through her nose.

"Yeah, I feel terrible but don't want to apologize either, so let's skip the deflecting," he said, and grinned when she laughed. "Here's the truth—I think I know what caused the dreams to change."

She made a strangled sound, and he groaned.

"Say it," said Phillip.

"I knew it was your fault!" Her clothes rustled against the grass. She must have sat down. "Nothing ever happens in my life, so it had to be you. I can't believe you're telling me the truth."

He laughed. "I haven't slept much, so blame it on that."

"Why haven't you slept? Are you all right?"

Even with them angry at each other, she was worried for him. Her concern made him pause, and Phillip sighed.

"I'm fine. It's related to what I need to tell you," he said, running a hand over his face. "I have magic."

"What?"

"Yeah, that was my initial response, too," said Phillip. "I've spent the last week learning magic."

She hummed. "Is that the important, real-life thing you mentioned?"

"Oh, well . . . there's probably going to be a war soon, so I have to do some things." Phillip winced. "If I don't learn enough magic, I might die."

"'Magic.' 'Some things.' 'Might die,'" said Briar Rose. "Are you sure that's not your dream world?"

"Well, you're not there, which is certainly a dream come true," he said. This wasn't as bad as he thought telling her would be. "I've been training, and it's exhausting. My point is that our dreams changed the night after my magic made itself known."

"Made itself known?" she asked. "Did it introduce itself to you?"

"By strangling Johanna," he said. Phillip explained what had happened with Johanna, meeting the three fairies, and some of his training. He didn't tell her about Maleficent but said that he would probably need to fight someone dangerous once he retrieved the armaments.

If he could.

"People have always depended on me," he said. "Thinking about failing, though, still breaks my heart each time."

"Hmm . . ." She took a deep breath, and he could picture her sitting in the grass, chin on her knees and nose scrunched in concentration. "I didn't know you had a heart."

The sound he made was entirely too embarrassing, and she burst into laughter.

"No one learns anything perfectly in less than a month. I think you're being a touch hard on yourself," she said. "What does this even mean for you? You're already a knight."

Right—she had no idea he was a prince and bound by even more responsibilities, like protecting a princess from an evil fairy.

"It means I have more to do, but also might have less to do in the future," said Phillip. "But it's more complicated than that. I'm a prince, and if I fail my training, my kingdom is doomed. That feels like a big enough reason for our odd dreams to change."

The thorns of the wall started to writhe more furiously when he spoke.

"I couldn't hear the second half of what you said over the vines," she said. "I'm sorry you're in danger, but magic is exciting, at least."

"I said that I'm a prince. You're speaking with His Highness, Prince Phillip of Artwyne."

The maze wall twisted and creaked, drowning out his words completely, and Briar Rose quieted.

"I just tried to tell you something about myself," he said, and this time the wall must have allowed it, because Briar Rose hummed in response.

"Curious," she said. "I guess it still doesn't want us to know certain things about each other."

"Clearly. More important, and something we can talk about: magic. I've got it," he said. He hadn't gotten a chance to brag yet. "I'm not bad at it, either."

"So you're actually trying to master it?" she asked. "You, who never wants to try at anything?"

Phillip scowled. "Oh, shut up about that. Like you've done everything ever asked of you."

She didn't say anything, and he threw one arm over his eyes.

"All right, so you do everything asked of you. The rest of us can't be perfect." He could feel her eyes rolling. Changing the subject, he asked, "Nothing happened with the thorns once I was dragged out of the last dream, right? You were fine?"

"I was. Thank you," she said. "My aunts did keep asking why I was so concerned, and I finally told them an injured bird got away before I could catch it and help."

"Ah, I'm your little injured bird now. I have never been so insulted in the entirety of my life, and I travel with a self-proclaimed poet." Phillip peeked up at the sky, remembering their last conversation. "What did happen? Why weren't you allowed to go to town?"

Best they dealt with it all now. Briar Rose hesitated, and then quietly said, "Nothing new really happened. Contrary to what you believe, I didn't do anything. My aunts just won't let me go to town. They smile and nod and tell me to trust them every time I bring up leaving. It's in my best interest, they keep repeating with no explanation. It's lonely even though they're here with me."

"Oh, an adult-who-knows-better-than-you situation. I know that one well," Phillip said. "Doubly lonely for someone as obsessed with travel and stories as you."

It was odd, feeling bad for her. He hadn't picked up on her loneliness when listening to her life, and that seemed like an oversight on his part. Listening to her now, it was obvious how alone she felt. They were both surrounded by people who thought they knew what was best for them and dismissed them at every turn.

"It makes me feel like a child," Briar Rose said, voice rough. She cleared her throat. "Don't say anything. I don't want you pitying me."

"Oh, that's the last emotion I feel for you." Phillip sat up and stretched, trying to sound as nonchalant as possible.

There was silence, save for the thorn wall, and Briar Rose sniffed. Phillip could picture her squaring her shoulders and wiping her face. She had always been strong and focused, but a person couldn't be like that all the time. It would wear them down to nothing.

"Briar Rose?" he asked softly enough to not shock her and loud enough to be heard. "Do you want to commiserate, or do you want a distraction?"

In the past, he wouldn't have asked—not that they had been able to talk to each other before—but it felt different these days. Their shared dreams had always been intimate, and they had grown more so since the maze appeared, despite their bickering and fighting. It was easier to connect the Briar Rose of his childhood dreams to a real person now. She wasn't a dream; she was right there and she was hurting. Despite their fighting and history, they were all the other had.

She inhaled and said, "A distraction, please."

"Zero pity and one distraction it is, then," he said. "Let this ruminate in your mind: I, Phillip the Feckless, have to rob a wizard soon."

"Oh, I would love to meet a wizard!" Briar Rose cleared her throat. "A real one, you know. Not you."

They were back to normal, then.

He muffled his laughter with a hand. "I'll make a deal with you—I will tell you all about my very fun, wonderful magical adventures once I beat you to the end of the maze."

At least these stakes didn't involve death.

"You're on, little bird," she said, and took off running. "Try not to get kidnapped by a plant this time."

No, they weren't back to normal. Their relationship had shifted, twisted by happenstance and the nature of these dreams until they weren't quite friends but were no longer enemies. They were something new and growing, as changing as the dream wood that had introduced them.

And that didn't bother Phillip as much as it might have once.

The noonday sun hung hot and bright overhead. Phillip wiped the sweat from his face, the stench of ash and oil clinging to him. Poena stood across the clearing, and her flames clung to her like a cloak. They left shivers in the air, burning away any vines he threw at her and withstanding any gusts he tried to knock them aside with.

"Come now, Your Highness. I know we are both ready to rest," she said. "We can if you defeat me."

But he couldn't touch her. It was now day six of fire training. Phillip had been working with Poena nonstop the past three days, to the point where he hadn't dreamed of Briar Rose once, and he was further from victory than ever. Poena was a terrible fighter, fumbling all manner of weapons and falling to pieces the moment a fist or blade went her way, but getting close to her was impossible. On his first try, he had punched her and gotten scalded so badly it had scarred, and the second day, he hadn't even been able to get near her without his hair catching on fire. She used flames like shields, defending and harming in equal measure. The air around her constantly shimmered with repressed, threatening heat.

Fire flourished with wind and plants, and he couldn't

control enough dirt to bury her. Every time he tried to sink her, she attacked him until he was too busy to focus. He had to smother the flames.

"Rain," he said softly so that Poena couldn't hear, and waved toward the sky. He had summoned storms before, but none strong enough to put out anything greater than a campfire.

A storm cloud gathered overhead. Poena glanced up, the flames swirling in her hands flickering. Sleet poured over her, hissing when it touched her skin, and she shook it out of her eyes. A veil of steam separated them, and Phillip took a step back. It wasn't what he wanted, but it was fine. No one could light a fire with damp tinder. He used the steam for cover.

"Hiding won't beat Maleficent," Johanna called out from her perch near the tents. She was watching, because of course she was, and she wasn't impressed. "Each time you get burned, I'm writing a poem about it and sending a copy to every town we've been through."

Phillip twisted to glare at her, and said, "You wouldn't dare!"

Phrike applauded as though it were all simply a stage play.

"Do not dare look away from me!" Poena's shout startled Phillip, and he spun toward her.

The snout of a great dragon, scales made of fire and eyes white-hot, emerged from the steam. It was made from the flames wreathing Poena and rested over her like a giant mask. A tongue flicked out between wavering teeth. Smoke poured from its mouth.

Phillip stumbled back, skin blistering. "More!"

The storm cloud followed Poena, but the sleet sizzled away before even landing on her.

"More?" she said, hand clutching at her chest. Fire covered her hands in the shape of claws. "I am not a candle or some silly little campfire. The flames and the power come from inside of me. You will never be able to stop them."

Phillip frantically summoned a sword of thorns. The air around her was so hot it rippled like water. She grabbed the sword, and it crumbled to ash. Phillip stumbled, chest tightening and throat aching. The dragon opened its mouth wide. He threw himself in the other direction and landed hard on his back, unable to speak or breathe or move.

Poena glided toward him, her wings unfurling flames. She lifted one foot from the smoking grass and pressed it into his chest. The dragon's tongue licked his cheek. Phillip screamed.

"Pitiful," she said, red curls alight. "All those years

of training to be a knight, and you can't even touch me without whining. You're a disappointment."

He gagged on the burning air. Smoke curled out of her sneering lips like serpents.

There was no point. All of it, his knighthood and magic training, was useless. He couldn't do anything to the flames without feeding them, and she had the upper hand so long as her fire raged. Attacking her would be like punching a flaming log to put out a fire. It was impossible.

But he didn't punch campfires to put them out. He smothered them.

He needed to smother her, not her fire.

Hope surged through him. Smother, smother, smother. How could he snuff her and her fire out? He couldn't drop a cup over her, could he? What did snuffing a candle even do?

"Air!" he choked out. Phillip reached for her throat. He couldn't touch it, but his magic had to know what he meant. He clenched his fingers as if he were strangling her. "Air."

A cold burst of wind swept over him. Phillip sucked in a deep breath, the black at the corner of his sight receding. Poena grasped at her throat, struggling to breathe, and her wreath of fire vanished in a puff of cinders. She collapsed. Phillip rolled to his knees.

"Do you surrender?" he asked.

Poena, pale skin turning blue, nodded.

"I can't wait to hear this poem of yours," said Phillip to Johanna as he stood.

"Neither can I!" came a familiar voice from behind him. "Well done!"

Phillip turned. Eris stood there, clapping quietly, and she came to stand next to him. Slowly, the air flowed back into the space around Poena. She coughed and crawled to her feet, muttering beneath her breath. Eris grinned at Phillip.

"Wonderful job," she said. "I think you're ready to rob a wizard."

10
The Tower and the Knight

*A*FTER A QUICK breakfast and even quicker planning the next day, they all huddled in around Phrike and let her yank her shadow over them. They were standing in the clearing one moment and staggering in an odd wood the next, Phrike shaking out her shadow like a traveling cloak. The fairy magic shivered off them like water from a duck.

The plan to steal the Sword of Truth from Old Barnaby was simple: Phrike and Poena would lure the wizard out of her home, and Phillip and Johanna would sneak in to retrieve the sword while Eris kept watch.

There was a town near the tower that paid the elderly wizard for protection. Extortion, Eris called it, and they were going to use that to their advantage. Phrike and Poena would fake an emergency in the town, drawing Barnaby to it, and with any luck they would be able to keep her there for an hour at least. The wizard's wife, Zohra, would be easy enough to avoid once Phillip and

Johanna were in the tower. The only remaining question was how they would get into it.

"What's our next step again?" Phillip asked the moment Phrike and Poena left in a puff of shadow magic. He wished he could have asked Briar Rose for her opinion on their plan. She had read a number of books and surely knew something useful about wizards or robberies.

Eris snorted and herded him toward Old Barnaby's tower. "Get in, steal the sword, get out."

"Is that the short or long version?" he asked, and swallowed as they left the forest and stepped into the shadow of a tall tower silhouetted against the pale orange sunrise.

"That rather depends on how quickly you find the sword and get out alive," said Eris.

Johanna pulled out the little journal from her chest pocket and jotted something down. Phillip glared at her. She shrugged.

"Don't you have other things to worry about than me and my writing?" she asked, and blew on the wet ink before putting the book back. "We don't have many days left. This has to go perfectly."

This was their only chance to retrieve the Sword of Truth. If they made a mistake, Old Barnaby would never let it out of her sight again.

"Don't remind me," muttered Phillip. "If we manage to do this, will I finally get to read what you're working on?"

"You can read it when you're dead," Johanna said.

"So tonight, then?" he mumbled, and she scowled.

Phillip turned his attention to the tower. It was a spindly building of russet stone that listed over the edge of a cliff above the sea, and so impossibly tall that it had to be held up by magic. A dark blue flag with a gold star crowned the top of it, and a large garden shaped like a half-moon encircled the grounds. Thick vines full of pale purple flowers grew around the spires of a wrought-iron fence, silver spikes glittering in the morning light. Tall hedges and lush trees kept the gardens hidden from prying eyes.

"White yarrow," Eris said, and nudged a fluffy bunch of flowers growing around the bottom of the fence. Smoke curled up from where the plant had touched her. "The old girl's thorough. I'll give her that. I definitely will not be able to join you, but you should have no issues with the house or the wife."

Phillip had known there were plants that kept fairies away—the gardens of Artwyne overflowed with yarrow, clover, and betony—but he had always thought them little more than an old tale, and something that only worked on evil.

"So disappointing Zohra stayed with her after she robbed your father," Johanna whispered to Phillip. "I heard her gardening was as good as her poetry."

"You should know better than to trust a poet," he said. "I never do."

She glared at him sidelong, and Eris sighed.

"Children, focus." Eris touched her wand to Phillip's chest. The sharp burst of winter air that heralded her magic swirled around them. A brooch, shaped like a cat rearing on white-tipped paws, appeared on his tunic, and the yellow gems of its eyes began to glow. "Should anything happen, this will allow me to find you."

"Thank you," he said, tapping its nose. He wanted to ask how it worked, but he knew there wasn't time. "This is it, then?"

"This is it," said Eris. "It should be a good old-fashioned robbery."

Johanna frowned at Phillip. "I'm not familiar with that sort of fashion."

She had never so much as stayed out a minute past curfew as a page and wasn't happy at all to be stealing the sword. Phillip had never been so glad that *wizard* would be hard to find a rhyme for.

"Your sartorial choices are fine," said Phillip. "And you are sure that there's no way we can ask Barnaby for the sword?"

The memories he had of her when she'd worked for his father were few and hazy, but he vaguely remembered her being aggressively serious during court and enchanting her tomes to flap back to her quarters like clunky birds the moment court was over. He didn't remember her being evil.

"She stole the sword from your father knowing that it was all he had to help against Maleficent," Eris said. "Stick to the plan."

"Good point."

"Phillip," said Eris, taking him by each shoulder. She glanced at Johanna, and the girl looked away. "You can do this. I believe in you."

"Oh." Phillip swallowed. "All right."

He felt light and full all at once, as if his chest would burst and cave in on itself.

A few moments later, a small shade unfurled from the forest floor and flattened itself against the uneven fence.

"Barnaby's here!" came Phrike's voice from the shade. She could use her shadows to talk to people across long distances, though they couldn't reply to her. "She teleported! Go! Go! Go!"

The shade slipped away, and Eris dropped her arms. "Well, you heard her," said Eris. "Go."

"I think we should slip around and climb up the tower," said Johanna. "If the cliff is the defense for that side, it might be our best bet for getting in undetected."

"Please do not climb up the cliffside. That's far too dangerous. You can fight magical guards. You cannot fight gravity and win," Eris said, and with a final piercing stare, she vanished like a fog in a breeze.

"Let's go for the garden first and decide once we know what we're up against," Phillip said, and touched the yarrow as Eris had. It was soft and fresh, and the vines twining through the hedges on the other side of the fence didn't move. An odd comfort, considering the snuffling of prowling animals they could hear from over the hedges. He laced his hands to boost Johanna over the fence. "You first."

The broken blackberries speckling the hedge left dark smears against their clothes. Phillip climbed over, whistling when he glimpsed just how tall the tower was. Lush gardens full of roses rustled in the sea breeze, and honeybees fluttered from chamomile to forget-me-nots. A creek flowed from a fountain in the south to the northern cliff, small spiraling rivulets branching off it into the garden. Guard animals, everything from weasels to lions, paced the garden paths.

"Are those . . . ?" Johanna glanced at him.

A large prowling dog made of thick, curling grape-vines and two bunches of grapes that looked like floppy ears sniffed at the air. There was nothing to its nose save for a leaf that might have looked nose-like at a different angle. It yawned, baring a mouthful of thorns.

"Yes," said Phillip. "They are."

Nearly every creature in the garden was made up of plants. A lion with daisies for fur sat by the creek, and a cat of rosemary batted at its tail. On the other side of the garden, a dog of dandelions barked at a completely normal squirrel. It chattered down at the dog from its perch in a plum tree.

"We should've planned better," Johanna grumbled.

Phillip shook his head. "Only eight days until the curse, and I was always better at improvising, anyway."

"Well, at least we know they're as divertible as normal animals," Johanna said. She watched the nearest dog with narrowed eyes. "Did you ever figure out how to summon fire?"

Even if he had, burning the plant animals felt wrong. They were so lifelike, and it wasn't their fault he needed to get past them.

"Not even a spark. We'll have to sneak around them and cross the creek. That will take us away from the lion, cat, and little dog." He nodded to the creature barking up a tree. "The other ones may scent us, if they can smell, but that's the path of least threat."

Johanna sighed. "This feels so underhanded."

"Look." Phillip sat down next to her. "I know this quest isn't as noble as in your books, but real life isn't like the stories. Barnaby stole the sword from my father and ran. We have to do this."

"I know that," Johanna snapped. "And stop mocking my stories. True love is real. Magic is real. How can you not be hopeful knowing that?"

"Easy for you to say," he mumbled.

"I wish I were in a cursed sleep right now," Johanna said, and elbowed him. "How are we going to do this?"

Phillip glanced over the hedge they were hiding behind and followed the grapevine dog. It ignored the other vine creatures, pawing at the dirt as it passed. Phillip took a deep breath, and all he could smell was the heady aroma of flowers blooming far out of season and cool, damp earth. An idea sprouted in the back of his mind, and Phillip sat down, his back to the hedge. The familiar bite of his magic filled the air, making his breath visible. Vines and grass began to coalesce around his fist.

"Johanna," he said slowly, "would you like to be the front of a horse or the back?"

She opened her mouth and shook her head. "You are not suggesting what I think you are."

"Oh, I am. I doubt they're smart enough to notice the difference between Barnaby's magic and mine," he said. "I would bet they're looking for anything that isn't a plant or Old Barnaby and her wife."

He directed Johanna's attention to the squirrel at the far side of the garden, and she squeezed her eyes shut.

"Fine," she said, "but I'm the front."

"Fair enough." Carefully, Phillip reached a hand out to direct the plants to take the shape he wanted. "Let's make a very pretty horse."

He couldn't create them out of nothing like Eris did with the leaves, but the garden provided plenty of plants for his use. Johanna stood and Phillip slumped behind her, one hand firmly gripping her tunic. The grass overtook them in a wave, covering them in the form of a horse, like a costume. They took a few hesitant steps.

It took a few minutes, but eventually they moved like a horse. It was difficult to keep all the plants covering them. He reached up and touched the vines of the horse's neck.

"Bloom," he whispered, and the vines burst into a bright peony mane. He nudged Johanna from the back.

"You have to lead. I'm watching our legs to make sure they don't get too human."

"Why can't you make us each a horse?" Johanna grumbled.

"I would rather not divide my magic between two constructs," said Phillip. "Besides, if anyone should be complaining, it's me."

Johanna took a loud, deep breath and started walking again. Their feet crunched down the mossy stone path with the odd cadence of a horse's four-beat gait. The wind rippled across them, and Phillip gestured again to make the horse toss the vines of its tail. The hairs on the back of his neck stood on end.

"Lion on the left," she muttered. "It's looking at us."

Phillip felt more than heard the rumble of its yawn and shuddered. "Unless it moves toward us, keep going."

They took a few more slow steps, passing over a small plot of flowers and an irrigation creek. The plants around them shook, and Phillip tightened his grip on them with a quick gesture. Johanna hesitated, and he touched her shoulder.

"We're passing a badger," she whispered.

From his hunched position, Phillip could spot the animal's thorny claws pawing at the dirt and a snout of pale purple thrift flowers snuffling at the horse's hooves. The badger scurried to its burrow.

"Good," said Phillip. They made it to the creek, minnows flickering beneath the water, and the gait of the horse slowed. He swallowed. "Steady."

"We're close to the front door, but it's got a lock on it," said Johanna. "There's two big windows flanking it with only shutters, though."

"Pick one and head for it."

Their path shifted left, and Johanna stiffened.

"The dog!" Johanna's muffled voice cracked. "The dog is coming toward us."

Phillip flattened his hand against her back and pushed her on. "Only stop if it attacks. The others let us pass. Keep going."

The legs of the horse Phillip had built moved jerkily, and he felt his fingers digging so deeply into his palm they broke the skin. The dandelion dog sniffed around them and padded across the stone. The flowers of its fur opened and closed in the corner of Phillip's sight. The horse tossed its head back.

Phillip hadn't told it to do that, but it made the dog scramble away with a *woof* of displeasure.

He felt Johanna relax and patted her back. "See? Keep going."

Eventually, the ground beneath their feet reddened and changed until they were walking on a path of stones instead of grass. The cool, calm breeze that always fluttered around Phillip when he was using magic faded. Sweat dripped down his neck, and the grapevine around his arm wilted. The rest of the plants began to die and dry out, dragging them both to a stop. Phillip tried to gather his magic again, but nothing happened. The plants he'd woven around them kept withering. He glanced down.

The eyes of the cat brooch had gone dark.

"Phillip?" Johanna asked, panic rising in her voice.

"Johanna," he said. "Get ready."

They were within running distance of the shuttered windows. The unmistakable roar of a lion rang in Phillip's ears.

Fear gripped him by the throat. "Go!"

They sprinted out of the dead plants. The lion's paws pounded, causing the earth to tremble as they ran. Johanna reached the tower first and leapt for the window shutters. She ripped them open, slamming them into the stones, and shimmied up to climb through. Phillip chanced a look back.

The lion was only strides away, and the others were a few steps behind it.

Phillip strained for the window opening. Johanna

was balanced there, grasping for his hands, and he grabbed her. She helped haul him up. The lion's claws tore through the bottoms of his trouser legs. Phillip fell through the window with Johanna.

The lion, despite its size and power, didn't leap through the window after them. A hawk of heather clawed at the window as if glass covered the opening. Phillip pressed his cheek to the cool stone floor.

"I don't know what happened," he said. "My magic stopped working."

Johanna kicked his foot. "Terrible timing."

"We're in. What more do you want from me?" He pushed himself to his feet and shook his head.

The entry hall to the tower was crammed with all sorts of interesting things—suits of rune-inscribed armor, tapestries of dragons and battlefields, books bound in everything from large oak leaves to what looked like the scales of a serpent. A little shelf near the front door held three pairs of shoes, and there was an empty place where a fourth would go. In the center of the hall, a circular staircase led up and down. Phillip nodded downward. "Let's start below."

Phillip expected some sort of trap, but nothing stopped them as they made their way down the stairs. The stone walls were cold and dry. Phillip fiddled with the brooch at his collar, tapping the dark eyes, and Johanna touched his arm.

"Barnaby must have set up a way to prevent the use of magic in her home," she said. "Eris couldn't come in here, so she couldn't know."

"It's fine. I'm only worried about what we should do if we need her." Phillip let his hands fall. "Let's see what we've got."

At the bottom of the stairs, wreathed by the flickering light of three candles, was a large stone door made up of small tiles. Each tile was painted with a letter from the alphabet. They were horribly jumbled and clearly able to move. At the top of the door was an inscription.

"I transcend with my feet on the earth. My soul is delible and indelible in equal measure, though my measure is not always equal. My body may crumble to dust, but I shall never be truly dead, for I shall always live on lips and fingertips," Johanna read, and looked at Phillip. "It's a riddle."

"You don't say."

She slapped his arm.

"What's the answer?" he asked.

Riddles were not Phillip's strong suit, though they were popular at court. It wasn't that he didn't like riddles; it was that he didn't like not knowing the answer from the start. Surprises were the worst.

Johanna shrugged and said, "I'm not sure. Hold on."
They each read it again.

"It has to be something to do with measure, though I've no idea what," said Phillip. This was exactly Briar Rose's sort of thing, and he wished he could ask her. "But what's delible and indelible? That's impossible."

". . . *live on lips* . . . oh!" Johanna let out a breathless little gasp and touched her heart. "That's so sweet."

"What?" Phillip asked. Whatever Johanna had discovered was lost on him.

"Her body may crumble to dust, but she will live on as words. Her measure is not always equal. Her metrical feet will remain on the earth while she transcends," she said, smiling at him as if that were the answer. "It's poet. The answer is poet."

Phillip groaned. Of course—Old Barnaby's wife, Zohra.

"That's fairly romantic." Phillip reached out and pushed the letters needed into place, and the door creaked open with a rattling groan. Phillip stepped back and grinned. Briar Rose would have loved that answer.

Lights flared to life in the room once the door was all the way open, and Phillip blinked. The vault was not a vault, and nothing was in the small room save for a tall statue holding aloft a double-edged longsword. The sword gleamed, untarnished and untouched by the thin layer of dust that covered everything else in the room, and the candlelight caught the blade in odd, twisting patterns. Power like lightning charged the air and left behind the taste of storms. Phillip took a hesitant step toward the statue.

Nothing happened.

He continued forward and stared up at the statue's hands. They were clenched around the sword as if they had been carved around it, locking it in place. Johanna paced behind him.

"No puzzle. No spell. What do we do?" She tapped her chin with a finger. "Perhaps there's another riddle."

There wasn't. There was no indication as to how to remove the sword, leaving Johanna speechless. Phillip tried to pull it free from the statue's hands despite knowing it was hopeless, and Johanna knocked on the floor and walls for trick panels or doors. Phillip even retreated to the riddle on the door and rearranged the letters into relevant words—*sword, truth, please, open, unhand*—to see if that worked. None of it did, and the sword stayed firmly grasped.

"It's the Sword of Truth," said Johanna. "Why did we think this would be easy?"

"That's not true. I thought this would be . . ." Phillip stared at the statue, his thoughts sputtering to a stop. "Truth."

Truth—it was one of the most important ideals, and they were making a mockery of it by trying to steal the sword.

Phillip stood before the statue and stared up at its inscrutable face.

"Hello," he said, and waved at it. "This is awkward, I know, but could I please have the Sword of Truth? I need it to defeat Maleficent."

It had been made to defeat fairies, though different ones from far longer ago, and it was the Sword of Truth. Surely it appreciated honesty.

A terrible grinding noise rattled through the room. Dust puffed out around the statue as its fingers furled and arms lowered. Phillip covered his nose and took a step back. The statue held out the sword to him in two open hands.

"I didn't know that would happen." Phillip took the sword, nearly gasping at the perfect balance and weight of it. "Thank you?"

Slowly, the statue shifted into a relaxed position, thick stone arms at its sides, and it looked as if it had never moved at all once the dust settled. Phillip stared down at the sword.

It had worked! He had worked it out! Phillip, without his training as a knight or prince or even in magic, really, had gotten the Sword of Truth. Joy tinged with triumph felt light and fluttery. The whole of him felt as if he'd float away, even with the heavy sword in hand.

"You're not very convenient, you know. No sheath." He gripped the sword tight in one hand and turned to the door. "Pretty, though, so I'll forgive you."

There came a ringing so low and quiet he would've missed it had he not spent so much time recently around magic. It shook his teeth and echoed between his ears. The sword, it seemed, didn't appreciate being called inconvenient.

"I can't believe that worked," Johanna said with a laugh. "I suppose thieves don't normally ask for permission."

"And we're exceptional thieves." Phillip elbowed her. "Come on. Let's get out of here."

They made their way up the stairs, but when they reached the top, Johanna froze. Phillip, a few steps behind, peered around her.

An older woman stood before the door leading to the gardens, her arms crossed. She was a whole two heads shorter than Phillip, crowned by a cloud of glossy black curls shot through with white, and shaking her head like the two of them were wayward children. Her visage struck some chord in the back of Phillip's mind, summoning up a memory of this woman dancing with another, whose face was obscured by a wide-brimmed, star-speckled blue hat. Barnaby's wife, Zohra, stared down her nose at him.

"You march down there right now and put that back," Zohra said, "if you know what's good for you."

It was a bold statement for a poet to make, doubly bold for someone to make when they were outnumbered by opponents if not by age. Zohra looked stern enough, but there were black ink stains on her fingers and no weapons to back up her threat. Phillip was fairly certain her hairpin wasn't even a real pin but a delicate glass quill.

"Never have known what 'good for me' is," said Phillip, adjusting his grip on the Sword of Truth.

Johanna hissed, "I am not fighting an elderly person."

"Fight her? Of course we're not fighting her. We'd kill her!" To Zohra, he said, "It would be better for all of us if you let us go through that door."

"Absolutely not," the old woman said. "I'll count to three."

"Please don't do—"

"One."

Johanna groaned.

"Two."

"All right," Phillip said to Johanna. "Here's my plan: let's just run past her."

"Three."

Zohra slapped the wall of the tower, the brick under her fist sinking into the wall with a flicker of magic. A loud *crack* shook the tower, and one of the armor sets on display stepped off its pedestal. Metal ground against metal, and the sound shivered through Phillip's teeth. Johanna took an unsteady step back. He nudged her aside.

Another set of armor leapt down from its display, and it ripped an old ax from the wall. Phillip could see no way around them.

Of course the wizard who had written a magical riddle in honor of her beloved wife hadn't left her defenseless.

"Up the stairs," he said, and shoved Johanna toward them. "Run!"

They took off sprinting. Phillip looked back only once, catching sight of the largest suit of armor carrying Zohra into what he could only assume was a safe room. All around him, suits of armor stepped from their platforms in the alcoves of the stairs and shook the dust from their joints. They moved with hollow footsteps, magic filling their empty forms, and a few drew swords from sheaths. Phillip reached the next landing first, Johanna at his heels. A small suit of padded armor took a swing at Phillip.

He ducked, stumbling into the wall. Johanna passed him and grabbed his shirt. She tugged him up the stairs.

"I've always been terrified of poets," he muttered. "But I think I have an idea."

Behind them, a set of scale armor climbed the stairs two at a time, and four sets of plate armor clanged after it. One carried an ax, and another had ripped a monstrous pike from the wall. Phillip lunged at the scale armor and rammed it with his shoulder. It teetered, top-heavy without a person inside of it. The scale armor fell, collapsing against the pike-toting armor behind it. They both slammed into the three other suits of armor.

"See?" he shouted. "Improvise!"

Johanna gulped down air as they sprinted. "I hate you!"

The stairs opened up around every bend, revealing living quarters and laboratories and libraries. Floor after floor they climbed, and on each floor, more objects joined the chase. A taxidermied fox nipped at Phillip's heels, and a kettle in a knitted cozy of orange, white, and pink spat tepid barley tea at Johanna. Phillip kicked the fox away, and at the next landing, an ermine-lined robe took its place. He swatted away the robe's sleeves.

"How many floors are there?" Johanna asked.

"Just keep going!" He leapt over a bearskin rug and dove past the tenth landing. "Find any landing with nothing on it!"

Johanna groaned. Their predators were a cacophony behind them, increasing in number and gaining on them with each step. Phillip gasped, chest tight, as they neared the top. The uppermost landing was a small circular room with a glass roof glittering with magic, two telescopes, and cushions on the floor. The door blocking it from the stairs was a flimsy wooden one, but Johanna shut it anyway. She jammed the long hairpin trying to stab her into the crack between the door and wall to keep it shut. The hairpin struggled but held.

"You owe us a rescue, Eris," Phillip said, tapping his fingers against the dark-eyed cat brooch.

Johanna prodded one of the telescopes with her toe. "We'll have to climb down the side of the tower."

"They could attack us from above. We'll be vulnerable if we're clinging to the side of the wall," he said.

The door behind them shook, wood splintering. Phillip moved to the opposite side of the room. There was a small balcony overlooking the cliff, and far, far,

far below them, the sea crashed against the rocks. Phillip rubbed his eyes with his shirt. The cat brooch glowed in the corner of his sight.

"What's wrong with you?" he asked it.

Behind him in the tower, the door shook so hard he winced. He darted back inside, wanting to grab Johanna, and the brooch's eyes flickered out.

He took one step onto the balcony. The brooch's eyes glowed.

"Vines," he muttered, and held his hand out. A few stories below them, a vine unfurled from its spot growing up the tower and reached for him. More began to move around it. "Good. A net works."

The plan in his mind was half-formed and deadly, and the only comfort was that if it failed, he wouldn't have to live with knowing he'd gotten them both killed.

"Johanna, come here," he yelled.

A gauntlet broke through the door, and Johanna scrambled away from it, backing up into him. A full suit of plate armor painted in the reds and whites of a long-gone noble house pulled the ax back and swung again, nearly cleaving the door in two. A dozen other enchanted objects dove for the gap, a handful wriggling. Johanna batted aside a small stuffed bunny with the flat of her sword.

"I have an idea," said Phillip, "but you have to trust me."

The suit of armor tossed aside its ax and gripped the two sides of the shattered door, prying them apart. The fingers of the gauntlets flexed, magic crackling between them like stitches.

"I trust you. I trust you," she said. "What are we doing?"

"We're jumping," he said.

"Never mind." Johanna kicked a chair away from them. "They have to go down if they're beheaded, right?"

"No, they don't."

The tower shook as the suit of armor took each step, a half dozen more suits behind it. All of them carried weapons as sharp as the day they had been forged. Phillip glanced down at the brooch—still a flickering yellow. He dragged Johanna to the edge of the balcony and wrapped an arm around her waist. His other hand gripped the Sword of Truth.

He hoped Briar Rose wasn't listening to this.

Johanna nodded. "Do it."

Phillip threw them backward off the balcony. Johanna shrieked, fingers digging into his arm. He held tighter, the wind rushing up behind him, and imagined the plants of the garden growing out along the cliff and weaving through the air like a web. Power thickened around them, cold and sharp. Phillip twisted to look.

The vines were covering the gap below, but through the holes he could see the waves of the sea eating away at the cliff and leaving behind jagged rocks poking up through the fog like teeth. He needed more vines, and he needed more *time*. They were falling too fast. He squeezed his eyes shut and held the sword as far from Johanna as he could. The chill of his magic stole his breath.

And everything went dark.

I I

So Familiar a Gleam

" . . . ONCE WAS a boy named Phillip, who dove and forgot to backflip. He landed on vines and—well, what rhymes with *vines* that we haven't used? Oh! *Times.* He landed on vines one or two times, and no one has heard from him since."

Briar Rose's lilting voice stabbed at Phillip's aching head. He groaned, awareness and pain washing over him. Even the quiet sounds of the thorn maze—the creak of vines and rustle of leaves—hurt. He tried to turn over and gave up.

"Did I land on them?" he asked, words scratching through his throat. "Feels like I missed."

She sucked in a whistling breath. "Oh, pity. I thought you might be dead."

Trying to determine just how sarcastic she was being made Phillip's head spin.

"Death can't hurt this much," he said, and forced open his eyes.

So Familiar a Gleam

The hedges towering on either side of him shifted, vines grinding the leaves to dust as if the wood and the thorns were at war. He rolled his head up and then touched his chin to his chest. That worked, so maybe he wasn't dead. He lifted his legs up and rolled his torso forward again. Slowly, he rocked into a sitting position and rested his elbows on his legs. His hands were so bruised it looked as if he were wearing gloves.

"Why did my injuries carry over to the dream?"

Usually, the dreams were a reprieve from the physical pains of the day—after all, Briar Rose hadn't figured out how to punch him yet—but the rules had changed. He flexed his fingers and hissed. From the other side of the maze, Briar Rose made a sound like she was about to speak.

"How much did you hear?" he asked.

Phillip couldn't remember what happened after the fall, and trying to recall anything only brought flashes of light and pain to mind.

"Enough," she said, and he could hear her swaying back and forth, clothes brushing against the grass. "I cannot believe you robbed such a nice woman. She gave you a chance to leave! I'm not entirely sure of the details. Johanna and you were very close-lipped during your heist, and the guards chasing you were horrendously loud, but I overheard your fairy tutors when they got you. You jumped out of a tower, Phillip! How did you even survive that?"

"Magic," said Phillip. He froze and nearly choked. "Is Johanna all right? Is she safe? Briar Rose, you—"

He expected her to draw it out or tease him more, but she quickly said, "She's fine, I think. Unconsciousness doesn't really count as sleeping, apparently, because I still heard bits and pieces of Johanna talking about what happened in the real world before you joined me here."

Phillip sighed. "Thank you."

"I'm not a monster," she said, and scoffed. "I wouldn't not tell you. I actually like Johanna."

"Yeah, and if she asked you something, you'd answer," said Phillip. "Me? Not so much."

Briar Rose laughed. He slowly stood, pleased she hadn't reverted to the titter she used with her aunts. Maybe he wasn't alone in pretending to be someone he wasn't in real life.

"Well, we can put to rest the question of whether we'll ever dream of the other's life again now that the maze is here," she said.

He stretched his arms. "What's the first thing you heard?"

"The riddle. It was very romantic, from the sound of it, just like in all those stories with knights and quests." She laughed again, and even though it was at his expense, he didn't mind. It *was* funny now that he knew no one had died. "I thought you were some sort of knight. Doesn't thievery go against chivalry?"

"I'm some sort, certainly," said Phillip. "You know that training I mentioned and the magic? This wizard stole a sword from the king ages ago, and I had to get it back."

She hummed. "Oh, that puts the riddle and guards in a new light."

"They weren't even guards. They were magical suits of armor with weapons worse than anything I can swing. What do you even know about knights?" he asked, knowing very well that she had spent an entire year being taught hierarchy and all the relevant details required for courtly etiquette.

"Having met you? Less."

With that, Phillip forced himself to walk down the path before him. The maze was as inscrutable as it had ever been, hedges thick with leaves and writhing vines covered in thorns. The deep gouge in the dirt he had made with his toe and left as a marker during the last dream was still there, but since he always stayed next to Briar Rose, he wasn't sure if either of them was making any progress. He didn't feel up to taking part in their competition tonight, though.

"There once was a boy named Phillip . . ." Briar Rose began again.

Phillip groaned. "Please no. I can't believe you're so bad at rhyming," he muttered loudly enough for her to hear. "You're worse than Johanna."

It wasn't much of an insult, because Johanna was quite good, even if she hadn't let him see her newer work all year.

She sniffed and stomped down her path. "My first five poems were better, but you weren't here, because . . . oh, what was it you were doing again? Stealing? No, *improvising!*"

She clapped twice, and he rolled his eyes.

"I can't believe you thought jumping from a tower was the best escape plan," she said.

"Did you forget it was a wizard's tower?"

"What do you mean?" she asked.

He could practically hear her heart stopping at the thought of being wrong. Worse, he was the one calling her out.

"The tower was bewitched, a fact even the fairies

missed, and my magic failed once we were nearly to the door." He whistled, pretending to think it over. "I got to do this fun bit with a horse and a lion."

"You saw a lion?" She sniffed, a wholly unfamiliar tone to her question. "A real lion?"

"Oh, no. The one I saw was made of flowers."

Briar Rose inhaled. Loudly. He could imagine her curious stare from the other side of the maze, and it made him want to continue. She sounded genuinely interested, and he wasn't sure why that pleased him so.

"I will tell you all about it later and describe it in as much detail as you want," he said, "but I really need to be in the waking world right now."

"Wait!" Briar Rose let out a little sound like she'd gotten too close to the wall. "I found this book I need to talk to you about."

Phillip sighed. "A book?"

"Yes," she said. "It's by a wizard. *Awakening the Dream Within*—have you heard of it?"

"You know I haven't." He was exhausted, hurting, and not in the mood for her pointed questions. "What about it?"

"It talks about magical dreams! Most of it's nonsense, but there's this chapter about how magic sometimes provides dreams as escapes to fairies and other magical individuals. It's the first time I've come across anything about dreams in a book!"

"Does it mention if sleeping here would wake me up in the real world?" Phillip asked.

"It might," said Briar Rose, oblivious to his annoyance. "I can check, but I'm mostly hoping this will point me in the direction of another book with more information. You started having the dreams before me. Do you remember ever having normal dreams?"

"No, but I hear they're far easier to wake up from," Phillip said, sighing.

"It's so curious the way this wizard talks about magic. There are a few wizards mentioned in the history books, but none of it is from the wizard's perspective. They're supposed to be all-powerful and smart. I mean, you would have to be to memorize all of those spells. . . ." Briar Rose's voice trailed off, but it was still too loud for him to block out entirely. "This one talks about magic like it thinks and makes decisions, and . . ."

Phillip pinched the bridge of his nose, a headache forming just behind his eyes.

". . . never studied magic before, but it must be exceptionally difficult. I'm surprised you're taking to it. How did it work when you found out?"

Phillip could barely think past the pounding in his

head. "Briar Rose, I'm sorry, but I need to wake up. I can't deal with this right now."

He heard her exhale sharply. "I thought you'd be at least interested in figuring out why for our entire lives we have dreamed of each other in a strange wood," she said, an edge creeping into her tone. "I know what you're doing is important, but—"

"It's me, so how important could it be?" he snapped, interrupting her. "I know what you think of me, but I'm not gallivanting through some forest doing as I please. If I fail to learn magic—no, not just learn it. If I fail to *master* magic, people will die."

She stomped around like a child not getting their way. "I wasn't saying it wasn't important. I'm just trying to figure out why we dream of each other and why we're in this maze."

"And then what?" he asked. "As optimistic as we were, let's be honest—there's no prize for us at the end of this. We don't get anything for figuring out why we dream of each other."

"I was only asking questions!"

The hedge responded to her, the thorns growing longer and thicker. They blotted out what little sky there was.

"Oh, please!" He pressed a knuckle against his eye

to try to ease his headache. "As if your questions are innocent. You think I can't do anything."

"Because you never do!" She scoffed and paced and smacked a vine away so hard that the hedge shook. "Would you rather I say nothing? You would, wouldn't you?"

"You could say nothing," Phillip spat, "and still your presence would smother me."

Her tone was sharper than the thorns between them. "Only you would think people being interested in your life is like pressing a pillow over your face. You said practically the same thing to your father after the tournament before you threw your life away. You're so scared to love anyone and disappoint them like you do your father that you don't even love yourself, no matter how self-centered you pretend to be. It's cowardice."

Fury flared in Phillip, hot and painful, more consuming than any other emotion he had ever felt. He covered his cry with a hand.

"I'm not one of your stories. I'm a person," he said so quietly he wasn't sure she could hear. He felt small, like a bug pinned in a shadow box. His anger was so still it unnerved him. Not a fire but smoke. "So what if I give up? So what if I don't try to live up to your impossible, naive standards? No matter what happened to me, it was never going to be good enough for my father, and I'm not going to be talked down to by some girl who is prattling on about dreams when important things are happening."

The final words were the only ones he shouted, and he grimaced.

"Of course I'm talking about it," she shrieked. "The dreams are the only interesting thing to ever happen to me!"

Phillip hesitated, furious mind barely catching what she had said. That couldn't be true. She told those animals story after story about traveling and adventure, and she'd had dozens of tutors growing up.

"You have no idea what it's like," she said. "These dreams are all I have."

The weight of it—of her idyllic life being compared to his, of her dismissing his concerns in favor of the dream, and of his panic over his escape from Barnaby's tower—crashed into his chest, and Phillip turned on his heel and took off down the path that led away from the wall they shared. "I'm sorry."

And whatever response she shouted was lost in the cackle-like creaks of the thorny vines.

Phillip awoke with a start. He didn't remember falling asleep in the dream maze or being dragged away by a vine. He had been racing through the paths, growling at dead ends, and avoiding Briar Rose. Based on the sound of her equally angry outbursts, no matter what path they took, they remained right next to each other, separated by only a single wall. He hated it.

He hated every part of it—the maze, her words, how angry he had gotten.

"There now," muttered Eris, patting his shoulder. "You're safe. You're well. Johanna is fine, too."

"What?" He stared at her before remembering that his fight with Briar Rose was a dream she didn't know about. "Oh, right. Sorry. I had a nightmare."

"Who wouldn't after a fall like that?" Eris said.

He was swaddled in what felt like every blanket he and Johanna had. The tent flap was open, a clear evening sky twinkling down at him. Eris sat on one of her leafy stools next to him, a damp cloth in her hands, and Johanna's bedroll was gone. Eris spotted him looking around for it and gestured outside. The camp looked the same, but they were in a different location. A northern wind nipped at him even through the blankets.

"We relocated while you rested to ensure we couldn't be found and decided that moving north, nearer to the shield, was the best plan," she said. "Phrike is with Johanna, and Poena is ensuring that Barnaby and Zohra did not follow us. How do you feel?"

"Like I jumped off a tall tower and caught myself with a bunch of plants." Phillip groaned and sat up. "How do I look?"

"Worse than you feel, I hope. Phrike has healed most of your injuries, though it will take time for the pain to ease." She slowly helped him into a proper sitting position, pressed the mouth of a waterskin to his lips, and helped him drink his fill. "What possessed you to do that?"

"I didn't know how else to get us out with the sword, and I wasn't going to let all of those enchanted objects kill Johanna," he said. He still had the full range of motion in his arms, but the muscles felt far too tight. He flexed his fingers and noticed that delicate little designs that matched the hilt of the Sword of Truth were now embossed in his hand as if painted in midnight blue and crimson red. "My magic stopped working once we got near the tower. I only noticed that I might be able to use it again on that balcony because of that brooch."

"And you trusted your magic to catch you," she said, staring at him with wide blue eyes. "Drink this."

She handed him a small bottle that smelled of honey and tasted of the bitterest, meanest flowers, and he gagged it down.

"That is a level of faith in magic I didn't anticipate you reaching so quickly. Or ever," said Eris.

Phillip's remaining fury at Briar Rose sharpened his tone. "You're the one who told me to have faith. You told me that magic was about belief and said I was doing well."

"Stop assuming I mean the worst," Eris said, and checked the bandages on his hands. "What if the brooch had been wrong?"

Guilt prickled over him, hot and shameful. He had assumed she simply doubted his tactics, not that she was worried for Johanna and him.

Phillip shook his head. "You made it."

Eris stilled. She drew in a shallow breath and gently took his injured hand in hers.

"Thank you for trusting me so deeply," she said slowly, "but please take better care of yourself. I am loath to say it, but I have enjoyed teaching you, and your death would be a blow."

"You're the only person who's ever said that who I know means it," said Phillip. "Everyone else wants me safe and sound for Princess Aurora's sake, not mine. I know you're training me so that I can defeat Maleficent, but you haven't made it all about her."

"Well, let me temper it by begging you not to die until you learn illusion magic and get the shield," Eris said with a soft chuckle. "I doubt the princess wants to be a widow so quickly."

"I wouldn't know," he said, and it sounded bitter even to him. "I'm tired of hating her all the time. Now, you and the others glided in with your magic and plans, and for the first time I don't feel like I'm drowning or being tugged along on a fishing line."

Eris leaned in close and tipped his chin up so that he couldn't avoid her gaze. "Phillip, you cannot live your life hating things simply because others think you should do them. Curses and gifts all come to pass whether we want them to or not. The curse will come, but you are in control of your reactions and the nuances of your life. Refusing everything you've been offered is a bit like cutting off your nose because someone you dislike said it was nice-looking."

She flicked his nose, and Phillip snorted, pulling away. The comment felt too much like a reprimand from his father.

"That makes me feel like a piece on a chessboard." Phillip wiped his face.

He didn't want to be controlled at all, though what she described wasn't really control. It was like setting a course through a wood. How he got to the other side was up to him, but he would get there. There was no turning back.

"We are all pieces on a board. Some of us are more aware of it than others and know how to play our parts," she said. "Your education, knighthood, and betrothal were all decided by someone else. They do not have to be. You can learn to play the part you want."

"The part I want?" The deep, aching dread eased a bit. "Like marrying someone else?"

"What?" Eris startled. "What do you mean? Have you met someone?"

He hesitated. The flash of golden hair through the maze and the image of violet eyes crossed his mind, and he winced at the memory of Briar Rose's furious last words.

"No," he said a little too quickly. "But that doesn't mean I don't want to love and be loved."

Eris let out a soft, breathless sound. "You've known about your betrothal since you were a child. You always knew you would not marry for love, so why should you love anyone else, much less yourself?"

That sounded far too much like what Briar Rose had said. *Yelled*.

Was he so transparent?

"I don't love the Phillip I'm supposed to be," he said, "nor do I like the person those expectations have created."

He hated the argument he'd had with Briar Rose. He shouldn't have lashed out at her when he knew it wasn't her fault. His frustrations and worries with the waking world were no excuse for him to yell at her, and he had to make it up to her. She had only been trying to help.

He was still angry and sad and desperate for something else, and he didn't want to be the sort of person who accomplished nothing and yelled at girls in mazes who might have been exasperating but weren't at fault.

And on top of all of that, he couldn't help thinking about how similar Briar Rose and he were. They were victims of circumstances outside of their control. He might have liked Briar Rose if they had met in real life. He didn't want to be so quick to anger, and that was up to him.

"I messed up," he mumbled to himself.

Eris's brows pinched. "With what?"

"It's a secret," said Phillip, looking away. He hadn't wanted his father's advice since he was a child, but he wanted Eris's. She would know what to do, or at least be honest with him. "A while ago, I met someone."

Eris's eyebrows drew into a single thin line.

"Not like that," he said, flushing. "We're not even friends. We mostly vent to each other and try to outdo the other at whatever we're doing, but we got into a fight last time we spoke."

"Oh." She blinked rapidly and leaned against a tree. "And you do not love this mysterious not-friend?"

He scoffed. "I barely even like her, and she definitely doesn't like me."

"You protest a little much," she muttered. "You like her enough that this fight is bothering you, though? How many friends do you have?"

"A few?"

Johanna and Briar Rose were the only occupants of that list.

"How many have yelled at you?"

"Two of them," he said.

"Being a prince is an odd sort of isolation, but isolation nonetheless, because you exist on a level many don't," said Eris. "You wouldn't kill Johanna for talking back to you, but you cannot ignore that you're in that position. I imagine the only people who have ever argued with you were your father, Johanna, and this girl."

"Thereabouts," Phillip said, shifting uncomfortably. "My father gave up on it a while ago."

"He has no idea what to do with you, does he?" she asked.

His father never tried to understand, and he had a terrible suspicion that Briar Rose's aunts were the same.

"He knows exactly what he wants to do with me," said Phillip. "Did you ever fight with your parents?"

"Oh, that was ages ago, but yes. I tried so hard to be good for them. I did everything they asked and was always worried about whether I was good enough. Then I met my mentor." Eris sighed and smiled, the sad tilt to her mouth making Phillip's heart ache. He wanted a teacher that made him reminisce like that. "I hated her at first, but eventually I realized that she was the only one who never gave up on me. She understood exactly why I felt how I did. How stifled I was. How hopeless. She offered me an escape and pushed me harder than I had ever been pushed, and I became the best possible version of the Eris I always wanted to be. She taught me what power I truly had."

Eris offered him her hand. She handed him another tonic and tapped his chin with a finger. "Chin up. Stop throwing yourself off the board and learn to play the game. Figure out what rules you can bend. That was the best lesson my teacher ever taught me, and she taught it well: there is always a rule waiting to be broken. I cannot grant you a wand and make all your troubles disappear, but I can teach you how to use your magic. How to become the Phillip you want to be. How to find the love you want. I will not make you worry yourself to death over being good enough for me."

Phillip hid his smile with a bow of his head. He had never been allowed to make mistakes or argue or question things, but Eris's permission felt like the acknowledgment he had always wanted from his father. She wasn't dismissing him.

She *understood.*

"Once all of this is done, what will you do?" he asked Eris.

The question startled her and made her breath catch in her throat. "Oh, well, there are so many things in motion that I hadn't considered it."

"I'm terrible at chess and will need help learning how to play my new part. I'll probably need more train-ing in magic," he said slowly, and then swallowed the tonic in one bitter gulp. "That would be best for humans and fairies alike."

She would understand what he couldn't say: that he wanted a mentor like her.

"To our parts and the moves we're forced to make."

Eris chuckled and toasted him with a bundle of bandages. "Now that we have the sword, you'll be studying illusion magic. Impress me, and I will teach you everything I know once all of this is over."

12

Heart to Heart, Thorn to Thorn

THE NEXT morning, Phillip awoke long after dawn. He felt beaten up even if he didn't look it anymore, thanks to the fairies' healing, and got ready as slowly as he could. Phrike's first lesson surely wouldn't be as bad as Poena's teachings, but he stalled and let his mind wander anyway. He had to apologize to Briar Rose even if it didn't fix anything. Dreaming would be far more restful if it didn't always include a tooth-and-nail fight. He had far too many of those to look forward to with Maleficent in his near future.

"My being a wizard is enough to make her green with envy," Phillip muttered to himself before going to meet Phrike. Eris's promise had filled him with an eagerness he hadn't felt in ages, and he couldn't wait to train. "More briar than rose, really."

"What are you whispering about?" Johanna asked, coming up behind him and shoving him out of the tent. "Get on with it, Your Wizardness."

Phillip stretched one last time and joined Phrike outside. She had many talents and decided to start with some of her others before moving to illusions. Phrike tested him only once before determining he had little skill for healing, and, unlike Poena, she didn't even have to set him on fire to do so. She tried to teach him to vanish his bruises, but he couldn't manage it at all. Poena scowled at them the entire time.

"Healing's a mite harder to manage for most," Phrike said, giggling, and patted his head.

"I don't think Poena likes me," Phillip mumbled to Phrike.

"Don't feel too bad, my boy," she said, the rasp of her voice swallowing the endearment. "She dislikes most. You're not special."

Phillip bit back his usual retort in favor of thinking over his next words. Pieces on a board didn't speak; they waited to make a move.

"Has she always been like that? The one other time I met fairies, they were quite . . ."

"Jolly? Unflappable? So happy that it worried you they weren't taking things seriously?" Phrike giggled. "Wouldn't know. Ran in different circles, we did. I'm only here for, well, myself, I suppose. And you, of course. Eris convinced us to help her help you steal the sword and shield. She and Poena never really got on. Eris is a bit too wild for her. Unpredictable."

Phrike giggled again, not a real laugh, but the most he had ever heard from her, and shooed him into the clearing to begin his next lesson.

Phillip had requested to learn shadow familiars next, Phrike's most interesting trick. But unlike her, Phillip wasn't suited for shadows. He spent an hour trying to detach his shadow from his body while everyone watched, and only managed a half-hearted ripple of the shade across the grass. It was probably for the best; Samson would never allow him to have more than one familiar.

"No time to teach you bones and muscles and the like, but there's emotions. Those are easy enough to influence without knowing everything about bodies," Phrike said, and clucked her tongue. "Ah! Slumber. That's a good one. Here—remember how this feels."

She stood on her toes and tapped his temple, and the world went black.

Phillip blinked up at the sky. He was lying on the ground. "What just happened?"

There had been no warning, no creeping sensation of tiredness, and no time between her touching his face and his waking up. It was as if she had gone into his head

and removed the last minute entirely without his being
the wiser.

"What did you notice?" Phrike asked.

"Nothing," said Phillip. "Absolutely nothing."

"I caught you," Johanna said from a step away.
"You're welcome."

"My knight in shining armor." Phillip winked at
her and ignored her eye roll.

"Children!" Poena snapped. "Pay attention. This is
all for your benefit."

It was for everyone's, but Phillip bit his tongue.

"Sleeping's a useful trick," said Phrike, motioning
for him to sit up. "Healing outright requires more knowledge than we could teach you even if you had the talent.
But sleeping spells take far less. How's your anatomical
knowledge?"

"I'm no physician, but I can keep my humors in
check," he said. "What do I need to put people to sleep?"

"For slumber, it's quite simple." Phrike raised both
of her hands to his head. He had to stoop to let her do it,
and his spine cracked in protest. "You must touch them
and then recall the sensation of sleep, so pay attention
to what it feels like. Decide on a gesture, too, my boy. I
suppose telling someone to sleep will do just as well. This
won't hurt a bit. . . ."

It was like dying from cold. Phrike knocked him out with little more than a nudge a dozen times before letting him try it on her, and it took him a dozen more to even make her drowsy. It wasn't difficult or exhausting work, but not instantly understanding it made his heart race and his shoulders tense. By the time he finally made Phrike snore, it was late in the evening and Phillip wanted to do nothing but sleep himself. He ate a late supper with Johanna and crawled into his bedroll without so much as a "good night." Natural sleep took him quickly.

Phillip awoke in the hedge maze. The thorns and vines had nearly overtaken all that remained of the old wood, tangling themselves so tightly in the evergreen hedges that the leaves were withering to a dull brown. The twisting crack of the thorns growing and tearing through the branches of the hedge split the silence every few seconds, and Phillip listened for Briar Rose's shouts.

He deserved to be yelled at a bit.

"We've had this conversation a thousand times, Briar Rose."

Phillip froze, trying to hear where the voice was coming from. It was one of Briar Rose's aunts; which one he had no idea, but if he was hearing her, that meant—

"And I'll ask a thousand more times," said Briar Rose. *"Let me go to town. Or with you to market. Or anything! I can't stay here. I have always done what you said. I have never left the woods. I have never fought you on this, but I am fighting now, because I cannot do this anymore."*

She was awake, and he was listening in on her real life.

Before the maze, when it had been him alone in the wood, it was like Briar Rose and her aunts were always behind the next tree. Their voices had been faint and far-off. Now they were further muffled by the twisting vines. The voices didn't come from anywhere specific. It was like they were simply around the next corner of the maze, but no matter how far Phillip walked, he couldn't reach the source. Phillip settled down as close as he could to the wall.

He must have misheard her. She had left the forest where she lived. She had all those stories and friends.

"I need to meet other people. I need to be around them. I have only ever spoken to you, and I love you all dearly, but I need more. Please!"

She sounded near tears, but her aunt only huffed. Phillip felt as if he'd been dunked in a frozen pond. Of all the things he had overheard, he had never heard Briar

Rose sound so defeated. The chilling depth of his discomfort at at that moment shocked him.

It was unfathomable that she had never left the forest where she lived. Could all those stories, all those adventures he had been so jealous of, have been lies? But was it really lying if her audience was only animals and herself?

It was unthinkable that she had never even spoken to anyone else. Even folks who lived in the most rural farmsteads still saw others sometimes. Avoiding everyone took work.

"Now, dear, it's for your own good. We know best!" said one of her aunts in an insultingly upbeat tone.

"Why?" he shouted as she pleaded the same question.

Desperation made her voice waver, but her aunts seemed not to notice. Phillip did.

One laughed and said, *"Oh, sweet girl, you know we'll explain it all to you one day, but you must trust us."*

"You know we're doing this to protect you," another said.

"What is the point of protecting me if my heart is broken before I'm safe?" asked Briar Rose. *"All I want to do is go to town."*

And she sounded as if she was drowning, like he was.

Phillip stripped off his cape and wadded it up against the thorny vines so that he could lean against the wall. Maybe he could hear the conversation more clearly if he got closer.

"It's too dangerous!"

That was one of the other aunts, the strict one. Phillip had always imagined her tilting her head and staring down her nose at whomever she was talking to.

"You'll understand one day."

"She doesn't need to understand. She needs you to listen," said Phillip.

He rubbed his face; he had a terrible feeling in the pit of his stomach. His father had often said similar things; Phillip was supposed to be a heroic knight, but his father had all sorts of rules he couldn't know for reasons his father wouldn't share, to keep him safe.

Phillip had always wanted someone who listened to him, and he had yelled at her. Said terrible things. Hated her because she listened.

It made perfect sense now, though. Briar Rose had never been anywhere or met anyone. She was trapped and alone, so it was no wonder she had a thousand questions for him every time they met. He had always been jealous of her travels, but his time as a knight journeying through Artwyne must have seemed like an unattainable freedom to her. If he were in her situation, he would ask a million things, too. It wasn't selfishness or nosiness.

Speaking to him was the only means of escape she had.

"I don't want to understand. Please, I cannot stay here alone. Let me go with you."

"Absolutely not," said one of the aunts. *"That's final."*

Briar Rose took a breath, sobbed, and hiccuped, and her aunts discussed how best to fix her splotchy face. She gasped, and slowly, the voices of her aunts grew quieter and quieter until the only thing he could hear was her footsteps as she fled.

"I'm sorry," he said. His disappointment that Briar Rose would not be joining him in the dream world was as strong and bitter as his anger at her aunts, but he pushed it to the back of his mind. She wouldn't fall asleep easily after that and would find comfort in her only friends, the animals. That would at least make her feel better. "I hope I get to tell you that soon."

Phillip threw himself into his training with Phrike the next day to keep himself from thinking about Briar Rose. He found illusions were far easier than nature magic or defending against fire. Phillip could create an image of a boulder to hide behind that no one would know was fake until they tried to touch it, or he could conjure a screech behind someone to distract them. The illusions weren't always exactly what he wanted, but they were close enough for his first real day of training.

"A distraction is a distraction is a distraction," said Phrike, applauding as he made an owl hoot behind her. "Keeping up multiple illusions is difficult, but you can overlay them with enough practice—visuals, sounds, smells. Try to copy your deer."

She pointed at Samson, and Johanna laughed from her seat, watching everything to find holes in his illusions.

"Horse, dear," said Eris. "Humans ride horses."

"Try to copy your horse, then," Phrike said.

Phillip glanced at Samson. He and Taliesin had been enjoying their time of rest, grazing and rolling about with little interruption. Phillip raised his hand and whispered what he wanted to do, and slowly an image of Samson appeared. Phillip moved his fingers as if modeling clay, and the real Samson snorted. Taliesin eyed the illusion, pawing at the dirt. Phillip twisted his hand to his mouth and imagined a stick of celery. A carrot appeared in the illusion's mouth.

"Close enough," said Phillip, dropping his hand.

Samson charged his copy and tried to yank the carrot free, snorting when he bit through nothing. Phillip laughed and beckoned Samson to him. He had no idea how to explain magic to horses.

Eris snorted, and Poena glanced at her.

"Maleficent will be less forgiving than we are," she said sharply. "You must—"

A loud neighing came from the illusion of Samson, and Poena jumped, clutching her chest. She glared at Eris.

"We have six days," Poena said, "and no shield as of yet."

"It's fine," said Eris, restraining her laughter.

"Phillip, try again." Phrike beckoned him nearer and circled his illusion of Samson. "You're lacking detail. You mustn't leave anything out."

They spent the rest of the day perfecting Phillip's illusions and the commands and gestures he used to summon them. He fell into a restless sleep after midnight, hoping to speak with Briar Rose. Instead of opening his eyes to the dream wood, he awoke to Phrike leaning over him, nearly nose to nose. He yelped.

He wanted to apologize to Briar Rose and make sure she was all right, not wake up to Phrike's shockingly bad breath in his face, but it must have been time for his test.

"Outside when you're ready," she said, "but be quick about it."

She flitted out the flap. A bleary-eyed Johanna peeked at Phillip from beneath her blanket.

"Sorry," he whispered. "Another challenge."

"It's fine," she said, and sat up. She pulled her book from her pocket. "I'm behind anyway."

It was a poem, judging by the lines he could see, but he couldn't make out what the words said. Dozens upon dozens of lines had been crossed out and rewritten.

"Johanna," he said softly, "why are you so interested in writing whatever that is?"

Owlishly, she stared up at him. "I don't think you'd understand."

"That's never stopped you from explaining things to me before," said Phillip.

"Not everyone gets remembered, but you will be. Royals always are." Johanna raised one shoulder. "Myths and legends and the people who tell them get remembered. I just want something nice attached to my name when I'm gone."

He definitely didn't understand. Phillip dreaded finding out what others said about him.

"You didn't have to come with me. You could've stayed somewhere to write whatever you wanted."

"No, even if I weren't your squire, I would have wanted to travel with you," she said. "You make such creatively interesting decisions."

So mistakes that had to be fixed, then?

"I hope you get ink everywhere," he muttered, grinning. "You're healed up, right?"

"Right as rain," she said. "No more bruises, though still hurts like one. Should be well enough when we go get the shield."

"Good."

He left the tent with a nervous shake of his head. It was likely there would be no outright fight during the test of his illusion magic, the fairies instead testing him to determine what was real and what was illusionary while he kept up his own illusions. There weren't many days left, and he didn't *feel* prepared, even though he felt more in control of his life. The three fairies waited for him at the edge of the clearing.

"The Shield of Virtue has been resting with its maker for the last two centuries, but it is well guarded. We have five days left to take it," said Eris. "It is possible Maleficent may make a play for the shield. However, the real threat is Amis, its maker. To claim the shield, you must defeat them. As we are fairies and cannot wield the shield, this is a test you must face alone."

"So you'll face today alone, as well," said Phrike. "Ready?"

"I think so," he said. "What do I need to do?"

Eris grinned, her wand sliding into her hand. "Incapacitate me."

She swung her wand up, and a blast of wind so cold he couldn't breathe threw him across the clearing. Phillip landed hard on his back, the shock and pain trembling through his body. He struggled to get to his feet. Samson and Taliesin squealed.

"Don't panic. Only training," he muttered to himself. Phillip raised one hand as if lifting something. "Wall!"

A stone wall as tall as his hips appeared before him, and Phillip ducked behind it, racing for the trees. His heart slammed into his ribs. He had expected to fight Phrike.

Phrike was a terrifying prospect, but Eris wouldn't hold back. She knew he wanted to be the best.

"Oh, for magic's sake," Eris muttered. "Hiding won't beat Maleficent."

He was in the cover of the trees before she dealt with his illusion, but a cool breeze rippled through the leaves. Nature magic made graveyards of forests. He had to get out of there without her the wiser.

But Eris was good. She was far better than he with magic, knew all the intricacies of it.

She definitely wouldn't fall for the trick he had used on Poena.

"What can I do?" he whispered.

The bitterly cold wind that foretold Eris's magic swept through the trees, and he sprinted away from it, staying in the tree line. Branches and vines clawed at his back as he ran.

"Come out, come out, wherever you are, Your Highness!" Eris called.

Phillip raised his hand and twisted it, mumbling, "Wind."

The gust shoved her encroaching plants back. He moved in a semicircle around the clearing, staying low in the bushes. Footsteps sounded behind him. A breath rustled his hair. Phillip elbowed whatever was behind him and hit nothing.

"You think you can touch me? That you're worthy of that?" a hauntingly familiar voice whispered in his ear.

He felt nothing, but a face leaned over his shoulder. The nose was sharp and delicate, the skin a pale green, and the lips bloodred.

"Oh, dear," Maleficent said. "Does our valiant prince doubt my presence? My power?"

She wasn't real. She was a nightmare summoned by Phrike or Eris to scare him into revealing himself. Phillip needed to distract all the fairies to even get close to Eris. This illusion was nothing to worry about.

"No, thank you," he whispered, and crept toward the side of the clearing where Taliesin and Samson were watching the fairies with wide eyes. Their ears were back, and Taliesin kept shuffling toward the tent where Johanna waited. Samson sniffed up toward the tree line. Phillip held a finger to his lips.

"Distract them for me," Phillip said quietly once he was close enough. He gestured for Samson to run. "I will give you a million carrots if you tear off through that clearing right now."

The creaking of plants slithering around the forest floor as Eris and Phrike hunted him down grew louder behind him, and the illusion of Maleficent still hovered in his peripheral field. Samson didn't so much as huff.

What he needed was something to spook but not hurt the horses, like when Briar Rose had lobbed those rocks at him. Phillip felt around in the grass and found two small pebbles. He hurled them at Samson and Taliesin.

One bounced off Samson's side, making him rear,

and one smacked Taliesin in the ribs. Taliesin took off galloping across the clearing toward the tent. Phrike turned to Taliesin, and Phillip raced back through the trees. He summoned a sword of thorns to his hands and commanded his magic to conjure an illusion of the Sword of Truth. The faint scent of smoke hung in the air.

If they were going to scare him with Maleficent, he was going to scare them right back.

Phillip got as close to Eris as he could without being seen, and when she hissed at Phrike to get Taliesin, he lunged.

A sliver of lightning struck his hand. Phillip leapt back, his skin smarting. Phrike vanished in a flicker of shadows. Cold and quick, a prickle of power rolled over him, and he flicked his fingers out as subtly as he could. A whip of grass shot out from his feet and slapped at Eris's wand. Her magic smacked it aside.

"Like that could kill me," she said, and flicked her hand like she was swatting a bug. "And it was entirely too predictable."

A vicious gust of wind sent him tumbling backward, and he rolled to a stop.

"Everything you've done could've killed me," Phillip said, and stumbled to his feet.

"Well," said Eris, her eyes narrowing, "what doesn't kill you and all that . . ."

Eris thrust her wand toward him and magic shot out from the point. Phillip ducked under it, the power grazing his scalp. Eris attacked again. He knocked the shot away with his thorn sword.

The magic crashed into a thick elm and toppled it.

"Excuse you?" Phillip asked, turning slowly toward her.

Eris twisted her wand, and the wind picked up, cutting through Phillip's tunic with cold. He stumbled and threw up his arms to protect his face. A shield of grass wove itself before him. Eris's blow crumpled it.

The force rattled through Phillip, and he stumbled back again. Phrike, at the ready, appeared at the far end of the clearing. He flung his thorn sword disguised as the Sword of Truth at her, and she shrieked. The sound hit Phillip's ears like flint striking tinder. He smelled oiled steel and sweat. He tried to create another thorn sword and found nothing in his hand. Eris approached slowly.

Phillip couldn't be a disappointment now, not when he was so close to mastering magic and saving himself without following the path his father had laid out for him. He was so close to being in control.

"What is left for you?" the illusion of Maleficent asked. "What is left but failure?"

But it bolstered Phillip instead of distracting him. He thought of Briar Rose, alone in the wood and in her waking life, of himself staring at the stars and waiting for the reprieve of sleep, and of everything Maleficent had taken from him. That soft, quiet moment between being awake and being asleep consumed his mind. Maleficent had stolen his dreams and left nothing but nightmares. He made a gesture at Eris as if gathering something in his hand.

Magic flared at his fingertips. Phillip closed his eyes. He felt, rather than saw, Eris slowly slip into unconsciousness. She gasped and flinched, and her eyelids fluttered. The plants around him stilled and the air warmed. Maleficent's illusion vanished.

"Your Highness?" Poena's voice was softer than he had ever heard it before. "It would be best if you opened your eyes."

There was something different about this magic. It had been hotter and angry, and his mouth tasted like ash.

"That felt different," he said.

Poena clucked. "It *was* different." But she did not elaborate.

"Did it work?" asked Phillip, cracking open one eye.

Poena scoffed and shook her head. Phrike, kneeling next to Eris, was tapping the sleeping fairy's cheek. Eris was splayed out in the center of the clearing, her wand hand over her head, and her eyelids fluttered. Phrike poked her face again, and Eris jerked awake.

"You put me to sleep?" she said, and shuddered. "You knocked me out cold!"

Phillip beamed, and Poena let out a raspy laugh.

"And what fun it was," Poena said. "Good job."

It was a good way to incapacitate without killing, and Phillip's joy at doing it successfully nearly tore out of him. He took a deep breath instead of whooping. Eris yawned and rose.

"That won't take out someone like Maleficent," said Eris, "but it will definitely work on her minions."

She noticed when Phillip smirked. "You're pleased, aren't you, that you need not kill her minions?" asked Eris, narrowing her eyes.

Knights and princes had to rationalize things like murder when it was "for the good of the kingdom." Never mind that who got included in the "kingdom" changed with the whims of the rulers. Phillip knew Johanna felt the same way about killing, though she had strong feelings about all the other laws as well. It was partly why he had wanted her as his squire.

"Astounding," Eris continued. "You robbed a wizard just a few days ago. Your moral compass is inscrutable."

Phillip shrugged. "Some things are worse than others."

But he was only getting better.

13
Seldom What They Seem

*T*WO HUNDRED years ago, when fairies and humans first came to a hesitant peace, when dragons and all sorts of magical creatures wandered the lands, the Shield of Virtue had been laid to rest with its maker. The tomb of the great blacksmith Amis was deep in the spruce-speckled foothills of northern Ald Tor, and though the location was well known, few had tried to take the shield. The hike through the hills was difficult, the paths lined with crumbling ruins overgrown with moss and foggy green sage. Irises dark as dusk spotted the forest floor.

It was Amis, though, who kept adventurers away.

"Metal sang beneath their hammer. There was no metal they couldn't work and no artist's eye they couldn't draw, but when the war reached their city, they stayed behind. They took up the armor of the knights who had already fallen in their defense and created a shield so strong it would last a thousand years," said Johanna, her eyes bright and her reverence infectious. "They died helping the last people get out of the city but refused to stay dead and remained to keep anyone from following the survivors. Even now, in the tomb built on the ground they gave their life for, Amis protects their shield from those who would use it for selfish means and only allows the worthy to win it."

"And that's definitely not me," muttered Phillip.

Yet Phillip was the keystone of their plan. An hour earlier, Phrike had transported them all south of the tomb using her shadow. She had scouted the area the night before and noticed nothing—a blessing, since the thick bramble and mist kept them from seeing more than an arm's length before them. Their plan for the shield was unnervingly simple, and worse, Phillip would be facing Amis alone. He would attempt to win the shield from Amis fairly, passing whatever test they gave, and the others would intervene only if that didn't work. If it didn't, they would have to steal the shield and escape. Unlike Amis, they could teleport.

And then they'd only have to look over their shoulders for Amis forever.

"Hush," whispered Eris. "You don't know that. Your reasons for needing it are quite noble."

The fairies were fluttering behind Phillip and

Johanna, utterly silent as they glided through the fog. The dreary, stifling weather was doing nothing to improve Phillip's nerves.

"The fact we plan to steal it if I don't pass feels less than honorable, though," he said.

Amis had instilled their virtue into their final creation and been so dedicated to helping others that not even death stopped them. Phillip had heard the story a dozen times and loved each retelling as a kid, but he had tried to stop thinking about it after knighthood lost its appeal. There were as many different stories about how Amis decided worthiness as there were stars in the sky. No one knew which were true.

Phillip had passed his final test from the fairies the previous day, but his confidence was still partly for show. It helped, though, that Eris believed he could do it.

"No one has ever been able to observe anyone challenging Amis," Eris said. "We've only been able to watch them as they enter and leave the tomb, and no one in recent decades has left with the shield. There seems to be some sort of enchantment that prevents those who fail from speaking of the trial."

"So no information on how to prove myself worthy of the shield," Phillip said. "Great. Easy."

That was terrifying. *Virtuous* wasn't a word Phillip would've used to describe himself.

Light glinted off something hidden in the fog, and Phillip stopped. He raised his hand.

"There's someone there," he whispered, ducking. "I thought no one was here?"

"No one was," said Phrike, wringing her hands.

Eris inhaled sharply.

"They've got a bow." Phillip eyed them: a stout person, facing the other way for now, with plain brown clothes but a bow worth serious money. They were clearly scanning the woods as a lookout. He waited for them to turn fully and didn't see a crest on any part of their clothes. "Could someone else be making a move for the shield?"

The Shield of Virtue was legendary, and it wasn't uncommon for knights from different kingdoms to try to prove their worth. Every few years growing up, Phillip had heard of some Artwyne page or knight attempting the journey to Ald Tor to take the shield and coming back empty-handed. There were even rumors that some brave thieves had banded together to try to steal it. They hadn't been heard from since.

The archer crept nearer. Phillip motioned for the others to hide. Johanna crouched low in the bushes, and the fairies vanished from sight.

"Gag them," Phillip whispered, gesturing for a vine to cover the archer's mouth. "Mouth first, then hands."

The vines slithered away from him through the underbrush. One shot out and wrapped around the archer's mouth. The archer flailed and struggled against the plants, but Phillip's magic dragged them quietly through the undergrowth to him. He tapped the archer's temple.

"Sleep well," he said, and they passed out. Phillip searched their pockets. "Their purse has coin from Ald Tor, but whatever crest they wore was torn off their cloak recently. Who do you think they are?"

Phrike turned her veiled face to Eris, and Eris leaned down over the archer, studying them.

"Mercenaries," she said, and rose, her hands clasped behind her back. "There are factions who support Maleficent. We can't be sure whoever is here is not working for her cause."

"Can we be certain it's a group and not just one or two?" asked Johanna.

"Phrike," Eris said, "go see how many they are."

Phrike vanished. Phillip looked over the archer again while they waited. The archer's clothes—a dark brown cloak over nondescript padded armor—didn't provide Phillip with much information about who they were, but they did give him a plan. Phrike reappeared with a gasp.

"A good dozen or so of them!" She sniffed and nudged the archer with her foot.

Phillip nodded, less scared than he thought he would be. Maybe Eris's insistence that he believe in himself was working. "I should disguise myself to match them and attempt to reach the tomb undetected. I doubt fighting a group, mercenaries or not, would be considered virtuous."

"That would get you to the tomb so long as no one notices it's you and not them," said Eris, gesturing to the archer. She tilted her head back and forth and finally agreed. "He is right. We cannot even get near the tomb given the protections against fairies, so his winning the shield outright is our best chance at getting it."

"Amis was always so straitlaced," muttered Poena. "We will ensure that the mercenaries do not return and enter the tomb. We can draw them away like we did Old Barnaby."

"It would be better if we didn't fight them," said Johanna. "There are plenty of myths about the area being haunted and Amis using magic to keep people away. We could scare them?"

"That's a good plan," he said, and knocked Johanna's shoulder with his. "Go terrify these mercenaries and we can regroup here in an hour or if something goes wrong."

"Send word if anything happens," Eris told Phrike. "Go."

"Did you really know Amis?" Phillip heard Johanna ask as she and Poena vanished beneath Phrike's shadow. Phillip knelt next to the fallen archer and started undoing their scarf. Eris laughed.

"Phillip," she said in that disappointed drawl of a baffled teacher. "Think with your magic."

"Right." He winced and mimed putting on a tunic. "Create an illusion of their clothes on me, please."

Magic rustled across Phillip, and his clothes took on the appearance of the archer's. Phillip grabbed the archer's bow and quiver.

"Excellent. Let's get you to the tomb." Eris nodded for Phillip to move and walked ahead of him. It was odd to hear her footsteps, but flying would have been too difficult in the dense forest. She hissed.

Phillip froze. "What's wrong?"

"Clover," she said, shaking off the hem of her yellow dress. The plant was hidden under the deadfall, and beneath her dress, her feet were bare. Tendrils of smoke rose from her soles. "Amis is from before my time, when we were at war, but we flew over the woods observing the tomb. I knew we would not be able to enter it, but I didn't realize the defenses against us would be so thorough. I'll have to bear it, but my magic will grow weaker the closer we get."

Phillip stayed near her after that. The tomb was among the crumbling ruins of an old city at the top of a woody hill, and a large fire was burning at the heart of the ruins. Mercenaries in nondescript clothes milled around the fire. A handful paced outside the entrance to the tomb.

"For a group of indistinguishable mercenaries, they're well armed," muttered Phillip. He touched his collar, his fingers passing through the illusion of the archer's clothes.

"Don't worry about them," Eris said. "You will enter the tomb alone. I will ensure that no one follows, and once you have the shield, rejoin me. Then we will regroup."

She laid a comforting hand on his shoulder, then faded from view like mist in the wind. Across the camp, a hazy image of Johanna appeared behind a mercenary and leaned down near their ear. Whatever she whispered made the mercenary scream, and she vanished as quickly as she had appeared. Another ghostly illusion appeared between the mercenaries and the tomb. It stumbled toward them.

The mercenaries scrambled into action. A warbling whistle called out from the north, eliciting shouts from those around the fire. They all drew weapons, hesitating as one swung at the ghost and the sword went through it, and the illusion herded them into the woods, away from the tomb. Slowly, most of the mercenaries dispersed as they tried to deal with the ghosts. Only a few remained, but they had moved away from the tomb to the middle of camp, where the ghost of Johanna had appeared.

Phillip calmed his breathing. He shook out his limbs and slouched, matching the archer's height as best as he could without arousing suspicion. He began to walk through the encampment and tried to match the worry of the others. One of the mercenaries in the middle raised a hand to him. Phillip waved back, pointed toward the tomb, and then tapped the corner of his eye. As a knight, that was how he'd been taught to signify he was keeping watch, and it was all he could think to do. The other mercenary nodded and gestured toward the woods where the others had run off.

"Well done," said Eris, looming invisibly over his shoulder with her magic like winter wind. "The tomb. Quickly."

Phillip neared the tomb. Magic prickled across his skin the closer he got, charging the air until the hair of his arms stood on end. A scent like scalding seawater and heated metal hung in the air, and the ground shifted from uneven roots to a hard-packed dirt path. Eris's footfalls grew louder.

He had known her magic would be of little use there, but it was still shocking to turn and see her, the magic that kept her from his sight slowly fading. There was a stark white scar across her left cheek he had never seen before, and her yellow dress was paler and streaked with grass stains. He stopped a few steps from the iron-encircled entrance to the tomb. They were out of sight of the others there.

"Eris?" he asked, looking away. He had never realized that she used magic to change her appearance around him, but their nearness to the tomb was clearly weakening those illusions. It felt wrong to look at her without them. "Can you even be here?"

"I can be here, outside of the tomb, though it is quite uncomfortable." Despite her confident tone, she raised her hand to her scarred cheek and frowned. "I will wait for you. If you do need me, I can enter the tomb. However, I cannot be in there for long, and my magic will be very weak."

"But I don't want you to get hurt."

She jerked, her face fell, and she shook her head.

"Some successes require sacrifices," she muttered, but it seemed like she wasn't saying it to him. "You're kind, but we need the shield. You're a prince, Phillip. You must be prepared for others to sacrifice for your goals, especially for such needful goals as this one."

The sentiment dropped to the pit of his stomach like a stone. "Did your mentor tell you that?"

She nodded. "Now go."

He hesitated, and she shooed him forward with her hands.

Alone, Phillip stepped into the dark of the tomb. The entrance was in a thick wall of solid stone. Pale light flickered at the end of the hall, which angled down. A hushed voice rose through the cracks of a second door, and Phillip hesitated outside it. The light was from a torch stuck onto the wall, and with it, he could see fingerprints in the moss on the door where it had been forced open. Offerings of milk jugs and coins rested in the corner outside, the dust atop them undisturbed despite the riches there. Liquid seeped from the cracks in the tomb wall.

Phillip touched it and sniffed his fingers, the familiar scent of linseed oil filling his nose. He listened at the door for a moment.

". . . not very noble to strike weakly and receive a weak strike in return," said someone in a small voice.

Whoever was speaking cleared their throat and then continued, "But I don't want to die in a year."

Phillip paused at the one-sided conversation. It reminded him of Briar Rose practicing her speeches, though he hoped she would never have to worry about being murdered. Maleficent seemed like the sort who would kill someone for failing one of her missions. He peeked through the half-open door.

A young woman, unlike anything he had expected a minion of Maleficent's to be, paced across the small room. She tossed a knife from hand to hand, muttering and shaking her head. The light caught her pox scars and brightened her brown eyes when she turned. All that was left of the crest on her tunic was the beak of a large bird sewn in fraying black thread. She tossed her braided hair to her other shoulder with a sigh, not noticing Phillip.

"But you might not mean it all literally," she muttered.

Phillip wasn't sure what the woman was talking about, but he slipped through the door and drew his sword quietly. She noticed movement and rounded on him, knife slashing toward him. He caught her by the wrist and squeezed. The knife clattered to the ground.

Her gaze dropped to the sword in his other hand,

and Phillip kicked her knife to the corner behind her. She was Johanna's age, if that.

"Don't swing at someone if your grip's not good," he said. "You could have downed me with a kick by now, by the way."

She shifted, and he shook his head.

"Too late." Phillip tightened his grip on her wrist.

She pulled back to hit him and then caught sight of something over his shoulder. She froze.

"They're awake again," she whispered.

Slowly, Phillip turned.

"Oh," he said, breathless. "You . . ."

The stories didn't do Amis justice. They were two heads taller than Phillip and broader than his father, the top of their helm scraping against the stone ceiling as they moved. The helm was dulled by age and dented over the temple from the blow that had killed them, but the shape of the wolf's head was still there. A single green eye stared out between the wolf's bared teeth, and linseed oil dripped from them like blood. It oozed from the cracks of the bronze scales of Amis's armor and left dark trails through the green patina. The surcoat over the scales was soaked through.

And behind them rested the Shield of Virtue. It was nearly as tall as Phillip, edged in gleaming metal, and lined with the same silver-and-blue detailing as the hilt of the Sword of Truth.

"Johanna's going to die of envy," he mumbled.

Amis tilted their head to the side, and the soft *ting* of bone against metal sounded from the helm. "Johanna of Shiraz has nothing to fear."

"That makes sense," Phillip said. Johanna was virtuous to her bones, and the fairies should have sent her in his place. She would have stood a better chance. He glanced at the girl. "What's your name?"

She swallowed. "Who are you?"

"Phillip," he said. "Your turn."

"Brenna," she said, and frowned, looking over her shoulder toward the door. "You can't have the shield. I got here first."

"I don't think it matters which of us got here first. I'm taking the shield."

"You can't just take it." She seemed so offended by the prospect of his not knowing something that she forgot to try to pull her wrist away. "You have to earn it. It's a beheading game, but you're not noble at all."

"I've been saying that for years."

Stories of beheading games were popular. The knight was forced to strike a blow against an immortal opponent that would be returned in kind eventually. Was it nobler to behead the opponent and meet your own beheading with grace, or was it better to give them a weak wound and then be scratched in return?

It was nobler to fight truly and with full effort, striking a mortal blow as would be required in a real duel, than to not fight well and only wound the opponent. The truly brave and virtuous met death with honor. Or something. Johanna probably understood and explained it better.

Phillip didn't get it at all.

He dropped her hand and raised his sword. "Don't move."

She swallowed. "Fine. When you fail, I'll have my turn."

Phillip kept Amis in the corner of his sight. It felt wrong to turn his back on them. Even Phillip knew that people didn't get turns in a beheading game. Once he played, he'd be locked into it, and Brenna was already losing by taking so long to consider. Amis, quiet and dripping, watched him.

"A mirrored duel, is it?" asked Phillip. "Is that what I have to do to earn it?"

"No, that is not quite your game," Amis said, their voice sounding like a rusted lock being forced open. "You require a different test, Prince Phillip."

Brenna's eyes widened, and she gave Phillip a look he couldn't read.

"Prince Ph—" Brenna's voice died with a strangled groan, and her head dropped to her chest.

Phillip spun to her and raised his sword, unease sweeping over him. Her limbs went limp, and then they jerked. Amis raised their arm and moved their fingers as if controlling a puppet. Brenna lifted her head.

"A game befitting the puppet prince," she said, but the voice was not her own. It was Amis's. "Duel me, and whatever wound you grant to Brenna of Ald Tor, I will grant to you in one year. But it is a wound you must grant, not mercy."

Fear prickled across Phillip's skin like lightning. This was not at all like the stories. Amis was supposed to be virtuous and honorable, but Brenna hadn't agreed to this.

Some successes require sacrifices.

Eris's words rang in his ears, but Phillip wasn't sure he could do it.

He forced himself to look away from Amis. Brenna took three steps back and picked up her knife. She moved with the ill grace of a freshly born deer, and she held the blade with a strength he was sure she didn't possess. It was an old style of grip, the sort used by fighters who had learned to parry attacks before armor was enough to defend a body. She beckoned him to attack her.

But her eyes, so young and bright before, were lit by fear now.

"No," said Phillip. "She's not part of this."

"You are the prince soon to marry her princess." Amis's voice came from Brenna's mouth. It didn't fit her, and all he could think of was how like Briar Rose she had been, working out her problems aloud. "She has been part of this since she was born, as all subjects are a part of their ruler's choices."

Brenna lashed out at him. He dodged her first blow, catching the second in the arm. The blade tore through his sleeve but not his skin, and he knocked her knife away with a swipe of his sword.

Phillip shook his head. "This is not fair."

"Your idea of fairness is not my concern," said Amis. "Accept or leave."

"No." Phillip stepped away and frowned when Brenna followed. "She's not you. I'm not hurting her to get the shield."

Brenna lunged, her knife aimed for his ribs, and he twisted. Her knife ripped through where he had been. It would have slipped between his bones and into his heart, but as good as her aim was, she was too slow. Phillip tapped his fingers to her temple and tried to put her to sleep as Phrike had taught him. Brenna didn't so much as yawn. Phillip backed away from her. Amis's presence must have negated his magic like it had Eris's.

"Whatever wound you grant her, I will repay to you in one year." Linseed oil leaked from Brenna's lips. "Make your choice."

Brenna swung again, her knife tearing through the air toward his neck.

"If killing her is what gets me that shield, curse the shield," said Phillip.

Brenna's knife stopped a hairbreadth from his throat. "Are you giving up? Running away?"

Humiliation burned in his gut. Not getting the shield would be as good as giving it to Maleficent if these mercenaries were working for her. Wasn't this what his father and tutors had always hammered into his head: that ruling required hard choices? If Brenna was working for Maleficent, she certainly wasn't a very good person. He tightened his grip on his sword.

What was Brenna in the face of whole kingdoms falling to Maleficent? If this was Amis's test, didn't it mean that choosing to wound her was the honorable answer? If he made that choice, he'd be worthy of all the responsibility he'd been granted. He would finally be acting like the prince he was supposed to be.

Brenna pressed the blade against his skin, drawing blood, and he grabbed her wrist again.

"Have I wounded your honor, Your Highness?"

Phillip held her in place, horrified by how Amis's voice sounded coming from Brenna's youthful face.

"My honor's not worth a life," he said. Then the words hit him.

Phillip had assumed Amis meant a literal wound, but people were wounded constantly in all sorts of ways. How many times had Phillip's father wounded his heart with words instead of a blade? The king of Artwyne was always going on about his errant son wounding his pride. A small spark of hope burned in Phillip's chest.

"Here's your wound: you lose, Brenna." He twisted her wrist and knocked the knife from her hand again, then backed her up to the wall. "I'm taking the shield out from under your nose, and you're not winning today. You're failing whoever sent you here. You're returning with hands as empty as your heart, you hear me? You lose."

The lesson of the stories about these games was always to face fate, head held high, but those were morality tales, not true stories. They were meant for teaching people to do the honorable thing, not for being followed without thought. There was no honor in dying and leaving your mistakes behind for others to deal with. Living made much more sense.

"Your pride will heal," he said, and stepped back. "Maybe slower than your skin, though."

Amis didn't answer. Phillip hesitated, his certainty fading. Amis was an old legend and perhaps had different ideas about honor and mercy. Silence reigned, broken only by the steady drip of linseed oil, and Phillip stared at Brenna's unnaturally still body. She wasn't even blinking, her eyes as glazed as the walls. A terrible groan sounded behind Phillip.

"Sorry, Briar Rose, for not getting to apologize," he whispered, regretting everything all the more. "If you're listening, thank you for never leaving me alone."

Phillip turned to face Amis, his heart in his throat. Then Amis knelt with a squelching rasp of damp flesh against metal, bowing so that their neck was bared to him. The skin beneath the armor was weathered like worn leather and stained pale green.

"One year," they said in their own voice from their own body. Brenna, her strings cut, slumped against the wall. "A wound for a wound."

Phillip inhaled sharply to keep from laughing. "Thank you." He took the shield from its resting place. It was far too light for its size, and the air around it felt thick and briny, as if it had recently been tempered.

"Go," said Amis, turning their gaze. "And be wary of your strings."

14
The Fairies' Plan

*E*RIS FOUND HIM FIRST. She materialized, her appearance still oddly human-ish, at the very edge of the iron that ringed the tomb, and her eyes widened when she caught sight of what he was carrying. It was impossible to hide the shield, and Phillip peeked around the fence to see if any of Brenna's companions were near. Eris beckoned him forward.

"Please do not take this the wrong way, but I cannot believe you are holding the Shield of Virtue," she said. "We've done it."

"We have," said Phillip, confused by her outstretched arms. "I thought you couldn't hold this."

"Put it down, you . . ." She gestured for him to drop it, and when he did, she threw her arms around his shoulders. "I am so proud of you!"

Phillip flushed and patted her back. "Thank you."

He didn't know what to do with the lighthearted joy inside him, and as much as he loved her words, he hated how happy they made him. He couldn't recall having been this happy in years.

Eris pulled away. "Let's get out of here."

They reached the meeting point a few moments after the others. The stench of smoke hung in the air, thickening as they drew near. Johanna was doubled over, her hands on her knees, and Phrike patted her back every few breaths Johanna took. Smoke still spiraled from Poena's mouth as she sneered down at Johanna.

"I said I would take care of it, and I did," said Poena. "The 'get out of my way' was implied."

"I don't think you know what 'implied' means," Johanna said, straightening up and groaning. Her gaze landed on Phillip. "No way!"

He held up the shield. "Your confidence staggers me."

The two fairies turned, and Poena's jaw dropped.

"I cannot believe the plan worked," she said, licking the ash from her teeth. "Well, I must eat my words, Eris."

"And I am sure they are bitter and sharp." Eris bowed and then gestured to Phrike. "We should leave before anyone comes after us."

"Doubt they can," said Johanna. She hugged Phillip and frowned when her hands came back oily. "They'll be putting out those fires for ages."

"Oh, no," Poena said. "My fires do not go out. What would be the point of that?"

Phillip shifted his grip on the shield so that he could stand next to Johanna and Phrike and said, "I guess that counts as a distraction."

"Faster we leave, faster we can celebrate." Phrike applauded, cackling, and clapped Eris hard on the back. "Oh, she'll be so pleased!"

Phillip shook his head, his brows knitting in confusion. "I didn't do this for Princess Aurora."

"Ignore her," said Eris sharply. "Phrike, take us back."

They returned to their camp with a flicker of shadow. Over an early supper, they discussed their plans for the upcoming three days. The curse would take hold on the fourth.

Their celebration was small, though Poena relented and let Phrike tuck a red dahlia behind her ear. The fairies were certain that Maleficent would want to taste the fruits of her labors and witness Princess Aurora's succumbing to the curse, but they had no idea exactly when or how the curse would be triggered. There were no spindles in Ald Tor, and no one knew where the princess was. It was likely the curse wouldn't happen until after she was returned to her parents, so most of the plan involved waiting for that to happen. They would simply have to keep a close watch on the princess and fight Maleficent once the curse activated. There wasn't much else to do, given how uncertain it all was.

After a few hours of plotting and a solid hour of worrying, Phillip yawned and Eris shooed him to bed.

"What if Maleficent stops me before I can defeat her?" Phillip asked while fighting another yawn. "What does she do with people like me?"

"People like you? Torture," said Eris. "People who talk as much as you? Instant death."

"I take offense at that," said Phillip. "I am a man of few words."

Without any bite, Eris muttered, "Not few enough."

He laughed, but she scowled.

"Magic is dangerous, Phillip. Maleficent is dangerous even if you have the sword and shield."

"I know," he said softly. "I'm not some guileless interloper who thinks he can swoop in and save the day."

"It's not that. I shouldn't . . ." She took a deep breath and shook her head. "I'm afraid for you, but it can wait. Go to sleep. We'll talk in the morning."

Phillip lay back. He did need to rest, even if an empty hedge maze full of thorns and silence was all that awaited him. He missed Briar Rose, talking to her and competing against her and the easy way they slipped into conversation, and he was still worried about her and her terrible isolation. There was no denying the anxious anticipation flooding his veins. He wanted to apologize for real, figure out why her aunts were so peculiar about her leaving, *and* talk to her.

Briar Rose would probably kill him for getting to meet someone as legendary as Amis. Her curiosity would keep her from attempting to kill him immediately, though, and give them a chance to talk.

He hoped. He couldn't remember ever before wanting so badly to talk to someone about their life and about his.

Phillip closed his eyes, and the weightless presence of the dream wood took over. There was something darker in his sleep this time, something he couldn't put his finger on, that made his neck prickle and his heart catch. He opened his eyes to the tall hedges of the maze.

"Briar Rose?" he called out, standing and getting as close to one of the thorn walls as he dared.

Footsteps neared the other side of the wall. "Phillip?"

"There you are," he said, and sighed.

"You deserve—" he started, but she cut him off.

"I'm sorry," she said. She quieted, and he laughed uncomfortably.

"Thank you," said Phillip. "But you are the one who deserves the apology. I'm sorry about what happened last time. I took out my exhaustion and frustration on you, and that was unfair."

"Thank you," Briar Rose said. She hesitated. "I heard you, in a dream, when you apologized while you were awake. Did you just walk around talking to no one, hoping that I would hear you?"

"Yes," he said, "but it wasn't really no one, because I knew you might be there."

And that was the crux of it all: he couldn't be aloof and hide behind an oblivious mask if she might always be listening. He used to hate that she knew the worst of him, but it was a blessing. She had never used his past against him until he did it to her, and he had taken her presence for granted. He had never had to face his nightmares alone. She'd always been with him.

He owed her the same help and companionship.

"I heard part of your argument with your aunts." He stretched and tried to think about what would make her feel better. "Why did you hide from me that you had never left?"

"Surely you understand?" He heard Briar Rose pacing. "It's embarrassing. You're a knight who's been everywhere, and I've never left these woods."

Each word sounded as if it ripped out another piece of her heart, and Phillip tried to think of a way to make their terrible situation more equal.

"It's fine," she continued. "I mean, it's not, but it's fine that you know."

It wasn't fine. Nothing between them was. Phillip slumped, running his fingers through his hair. His life was finally on the path he wanted it to take, but his dreams were still a mystery. Regardless of everything else, he didn't want to be her rival anymore.

"Why won't they let you go anywhere?" he asked.

She made a faint sound in her throat. "Because it's dangerous, apparently, and I'm a soft, silly girl who doesn't know any better."

"So what if you're soft? You are never more terrifying than when you're caring for someone. You're many things, but silly isn't one of them. They shouldn't have dismissed you like that," said Phillip, standing up. "They were your only teachers, so if you don't know any better, it's on them. Our fight was my fault, anyway. I snapped and set it all off, and I am sorry about what I said. It was unfair of me."

"Thank you," she whispered.

"Do you want to talk about it?" asked Phillip. "We don't have to, but we've made a lot of assumptions about each other. Most of what I thought I knew about you was wrong."

"You weren't wrong about some of it," she muttered. She took a breath as if about to throw herself into deep water. "I don't think you ever realized how jealous I was of you."

"I . . . what?"

Phillip had a lot of things. He knew that, and he knew he had access to even more. But Briar Rose had never expressed interest in knighthood or any of the other typical things that came with nobility. She had never spoken of him with envy, only derision.

Unless he had been completely mistaken.

"I know your father isn't ideal and you feel trapped, too, and I'm sorry, but you get to do so many things," she said, and, from the sound of it, sat down hard in the maze. "Of course I talk to the animals, of course I pretend all the stories are about me, of course I lie, even if it is just to myself—the truth is so dull and deadening. My aunts taught me to be proper and accommodating, but why do I always have to be the understanding one? Why do I have to relent and wait every single time? What is the point of my life if all I ever do is read and study and stare out into the woods, wondering if there's more? I want to matter, Phillip. I can't be this small much longer."

Phillip winced at the deep despair in her tone, the way her voice faltered as if acknowledging her defeat would break her, and he pressed his knuckles into his eyes to keep from crying.

"You're not small," he said. "My opinion might not count for much, but you take up so much space in my mind. All those dreams we shared—old and new—are some of the best and worst memories I have. I hate that you understand me so well, but when we were younger, knowing that you might have been listening was all that kept me going."

Briar Rose gasped as Phillip nearly stuttered, his words surprising him. He had never said them aloud. He had never admitted them to himself until the past few days.

His father's realizing he wasn't the prince he wanted had hurt Phillip, but his mysterious dream girl's realizing he wasn't perfect had been terrifying.

"Your life means something," he said. "You're *you*— bossy and demanding and so kind you forget to take care of yourself in pursuit of helping others. You once kept a rabid dog company after it was too far gone to help. You believe in things so strongly it makes me believe them, and half the time I don't even know what you're arguing for, just that you're convincing. You once told a rabbit to leave your garden alone, and it did."

She laughed.

"And do you know the worst part?" he asked. "I was so jealous of how you got to plan your studying schedule and how you got to decide everything you did and had no one setting expectations for you. It's easy to be envious of someone when you think you know their life, but you can't ever, can you? We've been there for so much of each other's lives, and look how we ended up! I was so wrong about you."

"Niceties don't suit you," she said, but let out one of those unrestrained laughs. "I know what you thought about me—that I couldn't be hurt because no one was around to hurt me and because my aunts love me dearly. But they had expectations for me. Unlike your father, they rarely voiced them, so I was always trying to guess what they wanted."

Phillip swallowed, remembering all the times he had wanted his father and then gotten him but had been unhappy with what happened. That sort of crowded isolation and unspoken rules was a deep ache.

"You terrify me," he said. "We are alone, but you are much braver and more accomplished than I am, and I'm never admitting that again, so don't even ask. When we were children, I thought you were the bravest, most interesting person in the world, and then you heard what happened at my first tournament. I was so excited for the jousting and fighting and finally winning."

"You were," she said. "It was cute, though. You were eleven and barely old enough to compete. Only being able to hear things left me terrified. It was difficult to figure out what happened."

Once, it would have killed him to have her call him cute, but now it made him feel safe. He hesitated when he heard the steady draw of her breath. He must have been near a thin section of the wall. He crouched as close as he dared and listened to the rustle of her feet against the grass—all the proof that she was real and there and she understood.

"It was terrifying," he said, breathing faster than he wanted. It was hard to think about even now, years out from the day. "I was jousting, and I was the youngest there. It was for show, I know, but I was still so much smaller and already afraid of these giant knights in full armor. I'd practiced before but never in front of so many people. That first bout, I could feel my heart in my chest, and the armor I was in was so stifling. It was like everything was louder and bigger, and suddenly even lifting my arms was hard. Then the match started," he said slowly. Phillip never talked about it. Recounting it seemed dangerous, as if the words would choke him. "It had been raining that morning, and when I got knocked from Samson, I fell face-first in the mud. One of his hooves landed on me, not hard and he moved immediately, but the mud got into the armor. I couldn't push myself up, and every time I breathed, I gagged on the mud. I was drowning."

The helplessness of being too weak and shocked to move and being able only to struggle as Samson stomped around him had lingered for years in the back of his mind. There was nothing like the powerlessness of waiting for your vision to fade completely.

Phillip shuddered and said, "I could hear them laughing and talking while it got harder and harder to breathe, and then my father came over and picked me up by the back of my armor. Dumped me to my knees right there in front of everyone and told me to walk it off. I vomited while still wearing my helmet."

"I heard him say that," she whispered, "but I didn't hear the rest. I mean, I did, but I didn't realize . . ."

"There was no way you could have figured out

exactly what happened," said Phillip. The story still made him taste bile and dirt. Phillip covered his mouth, the familiar rage and grief welling up inside him until he felt like he would burst. Maleficent had been terrifying, but the realization that he would never be able to live up to his father's expectations had been far, far worse. "No son of his would be cowardly enough to quit after getting knocked off his horse. That's what my father said. So I didn't see the point in trying to be what he wanted after that."

Briar Rose took a loud, deep breath that made him feel worlds better, because if even she, someone who cared for everyone, agreed that his father was unfair, it had to be true.

"You were afraid I would think that you were a coward," she whispered. "I don't now, and I wouldn't have then, if it helps."

"It's the worst insult for a knight." Phillip shrugged. "And I thought you were some girl rebelling against normal rules."

"I never thought you paid attention to me," Briar Rose said softly. "I know you had to, obviously, but I never thought you actually cared enough to remember."

"Yeah, well . . ." Phillip felt his face growing warm and covered his smile with a hand before remembering that she, fortunately, couldn't see. "I guess we're both wrong about some things."

The silence that grew between them, broken only by her barely audible laughs, was comfortable and calming. Phillip rubbed his chest and tried to pinpoint the flutter behind his ribs as he imagined her sitting on the other side of the thorn wall. He hoped she was smiling, too.

Telling the story hadn't felt good, but making sure she knew the details made him feel better.

"For the first time, my life is in my hands, and you deserve the same thing," said Phillip, pushing himself to his feet. "Let's finish this. Something else, magic or fate or whatever, threw us together in our dreams, but we deserve to live on our terms: me outside of my father's shadow and you away from your aunts' overprotectiveness."

The thorn wall crinkled, and through the thorns, Briar Rose whispered, "What if you're the only person I'll ever meet?"

He took a left but could still hear her. There was no running from this question. "Then that's my gain and your loss, but I don't believe that."

Suddenly, a pale white hand poked through the thorn wall, and he leapt back.

"Come here," Briar Rose said.

"How?" Phillip reached out, their fingers brushing, and he shivered. Her skin was warm, like the sun on a spring day. He grinned and traced the lines of her palm. A vine twisted around her wrist. He tapped her hand. "Get out of there before the thorns eat you."

She yanked her arm in with a hiss. "It was worth a shot."

They walked in silence for a while until she sighed.

"You wouldn't have told me that story a few weeks ago, and you never would have been that sentimental," said Briar Rose.

"You make it sound like everything is my fault."

She chuckled. "Was that not what you agreed to?"

Ah, there it was—the teasing rivalry without the weight of anger or secrets.

"Absolutely not." Phillip peeked around the corner of the maze. "I'm simply distracting you so I can reach the end of the maze first."

"Until recently I was worried you didn't know what a maze was," she said. "It's sort of nice. I had never been in one before."

He wished he could picture her more fully: the blush speckling her cheeks, the glint of her eyes in the forest light, or the gestures she made with each word. The way she spoke and cared was beautiful. He wasn't as much concerned about what she looked like as he was desperate to see how she moved through the world. The very idea of seeing her filled him with an exhilarating anticipation.

"Sorry. I have to know," he said, rubbing his face even though she couldn't possibly know he was blushing. "How is it possible that you've never met anyone else? Don't you need firewood or food or medicine? Have none of you ever gotten hurt or sick?"

"Hurt? Yes," she said, "but we have ways to stop us from getting sick."

Phillip latched on to the warbling uncertainty in her tone. "What do you mean? Haven't you ever caught a fever or sneezed?"

"Of course I've sneezed," she said, but her exasperation lacked the bitterness it would have had before. "Back in the old days people might get sick, but we have ways to deal with that now."

"Do we?" Phillip narrowed his eyes at the thorn wall. That was the most suspicious thing she had ever said, and he had once heard her refer to a bear as a good friend. "Don't you remember when I was sick two years ago and stuck in bed?"

"That was just for a day," said Briar Rose.

No wonder their assumptions about each other had led to miscommunication.

"For two weeks," he said. "I was in bed ill for two weeks."

"What?" she asked. "How is that possible? My aunts always make me feel better right away. Tonics, mostly. Surely you have them?"

"We have tonics but none that work that quickly," said Phillip. Her aunts seemed odder and odder. "Have you ever gotten a cut?"

"All the time. Why?" she asked. "My aunts always murmur over it and argue about what to do, but then they do the same thing every single time—wrap it up— and it's fine by morning."

"Huh." He tried not to sound as interested as he was.

He could practically hear her narrowing her eyes. "Don't get too curious. You're not going to abandon everything else on your plate and try to find me, are you?"

"I don't think I could do that without dying." He laughed and shook his head. "And what if we stop dreaming of each other when we meet in the waking world? These dreams are the most stable thing in my life other than Samson and Johanna."

He turned the next corner of the maze. The walls were thinner here, as if they couldn't keep up with the distance the vines were trying to cover, and there were gaps. They weren't large, but they were there and didn't snap shut on his nose when he peered through them. A vine whipped out, slower than normal. Phillip batted it away.

The thorns were smaller, too.

And then he saw it: a flash of hair, like burnished gold, and a plain pale dress.

"Phillip?" Briar Rose called, breathless. "If you turn right, what do you see?"

Phillip stepped around the corner. The end of the maze loomed. He could make out the old dream wood beyond the last hedge, trees looming over the twisting thorn walls that composed the maze. He sprinted, his heart pounding and his mind racing at what might be awaiting him, and skidded into the familiar wood. To his right, a young woman ran out another opening in the hedge maze. She gasped and spun to face him.

Briar Rose was more like a willow tree than a flower. She was tall and lithe, stepping across the grass as if she didn't want to crush it. Her hair was loose and free and tumbled over her shoulders with the same pale gold tint as late autumn leaves. The only part of her as bright as petals was her violet eyes, rimmed in red.

Phillip tried to speak and had no words. She was

distressingly real and beautiful and oh so near for the first time, and he was afraid to break whatever magic had gifted them this.

"Phillip?" she asked, staring up at him, and a half smile graced her lips. "Oh. I thought there would be a reward."

She was perfect.

"You *are* as prickly as your namesake," he said, raising a hand to his chest and then dropping it once he realized he was shaking. "Already you wound me."

She laughed. "I am a much better reward than you."

His imaginings hadn't done her justice, and he had to clear his throat to keep his voice from wavering.

"You're all right," said Phillip. It seemed wrong to see her there, as if the dream would fade any moment or she would vanish forever. Gingerly, he reached out one hand to her. "You know I'm teasing, right? You're more than all right."

"Don't flatter me too much." She mirrored his hesitation. "I won't know what to do with you if you stop teasing me."

"You'll never be in danger of me flattering you too much," he said, bowing until they were nose to nose and their hands were almost touching. "I don't care for that gleam in your eyes at all."

Briar Rose bridged the gap, barely lacing their fingers together, and Phillip's heart leapt. He couldn't recall the feeling, like the air in his lungs had been replaced with something lighter and he was one wrong step away from floating into the sky. He knew that he didn't hate Briar Rose, but he hadn't realized how long his feelings for her had been so soft.

And he didn't hate that.

"So you are real," he whispered, and pressed his forehead against hers.

Briar Rose closed her eyes and arched closer, her words a whisper against his lips. "Prove it."

And suddenly, with a grip as sharp as a dragon's claws, he was ripped from the dream and her touch entirely.

15

One Gift, Friendship Rare

"PHILLIP!" ERIS whispered fiercely, her fingers clenched around his shoulders.

He jerked awake, gasping in air as if he had been drowning, and she backed away from him. The tent was dark and the entrance drawn shut. Night birds called out across the clearing. Crickets chirped in the distance. Johanna snored.

Phillip rubbed the hand Briar Rose had been holding, the feeling of her fingers lingering, and took a breath to avoid snapping at Eris. For the first time in ages, he had wanted to stay in the dream and spend as much time as possible with Briar Rose. They had only just cleared the air and met. He started to protest being awake, but Eris held up a single finger to her lips. Her fear made him hesitate.

"Eris?" Phillip asked, his voice raspy from sleep, as he slowly refocused his attention on the fairy in front of him. "What's wrong?"

"I'm sorry," she whispered, "but I have grown quite fond of you."

"Oh, no?" Phillip sat up.

"Save your sarcasm for the next part of this conversation," she said, then glanced at Johanna and touched her temple, putting her into a much deeper sleep. "You remind me of myself when I was younger—uncertain and forgotten, forced into a role you had no desire to take on, and desperate for someone to believe in you. I tried to be good for so long, but I was never good enough."

"Until your mentor," Phillip said quietly.

"Until my mentor, I thought I would never be good enough for anyone." Eris lit the tip of her wand with a pale light, shadowing her face from below. Her eyes reflected gold in the dark. "For her, I was good enough."

"Eris, what's wrong?" he asked. "You're acting oddly."

"You must listen to me until I am done, Phillip," she said, wringing her hands and glancing toward the tent flap. Each look made his skin crawl with fear. "Promise me that. Do not interrupt me. Do not doubt me. Trust me as I trust you."

His breath caught, and he nodded.

"Phrike, Poena, and I are Maleficent's apprentices. We disappointed her during the last war, and we have been doing this to get back into her good graces," she said in one breath.

A buzz like a thousand bees filled his ears. He must have misheard her, or she was joking. Eris had promised to teach him magic. She had taught him magic. Maleficent would never want that.

"We needed a way to steal the Sword of Truth and the Shield of Virtue so that they could not be used against Maleficent once Princess Aurora's birthday arrived, and you were our way. We assumed having you do it would be a boon to Maleficent. She would find it much more vicious to use you to hurt the kings than to simply use any human to get the armaments."

Phillip couldn't stop himself from laughing. "What?"

It was a joke. It was the worst joke anyone had ever told.

"Maleficent will kill you," said Eris. "But if you are gone and if I have time to convince her of your usefulness, she won't. She took me in, after all, but I need time. We can only get that if you run."

"She can't kill me," he said. "I have the sword, I have the shield, and I have magic."

Eris's face fell into an expression he hadn't seen from her before, and she shook her head. "Oh, Phillip.

Everything was a ploy I devised to get the arms and distract you from preparing for the curse with your father. You don't have magic. You never did."

Phillip had been stabbed before. He had been knocked unconscious, on accident and on purpose. He had even heard the snap of his own arm bone as it broke after he fell from a horse. The pain didn't hit until long after each of those hurts. The dark hole of wild terror always overtook him first.

It wasn't like panic or fear. It was something deeper, like swimming in a lake and looking down only to notice that you couldn't see the bottom. There was a sharpness to the world that terror and pain brought that let him move forward and get to safety. He knew in those moments that there was an escape for him so long as he kept going.

Phillip focused on a blade of grass near his feet and urged it to grow and curl around his ankle. It was such a simple magic, the first thing he had been able to do, but nothing happened. He held out his hand and coaxed it forward.

Nothing.

And the look Eris gave him when she noticed stopped his heart.

There was no escaping this. There was no swimming to shore. Phillip's chest tightened, and breathing became hard. This was swimming in the depths of a lake of dingy water without being able to see even his hand before his face or the predators lurking around him. This was drowning.

"I'm sorry. I regret lying to you and giving you hope, but there are ways to fix this." Eris drew in a sharp breath through her nose and cracked her knuckles. "It's ridiculous, really, but Maleficent went against her principles to train me, and here I find myself going against mine to save you. I was in your position once, and Maleficent offered me her hand. I took it."

"No," he whispered, and shook his head. He tried to call a breeze, but nothing happened. "No, we retrieved the Sword of Truth and the Shield of Virtue to defeat Maleficent."

"No, you stole them from King Hubert's wizard and King Stefan's mercenaries so that I could deliver them to Maleficent and they could not be used against her," said Eris. "Fairies cannot wield them. To hold them, even, is painful. To move them with magic is something only the most powerful can do, and they cannot do it more than once or twice. That I did not lie about."

A hot, jittery feeling filled Phillip's skin, coating his

palms in sweat and clenching his jaw. His tongue was thick and useless. Words cluttered his throat. "You're joking. You must be joking. Why would anyone spend so much time and effort on a simple robbery?"

"That was the point—we didn't just need you to steal the sword and shield for us. We needed to stall you and keep you away from your father and Ald Tor until Maleficent returned to these lands and we could turn you over to her. Maleficent loves nothing more than heartache. Lying to you about magic was the easiest way to get your attention and keep it, and we thought it would be the most fun for us. A cruel act, I know. I'm sorry, but you were only the prince then, and now you are Phillip," said Eris, shaking her head. "Not only did you not have time to prepare for Maleficent, but it was you who stole the sword and shield. It was you—"

"Tricked," he said. "Taken in. Lied to."

It was all nothing more than a feint designed to waste his time and break his heart. Was Briar Rose . . .

"Maleficent cast us all aside when we could not prevent her defeat," Eris carried on. "We had to make her trust us again."

"By lying to me. Was any of it real? The talks and promises? Your specialties? The training?"

Eris flinched.

She had been so kind to him. Poena hadn't been, but she had still taught him. Phrike had healed him. She had—

Phillip brought his hand up to his shoulder, still sore from his fall off the tower, and prodded it, gasping at the pain. The bruise was gone, but it still hurt. It still hurt because the bruise was still there—because evil fairies couldn't heal.

"It was all an illusion," he said. "The healing. The teaching. The friendship. The promises."

The healing should have been his first indication, but he had been so enchanted by the magic and the promise of mentorship—the simple idea that he could exist outside what his father wanted for him—that he hadn't even noticed it.

"You knew exactly what I wanted." Phillip pressed his fist into his chest, his heart beating unbearably hard, and thought he might be sick. "I could never feel my magic because there wasn't any. It was yours."

He hadn't been able to handle fire magic without being burned. He had to tell Eris what his gestures and commands meant before he could do magic. He developed it suddenly for no discernible reason.

He wasn't a wizard. He was a jester.

"You are as human as the rest of them," Eris said,

and took his hands in hers. "I'm sorry for giving you that false hope. You are talented and clever, but you have no magic."

Phillip was nothing more than a pawn—always had been and always would be. The carefully built future he had imagined for himself crumbled. There would be no comeuppance for his father, and Phillip would not save the day. Eris had elegantly placed him on the board of life and had removed him as quickly.

If he had finally found happiness here and it was all a lie, were his dreams fake, too? He had been dreaming of Briar Rose for over a decade, but could it all be fake? Was every joy in his life a lie?

"These weeks may have been a plot, but my warning you now is not," she said sharply, and took him by the shoulders. "If you leave and do not return, if your part in this plot against Maleficent is not certain, I can protect you. Maleficent will not follow if you go now. Let the others deal with her. Or not. It was never your fight."

"You want me to leave?" he asked, still trying to wrap his mind around it all.

"Yes! You went on your journey with Johanna. I am simply asking you to go on another one. To Maleficent you are King Hubert's son and Princess Aurora's future husband, nothing more, and she will kill you for that unless you do exactly as I say. Abandon this fight against her. Save yourself."

"Nothing more," he muttered.

"Like I was. So desperate to do good and always coming up short." Eris patted his cheek. "You will never be good enough for them—not as you were and not as you will be, no matter what you do—but you are perfect to me now."

"Now," said Phillip. "Now I have nothing. I have less than nothing. I have mistakes."

"Don't be ridiculous," Eris said, pulling away. "You still have me, and I am telling you to flee."

"I do have to leave," he said, his voice soft and distant, as if he were falling far away, sinking deeper into the murky lake of himself. "We can't stay here."

He glanced at Johanna, asleep and unaware, and Eris startled.

"Yes, take her," she said. She reached for him again and fiddled with his shirt, fixing his collar and brushing down his hair. "Travel away from here."

Let Maleficent win, she meant.

Should he? All of it, the last few weeks, had been for nothing. He had ruined his father's plans. He had ruined everything.

He could finally envision the life he wanted, and it was all a lie. All the things he had grown to like about himself were lies.

"I always run away," he muttered. "I thought I was changing, becoming a better Phillip. The person I wanted to be."

He'd had so many opportunities to do better, and when he had finally taken them, it had all gone wrong.

"So you are a work in progress," said Eris. "Live to be the finished product."

The words struck him. Only a little while earlier he had said nearly the same thing to Briar Rose, but from Eris it sounded like mockery. Had he really changed much?

It didn't matter. He wasn't a product. He was Phillip, and he couldn't run away—not after everything that had happened. Everything that happened after this was on him whether he liked it or not. He had to do something to set it right.

He had told Briar Rose his life was in his hands, and he would keep his word.

No magic, no way out of his marriage, and nothing to do about Maleficent. Well, at least he wasn't the knight in shining armor he had never wanted to be.

Except he had the sword and shield within closer reach than Maleficent did, even if they were in the tent with the fairies. He could fix one mistake.

"Take some time to gather your things, and by the time Johanna awakens, the others and I will be asleep. Leave then," said Eris. "Separate yourself from these troubles."

"Eris, wait," he said, and grabbed her arm. "Is Briar Rose real?"

Her eyebrows pinched together. "Who?"

Never before had one word given him so much hope. "Never mind."

She hesitated. "You worried about me once, Phillip. Sincerely worried about me. I am repaying that concern with my own. Leave tonight while my companions and I sleep, and stay out of your father's fight."

She left the tent, and Phillip collapsed, letting out a muffled scream into his hands.

Phillip couldn't face Johanna yet. Not with his eyes still stinging and his shirt wet where he'd wiped his face. He wasn't sure how he would explain to her—or if he even could—that the fairies were on Maleficent's side and Eris was betraying them. How would he say that the past weeks of their lives had been not only a purposeful waste of time but also detrimental to their success?

In one fell swoop, he had ruined everyone's plan except Maleficent's. He had robbed his father, effectively, when he took the sword from Barnaby—whom he definitely owed an apology to—and lied to Amis. Even though he had thought he was stealing the shield to defeat Maleficent, he doubted virtuous legends cared much for particulars. He'd gifted Maleficent exactly what she needed to win the upcoming war.

He had to get the sword and shield. Eris's confession had changed everything, but leaving the sword and shield with the fairies was as inexcusable as everything else he'd done. They had magic and he very much didn't; simply running away was easy and reasonable.

But Phillip had never been described as reasonable.

He quietly gathered up his and Johanna's belongings, trying not to wake her, and waited for a little while. It was still a long time until dawn, and Eris was sure to go back to sleep. The sword and shield were in the fairies' tent. He could get them once she fell asleep.

They had won—or so they thought—so surely they would be celebrating with a full night's rest.

"Need enough energy for the gloating," he muttered, easing Johanna's book out from under her head.

It was open, and the first few pages were folded in on each other. Carefully, Phillip fixed the pages and smoothed them out against his chest. The first page was crinkled but readable.

Unlegendary: Untold but Not Unimportant
Not all great knights live on in stories, and not all great stories are truthful tales of good knights. Who we choose to forget says as much about us as who we choose to remember.

Phillip stopped reading, ran a thumb across the title scrawled in her overly careful hand, closed the book, and placed it into a secure little flap inside her pack. He had never taken Johanna as someone who would want to write histories, but many of the epics were history embellished. This fit her nearly perfectly.

And it meant she wasn't writing about their own misadventures.

Certain Eris would be asleep by now, Phillip made

his way outside with their belongings. Everything was packed save for Johanna's bedroll. She could do that easily enough. The horses were Phillip's main concern, and he approached their sleeping forms slowly. Sprawled out on his side in the grass, Samson was chewing some dream food in his sleep, and Taliesin was standing a few strides from him. Phillip clucked at him, and the horse opened one eye. Phillip showed him the pack.

"We're being sneaky, all right?" Phillip whispered, and let Taliesin shake himself out before loading him up. "We need a quiet and quick exit in a minute."

Taliesin huffed. Phillip patted his neck, promising to get Johanna as soon as it was safe. Taliesin nudged Samson with a hoof, and Phillip shushed the large courser as he rose. Samson snuffled against Phillip's shoulder. Phillip kissed Samson's snout and set his pack and shoes next to him.

"Wait here," he said, and pointed at Samson. "Breakfast once we're safe."

Samson let out a soft nicker, and Phillip turned to the fairies' tent.

Without magic, he would have to move slowly. If anything went wrong, his only saving grace was that he could wield the sword and shield against the fairies and they couldn't touch them. Since being near the armaments didn't bother them, sleeping near them was the easiest way to protect them. Phillip hadn't questioned why they wanted to protect the arms when it was only the five of them. Eris's confession made it very clear, though.

Phillip had never been inside their tent. They kept the flap tightly drawn, the whole thing still prickling with magic whenever he went near it. At least he could still sense magic, but that didn't help him much. He knelt before the flap with his ear to the crack, and he listened. The muffled sounds of sleep—snoring and breathing and shifting blankets—drifted to him. Slowly, he was able to pick out three different breathing styles. All three fairies sounded asleep.

Phillip took a deep breath and opened the tent flap. The fairies did love their beauty sleep: Eris was stretched out on her back across a pillowy-looking bedroll, and a silk scarf was tied over her eyes; Phrike snored like a horse stampede while curled up in a nest of blankets that looked as if they were spun from the softest storm clouds; and Poena slept on a comfortable cot, tendrils of smoke curling out of her mouth with each exhale. They were on opposite sides of the tent, as if they couldn't stand to be near each other even when sleeping. In the center of the tent were the Sword of Truth and the Shield of Virtue, swaddled so tightly in blankets and rags that he could barely make out their shapes. The only light in the tent came from the sliver of shield still visible.

Phillip swallowed. The silence seemed brittle, as if the slightest sound would shatter it. He held his breath and stepped fully into the tent. His bare feet rustled across the rugs laid over the grass, and his heartbeat pounded in his ears. He stayed closer to Eris, certain she would be mad if she woke up but wouldn't outright murder him for not following her directions. He took another slow step toward the center of the room, and the fairies didn't wake. Carefully, he began to unravel the sword and shield.

They glittered in the dark, starlight flickering across their silvery surfaces, and he slid his arm through the straps of the shield. It was warm despite the cool night air, and the sword grip seemed to mold to his hand. Phillip turned to leave.

The rug beneath his feet rippled, and he froze.

Eris shifted, raising one hand to her face. Phillip prepared to run, but before he could, Phrike choked and cleared her throat in her sleep. Eris sighed and threw her arm over her covered eyes. Poena didn't so much as move.

Phillip stayed still, his heart little more than a

hollow knot in his throat. He had already failed terribly. He had to get the arms out of there and fix it.

Being a useless knight was one thing; being the downfall of humanity was another.

He took a painfully slow step toward the tent flap, and no one moved. Another step. He held his breath again. A final longer step. Nothing.

Phillip slipped sideways out of the tent, the sword and shield safely with him, and dashed to the horses. His hands shook, and fear scratched at the back of his neck. He listened for the fairies to give chase.

They didn't.

Phillip kept the sword and shield in hand when he woke up Johanna. She took the betrayal as poorly as he had, stalking out to Taliesin with a scowl so frightening the horse backed away. Phillip felt hollow explaining it, each trick and lie obvious now.

"Look—the most important thing we can do right now is get the sword and shield to Ald Tor and far away from Maleficent," he said, desperate for her to know that he wasn't simply running away. He shoved the shield into her arms. "We have three days until Princess Aurora's birthday, and it will take us that long to reach King Stefan's castle. Poena and Phrike, maybe even Eris, will come after us once they realize we took the armaments. I don't think they can track us, or they would have found us immediately after the robbery. It will be safer if we split up. Then, if they do catch up, at least one of us will get there with one of the arms. Or you'll finally get to punch Poena in the face."

That he wasn't going to do exactly as Eris wanted was something he could deal with later.

"Absolutely not," said Johanna. "I'm not leaving you alone."

"You will. I'm not asking you to do this. I'm telling you to," said Phillip. "There are two roads to Ald Tor from here—one around the woods and one through it."

Johanna inhaled sharply and clenched her teeth. She held up a finger between them. "Fine. But I'm going around. It's the easier, more common path, and they'll expect us to go that way," she whispered, poking him between each word.

The pair led their horses from camp and waited until they were far away before mounting up. Phillip kept the sword, and Johanna carried the shield on her back.

"Do you trust Eris?" she asked. The concern in her voice killed him. "Could this be another ploy?"

"No and no," he said. Every time he had raised his hand to call forth his magic, had Eris been laughing at him? Every time he had confided in her about his fears and goals, had she made note of it to use against him later?

Phillip swallowed. "But we'll find out how she feels once she notices the sword and shield are gone. Hopefully, that won't be until dawn and they won't be able to find us. Phrike usually moved us to places. She never moved us magically to people. Maybe they can't track humans."

Johanna took a deep breath and mumbled, "Hopefully. How are we going to explain this to your father?"

"Quickly, without leaving any pauses during which he can yell at me."

He knew he deserved a reprimand, but he felt so empty that he wasn't sure it would make a difference.

"Phillip, be serious," she said.

"We'll tell them everything," he said. "That's more important than my pride."

Johanna opened her mouth, stared at him, and closed it. Samson snorted.

"You can all remark on how unlikely I was to ever utter those words once we're safe in Ald Tor," said Phillip. "I got us into this mess, but I can't leave us in it. Not now."

He wanted to run and hide and never admit to any

of it, but he couldn't. The Phillip of a month earlier could have. Even with the lies and betrayal, Eris was right. Only he could control how he reacted to his circumstances and take charge of them. Eris had ruined him.

He believed in himself now.

16

Once Upon a Dream

PHILLIP AND Johanna reached the crossroads
an hour before dawn. She took the main road
that led around the woods surrounding Ald Tor and King
Stefan's castle, and Phillip bid her farewell with a promise to be safe. He ventured into the old woods, the trees
as crowded and dark as his thoughts. He spent the next
three days trekking through them in near total silence.

There was no world in which he could ever stomach what he had done. Phillip had been tricked and had
cursed them as effectively as Maleficent had. His only
hope was getting the armaments back to Ald Tor. Phillip
had never shown an interest in ruling—not since he was
a bright-eyed, naive boy—so it was no wonder his father
had never told him about Old Barnaby and the Sword of
Truth or King Stefan's plans to get the Shield of Virtue.
All those times Eris and the others had applauded his
progress had been little more than a prank. He wasn't
gifted at anything.

If Phillip had paid attention, refused to learn magic, or been a son his father could trust, then none of this would have happened. Instead, he had spent the past three days traveling and looking over his shoulder for furious, murderous fairies. It was his final day in the forest, and he had seen neither wand nor wing of the fairies. Hopefully, this last morning of travel would be as unexciting as the others.

"Today is Princess Aurora's birthday, and at dusk, Maleficent's curse will take effect. We have to get to the castle before that," he said to Samson, combing through the horse's mane with his fingers. "This is what I get for learning."

Samson flicked his ears and shook his head.

"Not that you have to worry about that." Phillip patted Samson's side. "There's not much horses can learn."

At least Phillip knew how to travel inconspicuously. He had tossed aside the cat-shaped brooch Eris had given him that first day before he entered the forest. Abandoning it felt oddly final.

Walking along with Samson eased some of his sadness and rage, but they were still knotted up inside him like a bramble growing around his heart. The nights had been the worst.

He hadn't been able to sleep much, and in the few

hours he had gotten, he hadn't dreamed of the forest, Briar Rose, or anything else. The fear that she was another trick lingered in the back of his mind. As he lay in the dark with no one but a snoring horse and the stars for company, his thoughts spiraled into all the different what-could-have-beens that would never be and all the moments when the people he had trusted were actually laughing at him. Eris at least liked him enough to turn on Poena and Phrike to protect him.

But he had learned she also wasn't the sort to tell the truth. If she had really been working for Maleficent the whole time, he wasn't sure he could trust anything she had said. And then there was the fact that he'd used her confession not just to escape but to abscond *with* the sword and shield.

"It's not even that she believed in me," Phillip muttered to Samson. He collapsed over the horse's back and let his arms fall to the sides. "She figured me out so quickly and knew exactly what I needed and wanted. Why hasn't anyone like my father been able to do that?"

If someone bad enough to side with Maleficent was the only one who knew him that well, was he bad?

She had seen him fall head over backside into the mud, leap from a tower, and shout "vines" many times.

He had been vulnerable with her like he was with few people.

"Briar Rose knows me as well as she does, I guess," he mumbled into Samson's neck. "And she's not even a little bit bad."

At his meanest, he would have called Briar Rose aggressively kind. Knowing that someone as good as Briar Rose could see him at his worst moments and tolerate him—maybe even like him—eased some of the pain.

Shaking his head, Samson bumped Phillip back all the way into the saddle and snorted.

"Come on," said Phillip. "Only a few more hours in these woods until we can stop for the day."

This far northeast, the landscape was craggy hills speckled with thick old forests. Trees older than time shaded them from the sun, and the river they were following had cut through the earth so long before that the shoreline was smooth and overgrown with moss and ferns. Spring was already in bloom here, flowers taking hold in the rug-like grass and bees fluttering from bush to bramble. Birds sang overhead.

It reminded him of what the dream wood had looked like before the maze appeared. There was a peacefulness to it that made him want to linger.

He wanted to talk to Briar Rose so badly it hurt.

She knew him, and she would understand how hurt and terrified he was. He needed to know that she was real and was all right.

Phillip closed his eyes and took a steadying breath, leaning down over Samson's back again.

A familiar voice rang out through the woods. Phillip blinked and sat up. Had he fallen asleep while riding again?

"You hear that, Samson?" he asked, and pulled the horse to a stop. "Beautiful."

Samson paced backward and shook his head, huffing. He tugged the reins forward. Phillip twisted in the saddle and stood, trying to see where the singer was or get a better angle to hear them from. Samson tried to walk on.

"What is it?" Phillip had to yank the reins to pull Samson around. "Come on. Let's find out."

Samson snorted, shook his head, and dragged them to the path they had been following.

"Oh, come on!" Phillip held the reins tight and tried to turn him, but Samson held firm. The horse walked them a few more strides. Phillip leaned down and patted his neck. "For an extra bucket of oats?" Phillip nearly laughed when Samson's head bobbed. "And a few carrots?" Samson nodded, and Phillip sat back in the saddle. "Hup, boy!"

They rode back the way they had come, toward the voice. Samson, at least, would forever be predictable and bribable. The horse's motive was always clear: food.

The person singing moved through the woods at a steady pace but was clearly across the river. Samson charged on with single-minded precision, and Phillip tried to squash the hope blooming in his chest. It couldn't be Briar Rose, no matter how much he wanted to talk to her right then.

"I can't get my hopes up," he mumbled, ignoring the disappointment that gripped him. He just wanted to talk to someone who knew what was going on, and he was clearly imagining Briar Rose's voice. "It's not her. It can't be her."

Samson pulled up near an outcropping of rocks as the voice echoed around them, and suddenly, he was off, galloping through the underbrush. He leapt over a fallen tree on the riverbank, and a branch caught Phillip in the chest. Phillip scrambled for a hold on the tree but lost it. He plummeted into a shallow offshoot of the river.

"Whoa!" he shouted, and spat out a mouthful of leaves and water.

Samson's frantic hoofbeats stopped. Phillip groaned, pushing himself up into a seated position. Now both his pride and his back ached. Samson picked his way through the water to Phillip with delicate little splashes. He pulled off Phillip's sopping wet hat.

Phillip glared up at him. He and Samson had been in tournaments and ridden through far denser woods, and it had been ages since Phillip had fallen off. He splashed Samson.

"No carrots," he said, taking his hat. "We'll see about the oats."

Samson huffed, and Phillip rose, rolling his eyes. Phillip leaned against Samson and dragged himself from the water. He was lucky it wasn't still freezing.

Phillip peeled off his damp cloak and set it out on a branch to dry. The singing had stopped. Phillip sat down on a nearby rock to dry off and get control of his thoughts.

It couldn't be Briar Rose. There was no way her aunts had kept her that close to civilization when they thought it too dangerous. It could be a trap, some new torture Maleficent had orchestrated on finding out he had slipped away from her minions with the sword and shield.

Eris might have changed her mind about helping

him once she realized the armaments were gone. Those were ultimately what she had been after.

"What do you think?" he asked Samson.

Samson huffed and nudged Phillip's foot.

"I'm not arriving home damp *and* disappointing." Phillip waved a hand at the sun. "I'll dry out soon enough and we can go then. I know you're excited to be stabled, but I am not thrilled about seeing my father."

Or Princess Aurora's parents.

Or Princess Aurora.

Phillip lay in a patch of sun. Even if he did find Briar Rose, would she want to talk to someone so self-absorbed he had fallen for Maleficent's tricks? Over the past few days of travel, his anger had cooled to a grief-tinged defeat.

"I'm wallowing," he said, eyeing Samson. "You made me wallow."

Phillip tossed his hat up onto the tree with his cloak and crawled up to sit on the roots of a gnarled old tree. Samson drank from the river, ignoring him.

"You know, Samson," he said, and emptied the water from his boots, "there was something strange about that voice. Too beautiful to be real. Maybe it was a mysterious being. A wood sprite or . . ."

Samson snorted and neighed, staring at something behind Phillip, and Phillip spun. It would be just his luck for—

Two rabbits were running off with his boots, and his cloak was flying away, as if even his clothes had grown tired of him. He stumbled to his feet.

"Hey!" he shouted. "Stop!"

He chased after them. The hat and boots hopped up a steep hill and vanished. The cape fluttered far too high for him to reach, tail feathers sticking out the back. Normal animals didn't rob humans of their clothes, but there was no charge to the air that came with magic. Samson cantered after Phillip. If it was magic, it didn't affect horses.

"No one finds out about this," muttered Phillip. He spun, grabbed Samson's head, and bumped his nose against the horse's. "I can't be the prince who got robbed by a pack of rabbits."

Samson huffed. The singing started again, slight and near. It was over the hill where his clothes had vanished.

Phillip crept toward the hill. "Wood witch?"

Samson let out a shallow groan.

The singing trailed off, and someone babbled behind the thick greenery. Phillip snuck as close as he dared, hiding in a tangle of plants beside a tree. He pushed the leaves out of his way.

Briar Rose—awake and real and looking as she had at the end of the maze—danced through the woods and sang to a small choir of creatures ambling after her in Phillip's stolen clothes. It was her voice. It was her face.

And it was definitely her floppy-eared rabbit Ears hopping in one of his boots.

Her bare feet shuffled over thick grass. As she bowed with the rhythm of the song, pale gold hair spilled over her shoulders and curled like ferns at the ends against a plain linen dress. The arch of her arms as she danced was as self-assured as her words had been all those times they had whispered through the wall, and an owl in Phillip's cloak gathered itself up until it was her height. It and the other creatures danced around her. The words of the song pierced Phillip's heart like an arrow.

"Once upon a dream," he muttered, and hit Samson's shoulder. "She's singing about me, right?"

Samson snorted.

Oh.

He wasn't certain this quiet, creeping feeling was friendship, but it was something akin to it that he didn't know. Sweet and bitter. His admiration of her studies.

His prior fury at her seeing his most vulnerable and embarrassing moments.

There was absolutely no anger now.

He hadn't appreciated her at once. She had grown on him, the way certain mushrooms grew on roots and allowed both plants to thrive.

Oh, no. That was a terrible metaphor. He'd have to ask Johanna for a better one.

Briar Rose spun away. Phillip darted forward, seizing his chance and the back of his cloak. He gently moved the owl aside and waited for the steps of Briar Rose's dance to return her to him. She twirled into the circle of his arms, and Phillip caught her wrists in his hands loosely, so as not to frighten her too badly. It was an old court dance, one he hadn't seen since he was a child but remembered enough of the steps to.

He stepped behind her, interrupting her song.

She stiffened, glancing at the owl in his cloak off to the side, and gasped.

"Oh," she said, pulling away from Phillip and then hesitating.

Her brows were pinched together in confusion, but she wasn't scared or angry. She was meeting his eyes as if waiting for something from him. Slowly, almost imperceptibly, she lifted one brow.

"I'm awfully sorry," he said so sincerely it was clear he didn't mean it. "I didn't mean to frighten you."

"It wasn't that," she said, and dropped her gaze. "It's just that you're a . . . a . . ."

He narrowed his eyes, ignoring the sting of her not recognizing him. Had his dreams been only that? His dreams alone?

"A stranger?" he asked. She hummed, and he laughed softly. "But don't you remember? We've met before."

He needed her to know him. Briar Rose had been his constant companion even before they could communicate. Friend or foe, he wanted to know her in real life.

"We . . . we have?" she asked, still poised to leave.

But despite her stance, there was a quirk to her lips and a glint in her eyes that let him know she knew exactly who he was.

He swallowed his retort. No more assumptions. This was Briar Rose, who had *never* met another person in real life. Of course she was nervous.

"You said so yourself." He held on to one of her hands, lacing their fingers as she had when they met at the end of the maze. Her hand felt nearly the same, though there were calluses he hadn't felt before. A few dark stains, from ink or berries, marred her skin. He liked how much more real it all made her. He tugged slightly, and she took a step closer. "Once upon a dream!"

Her violet eyes widened. Her hand squeezed his. She pursed her lips to keep from smiling and darted away from him, then hid behind a tree. Barely in sight, her fingers crooked and beckoned him.

"I know you," he said.

He went around the side of the tree and touched her hand. She inhaled, her mouth pinched and surprised. Slowly, she raised her eyes to his. Hope lit them from within.

He offered her his hand.

She smiled widely and for real then, truly happy to see him. She took his hand, and they spun into the dance again around a small lake. Her fingers tightened around his shoulder, and a flush as pale as sunrise was spreading across her cheeks. "Phillip?"

"Ah, ah, ah," he said, and pulled her close. "I'm your dream prince with . . . well, you're the one with a mischievous gleam in her eyes."

"Are you real? How are you here?" she asked, laughing and sliding her hand over his shoulder.

"Am I real, asks the girl who didn't recognize the boy she's been dreaming about all of their lives," said Phillip, pulling her closer. "It's been only three days since we spoke last."

It seemed ridiculous now to have ever read malice into her words. He had ascribed the feelings he felt about himself to her.

"Oh, hush." She squeezed his hand as he spun her again. "This feels exceptionally dreamlike."

They walked toward the edge of the cliff hand in hand, letting the few minutes pass in silence. In the distance, the tall white towers of King Stefan's estate glittered against a foggy lavender sky.

"Dreamy, am I?" Phillip grinned. "A lot happened. I'm traveling to Ald Tor to speak with my father and King Stefan. I can't believe you live so near to King Stefan's castle. How have you not walked over there?"

"I'm not supposed to," she said, and he remembered how often her studies had been about obedience, honor, and trust. "My aunts always find me first anyway. Aren't you supposed to be training?"

He winced. "That went quite badly, actually. I seem to have been tricked."

"What?" she asked.

Once, he would have mistaken her tone for one of judgment, but the look on her face made it clear she was worried for him.

"It's a long story," he said. "How much time do you have?"

"I live alone in a wood that I'm not allowed to leave." She gestured for him to sit. "How much time do you think I have?"

"Well, it's not that long." He helped her sit and then joined her in the grass. "You're smart. You might have a better plan than me."

Phillip told Briar Rose mostly everything. He was scared to tell her of all his failures, but she looked at him with such trust and curiosity that his worry faded to comfort. She would understand better than anyone how he felt, and it made him feel safe. Their meeting was a respite in the middle of the disaster that was his life.

Beneath his comfort stirred another emotion, one he didn't recognize and couldn't name, that warmed his heart and reassured him that he wouldn't be facing his uncertain future alone.

He didn't tell her that he really was a prince, afraid her etiquette lessons might take over her reactions to him. He also didn't tell her that he was betrothed. Already he was revealing so much. He didn't want to overcomplicate their first real-life meeting with every little detail of his life. There would be time for those conversations later.

And the idea of telling her he was promised to another made his heart ache.

"If someone told me they could get me out of this forest, I think I would do anything they said," she muttered, staring unseeing into the canopy of leaves. "Magical lessons, gifts and curses that always find a way to come true, an immortal guardian who tested you and found you worthy. If it's any consolation, your life is far more interesting than any of my stories."

He laughed. "I'd rather hear those."

Briar Rose explained more about her life with her aunts and the sheer loneliness of it all. The most recent argument she'd had with her aunts had been sparked by their insistence that she remain at home for her birthday and that they would handle any celebration. They were obviously keeping secrets, but instead of admitting it, they were breaking her trust. All she wanted was honesty and freedom.

"Today they sent me out for berries, but it was clearly a lie that they needed them," she said, and huffed. "I'm so tired of the lying."

"We could run away together. I've got a horse, and you've got a dozen maps and languages up there," he said, and tapped her temple. "We could make it pretty far."

She leaned into his touch, giving him goose bumps. "I'm afraid I am otherwise engaged tonight."

"You know I heard your aunts teach you that as a polite way to avoid meetings you don't want to be part of," he said, cupping her cheek in his hand. Phillip had wanted to meet Briar Rose, if only out of curiosity, before their dreams had brought them closer together. Now that he had, there was something new and burning beneath his skin. He traced the line of her jaw up to the curve of her ear. "We have known each other for so long, and you're still so upright and honorable. It's very frustrating."

She laughed softly and reached up to grasp his hand. "I promised my aunts I would spend the evening with them, and you have your own responsibilities to take care of."

"Run away with me. Spare me having to explain to my father how I was tricked, and I will spare you from having to feign joy at whatever surprise your aunts have for you," he said, and leaned his forehead against hers. "Two birds with one stone and all that."

The idea of traveling across the world, only the two of them, wasn't wholly unappealing.

"Are we the birds?" she asked, her nose bumping his. "Or the stones?"

"I think we're all birds to Maleficent, and she's very good at throwing stones." He drew back, stroking her hand with his thumb. "So do you dream and dance with mysterious men in woods often?"

"Only the good-looking ones!" She winked, and then she stood and pressed the back of her hand to her forehead. "Oh, I can't reveal such personal secrets to a stranger."

It wasn't a dismissal so much as a promise that they would finish playing their roles of strangers meeting in a wood again one day.

"Of course, miss. I understand completely," he said, rising as well. "However, I suppose since you will not run away with me, I need to get to that castle by sundown, and seeing you again would be a dream."

She covered her laughter with her hand and then stopped. "Sundown?"

"It's when the sun goes below the horizon and night begins."

She rolled her eyes and groaned. Her fingers laced through his, tugging him toward a tree so like the ones from their dreams. She wrapped her arms around his shoulders, leaning against his chest, and Phillip wrapped one arm around her waist. The other rested against the nape of her neck. She kissed his cheek.

It took everything within him not to startle from the touch, and Phillip tightened his grip on her waist. More than anything, he did not want to leave her.

What if this was only another dream?

"This is real. I can feel you doubting it," she whispered, the rustle of her breath warm against his skin. "We'll meet again, Phillip."

The warmth of her, the weight of her, the realness of her against him sang in his veins.

"Well, I need to leave soon or my aunts will never let me out of their sight again," she said, smiling and gazing up at him through her lashes. "This may be the first and only time we've met, but I would prefer it not to be the last."

Phillip wanted rather suddenly, desperately, to have her in his sights again.

"Forgive me, stranger," Phillip said and laughed at her charade. "Who are you? What's your name?"

"Hmm?" She lifted her head. "Oh! My name. Why, it's . . . it's . . ." She gasped and pulled away, clutching her heart. "Oh no, no. I can't. I—"

She dove back under the branch and gathered up her skirts, the image of panic. Her violet eyes were glinting with laughter. He nearly rolled his.

Now that he knew how lonely she was, it made perfect sense for her to cling to playacting like this. It was fun, too.

"Goodbye!" she shouted.

She had been alone too long. But then again, so had he.

He reached out for her but didn't give chase, like a player on a stage. "But when will I see you again?"

"Oh, never!" She threw up her hands. "Never!"

The smile never left her face, and Phillip nearly cackled.

"Never?" he called out.

She leapt from stone to stone, descending the small mountain far faster than he could, and crossed the stream in a graceful hop from shore to stone to shore. He skidded to a stop across the water from her.

"Well," she said, and glanced at him over her shoulder, "maybe someday."

"When?" he asked. "Tomorrow?"

He would be desperate to escape by then and ready to share with her all that had happened before he had to face Princess Aurora's birthday, the curse, and his betrothal.

"Oh, no." She stopped to pick up her cape and

basket, a wake of small animals chasing after her. "This evening."

Well, at least she knew what she wanted, and she was giving him a reason to escape the celebrations that night if everything went well and Maleficent was defeated quickly.

He waved to her. "Where?"

The woods were far too large for them to count on a chance meeting again.

"The cottage, in the glen." She looked back once more, smiled at him, and was gone, vanishing into the forest. Phillip lingered, his arm in the air and a pull urging him to follow her, and tried to calm the odd feeling fluttering about his chest. He definitely didn't hate his dream girl anymore. This was deeper and fuller than siple affection.

That meant he needed to speak with his father about Maleficent and his impending marriage. Eris might have lied to him, but she was right: it was time for him to be in control of his life. Even without magic, he didn't need to marry Princess Aurora. He could help without the betrothal.

Phillip sighed and let his arm fall, knowing how much his father would hate that. Samson moved up behind him.

"There's nothing left for me to do but face my father, is there?" he asked.

Samson huffed, sniffing the spot where Briar Rose's basket had been. A smear of blackberry juice stained the horse's mouth.

"You thief," he muttered, and patted Samson's neck. "All right—not everything is terrible. One thing is good, so I'm going to celebrate that for a moment."

Phillip whooped and leapt up, letting free the trembling joy he had kept restrained. He had never been this happy, and he couldn't control it. He hadn't wanted to be wild and screaming when he met her, so he did it now. The few birds lingering around him scattered with his shriek. Samson snorted.

"I found her!" He jumped to ease the energy flowing through him and bowed over, laughing into his hands. "It went better than I thought, she doesn't hate me, and talking to her was fantastic. I feel better. I think she feels better. Finally, something went right."

Slowly, the anxiety of how poised he had wanted to be before her faded, and he beamed at Samson.

"Don't ever tell anyone what you just saw," he said to the horse. "All right. Good. We're good now."

All he needed to do was confess to his father and

King Stefan and deal with Maleficent and Princess Aurora, and then he could return to Briar Rose.

He might not have magic, but he was going to live for himself, not his father, from then on.

Phillip took a deep breath, holding tight to the hope that meeting Briar Rose had brought to life in him, and nodded.

"Let's go," he said. "Time to be brave and finally be Prince Phillip."

17
The Fish and the Shark

*P*HILLIP HADN'T visited King Stefan's castle in years. As he was growing up, his father had wanted him to develop a relationship with King Stefan and Queen Leah, since they would eventually be family, but Phillip's few visits had been haunted by the memories of Maleficent and the looming absence of Princess Aurora. The white stone was brighter than he remembered it, or perhaps they had tasked some unlucky servant with scrubbing every nook and cranny of the place clean before the princess's return. Phillip lingered in the long shadow of the castle for as long as he could.

The Sword of Truth was burning a hole in his pack atop Samson, and Phillip glanced at the horizon for Johanna. He had seen no sign of her since they parted.

"Father!" Phillip said, greeting a fallen tree as he might have the king. "Funny story: I was approached by three fairies who claimed I had magic, and they trained me so that I could steal the Sword of Truth and the Shield of Virtue to defeat Maleficent, but it turns out they were working for her the whole time. Thankfully, I have the sword and shield. No magic, though. I'm still only Prince Phillip, Princess Aurora's future husband. However, I'm having second thoughts about that last part."

It had been easy to give in to the betrothal when everything was out of his hands and going against the current didn't seem worth it. Now, though, Phillip wasn't sure he could go through with marrying Princess Aurora. She needed someone to keep her safe, but knights had been keeping people safe for ages without marrying them. The curse was a different story.

For all their lies, the fairies' reaction to Johanna's and his thinking the curse could be avoided seemed genuine. If it would come to pass no matter what, that was even less reason for him to marry Princess Aurora. Anyone could guard her while she was in her cursed sleep. She would be protected, and someone else could try to find her true love, whoever that was.

Maybe Phillip's father wouldn't mind that.

And maybe Samson would learn to fly.

Meeting Briar Rose made the future seem less daunting, as if something in the universe was on his side, and he wanted her on his.

The Fish and the Shark

If King Hubert and King Stefan had needed so badly to unite their families, they should have done it themselves instead of sticking the responsibility on their children. Phillip could find a different solution to help Princess Aurora.

"Who needs marriage when you have understanding and friendship and a horse that understands sarcasm?" he asked Samson, glancing once more to see if Johanna was approaching from the road. Her absence made him anxious. "All right, boy. Let's go."

Samson nibbled at Phillip's pack, and Phillip nudged him away.

"You get carrots once my feet are fully dry again."

Samson huffed and took off toward the castle at an uncomfortable trot.

The lands around the castle were bustling with life. People ran from the castle to the farms and homes surrounding it, with bolts of fabric and baskets of food bundled up in their arms. Phillip sidled Samson into the queue of people waiting to pass through the first gate of the keep and kept his head down. The last thing he wanted was to be recognized and mobbed in public, and he also had no desire to reveal his foolishness to everyone.

Phillip left Samson in a small alley between the castle and the stuffed stables, placating him with an over-eager stable hand who would surely spoil him. Phillip didn't know his way around the castle very well, but he suspected his father would almost certainly be in the hall where court was held.

And that was the direction every servant was heading in with platters of food and jugs of wine, so it was a safe bet.

Phillip slunk inside with a handful of guests and servants. Everyone was gossiping about the birthday and wedding, placing bets on when Princess Aurora would show up and whether Prince Phillip had run away. Phillip slithered into one of the alcoves meant for servants to wait in during feasts, and cracked open the door. Inside the hall, his father and King Stefan were in the middle of a drinking game, with not a care in the world. A jester serenaded them with his lute and snuck drinks right beneath both of their noses. Phillip didn't even need the shadows of sunset to conceal his hiding place.

He was supposed to have arrived days earlier. Princess Aurora was going to meet her parents for the first time. Maleficent was coming with the intent of destroying them all.

And the two kings were playing a game.

". . . nest of their own, what?" his father was saying. "Place to raise their little brood, eh?"

Phillip furrowed his brows. Nest? He had never taken that much interest in falconry outside sport.

"Well, I suppose in time," said King Stefan.

"Of course!" said his father. "To the home!"

Phillip peeked around the corner of the alcove as his father poured out another round, laughing loudly. And Phillip was the irresponsible one? If they didn't even notice the jester's drunken state, how would they notice Maleficent?

"They don't know about the curse or Maleficent's plans," Phillip whispered, trying to rein in the fury smoldering in his chest. "They don't know it's all so dire."

Phillip stood on tiptoe to see the parchment rolled out on their table. It was building plans for a large castle, and the ramifications of his father's words hit him. The king had built a home for Princess Aurora and him, and he had done it without any input whatsoever from them. The design was huge and sprawling, fit for royalty but far too big and self-important for Phillip. There was even a separate wing for the parents. Phillip's heart beat so furiously in his chest that his father's words were garbled in his ears.

"Lovebirds can move in tomorrow," King Hubert said.

Lovebirds? They had never even spoken, and why would Princess Aurora want to leave her parents and home after only just meeting them?

"Tomorrow?" asked King Stefan, looking as horrified by the idea as Phillip felt. "But, Hubert, they're not even married yet!"

His father laughed. "Take care of that tonight. To the wedding!"

Phillip leaned farther out of the alcove and was horrified to realize that the plans contained labeled nurseries. Phillip recoiled.

His father was unstoppable in the worst of ways.

Here was a man who hadn't seen his daughter since her infancy, since he had swaddled her up and handed her over to three fairies for her own safety, and Phillip's father was already making plans for her to move out. Not to mention Phillip's well-known dislike for his betrothal and princely future. Yet King Hubert was barreling on as if Phillip's thoughts didn't matter, as if Princess Aurora's opinions didn't matter, and as if all these decisions were his to make and not theirs.

Phillip jammed a fist beneath his chin to keep from shouting at his father. Eris had betrayed him, but at least she had eventually been up-front about it. She had acknowledged the knife she planted in Phillip's back and treated him as reasonable when he took offense to it.

King Hubert poured King Stefan another glass of wine, but King Stefan swatted his hand away.

"Now hold on, Hubert," King Stefan said. "I haven't even seen my daughter yet and you're taking her away from me."

"You tell him," muttered Phillip.

Neither of them noticed the jester collecting the spilled wine in his lute, and Phillip suddenly understood the desire to drink floor-wine from a lute. This conversation and these assumptions were unbearable.

"Getting my Phillip, aren't you?" King Hubert said.

Phillip groaned. What was he? A consolation prize?

King Stefan sighed and said, "Yes, but . . ."

"Want to see our grandchildren, don't we?" asked Phillip's father, and Phillip had never wished more to be disowned. His father barreled over King Stefan's half-hearted response and flicked his beard. "There's no time to lose! Getting on in years. To the wedding!"

He toasted his friend, and Phillip glared from the alcove. Phillip had always thought he had been obvious about his feelings, but apparently the two kings wouldn't have noticed Phillip's presence or discomfort if their lives depended on it.

King Stefan pressed a hand to his friend's shoulder.

"Now, be reasonable, Hubert. After all, Aurora knows nothing about this."

The jester fell back under the table, and Phillip collapsed as he did, drawing his knees up to his chest. Hiding under a table was a tempting thought.

"Well?" his father asked without a hint of concern.

"Well," said King Stefan, trying preemptively to console him, "it may come as quite a shock."

That showed what King Stefan knew; there was no calming down King Hubert of Artwyne when he got going.

"Shock?" His father spat out his wine and pounded his goblet on the table. "My Phillip a shock? What's wrong with my Phillip?"

Phillip nodded. It was nice to be defended, but King Stefan wasn't disparaging Phillip. He was talking sense!

"Nothing, Hubert." The other king backed off as if he weren't a seasoned warrior, and Phillip rolled his eyes. "I only meant . . ."

"Why doesn't your daughter like my son?" said his father, closing in on King Stefan.

"Now, now," King Stefan said. He tried to stop King Hubert.

"I'm not so sure my son likes your daughter!" King

Hubert threw off King Stefan's hands and prodded him.

Harsh but true.

King Stefan straightened his crooked crown and drew himself up. "Now see here!"

"I'm not so sure my grandchildren want you for a grandfather!"

Phillip shook his head. Grandchildren again!

It was oddly pleasing to hear his father defend him, though.

"Why, you unreasonable, pompous blustering old windbag!" shouted King Stefan.

"Unreasonable! Pompous!" Phillip's father tore a fish from the table and wielded it like a sword. "En garde, sir!"

Phillip rose, no longer trying to hide, and sighed when they still didn't notice him.

"I warn you, Hubert, this means war!" King Stefan picked up a plate and brandished it like a shield, parrying each dull slap of the fish.

Phillip turned away. They sparred with the fish and the plate and made a mess of the dining hall. They probably wouldn't worry even if they did know what had happened to Phillip. All they were concerned about were cradles, uniting their families, and wine.

Phillip would have to fix everything, because they

were too far gone to help. Too joyous. Too in their cups. Too confident.

They had to know that the sword and shield had been taken by now if they had their eyes on it, and would they even believe Phillip when he told them about the curse?

No, probably not. Phillip had been the disappointing prince for years. They would never trust him over the princess's fairy godmothers.

Laughter rang through the hall, and Phillip couldn't even look at his father and King Stefan.

"What's this all about, anyway?" King Hubert asked, and Phillip shook his head. Hopefully, he had put the fish back.

"Nothing, Hubert," King Stefan said, chuckling. "Absolutely nothing."

And just like that, they were friends again and their problems were forgotten.

"Children bound to fall in love with each other." His father's words were a touch slurred.

"Precisely," said King Stefan. His speech was much further gone, and Phillip could make out the babbling of more wine being poured. "And as for grandchildren, I'll have the royal wood-carvers start work on the cradle tomorrow."

Phillip closed his eyes, covered his ears with his hands, and tried not to scream.

Hang it all—his duty, the betrothal, the curse. Phillip might not have taken his role seriously in the past few years, but recently he had resigned himself to obeying. He had decided to put his own desires aside for the better.

No more.

If he and Princess Aurora, by the sound of it, weren't worthy of having a say in their lives, then Phillip would live his life elsewhere.

Trumpets blared outside, and he startled, then darted back through the little door he'd slipped in through. Had Princess Aurora finally returned?

"His Royal Highness Prince Phillip!" called out a herald on the wall.

No, no princess. The stable hand must have told someone he was here. Phillip would have to speak with his father now and get rid of him as quickly as possible so he could find Johanna. They had to prepare for the curse on their own.

Phillip raced to the stables. Samson was surrounded by a group of well-meaning stable hands all trying to coax him into a stall. Phillip whistled, and Samson perked up. Phillip shoved his way through the crowd and climbed into the saddle. He needed to look as if he were just galloping up to the castle so that his father would assume the trumpets had sounded when he passed through the first gate.

Phillip was done being a pawn. He was done drifting through life without taking control. He was done letting his father dictate his future.

And he was going to teach his father how infuriating he could be.

Phillip pushed Samson into a gallop, weaving through the visiting crowd, and raced for the stairs of the castle. His father trotted unsteadily down them, glittering in his full King Hubert of Artwyne regalia.

"Phillip! Phillip!" King Hubert shouted, raising his arms in greeting. "Phillip, ho, Phillip!"

Phillip tried to bite back his frustration and schooled his expression as he dismounted from Samson. He knew the perfect thing: the only topic that had ever drawn out King Hubert's ire at King Stefan.

"Hurry, boy. Hurry! Change into something suitable. Can't meet your future bride looking like that."

"But I have met her, Father," said Phillip, smiling as widely as he could. He embraced his father briefly and pulled back.

King Hubert huffed. "You have? Where?"

"Once upon a dream," said Phillip, and even though he was joking, the idea was comforting. Marriage had always seemed like an inevitable disaster before, but the idea of marrying Briar Rose seemed as pleasant as she was. He picked up his father by the armpits and spun him around, humming the whole while. Phillip never should have taken any guff from a man he could throw over his shoulder.

"Oh, Phillip! Stop it. Stop that! Phillip! Put me down."

Phillip did and stepped back. There were two angry spots of color on his father's cheeks, and Phillip grinned.

"Now," said his father. "What's all this dream nonsense?"

"Oh, it wasn't a dream, Father." Phillip sighed. "I really did meet her."

"Princess Aurora?" King Hubert asked, practically salivating. "Good heavens! We must tell Stefan."

It took everything within Phillip for him not to roll his eyes, but over his father's shoulder, Samson did.

His father moved forward. "Why, this is the most—"

"I didn't say it was Aurora." Phillip pushed his father away.

Briar Rose would forgive his use of her in this so long as it got them both out of there.

"You most certainly did," said his father. "You said—"

"I said," Phillip stated very slowly, then stressed the part his father would hate the most: "I met the girl I was going to marry. I don't know who she was. A peasant girl, I suppose."

The look of incredulous fury on his father's face was the best vengeance of all.

"A peasant girl?" His father choked on the words. "You're going to marry a ... Why, Phillip"—he laughed and took Phillip by the shoulders—"you're joking."

Yes, a peasant girl. That was the truly terrifying part of the whole ordeal. Not the evil fairy set to curse the princess come sunset. Not the missing sword and shield. Not the looming threat to humanity.

Phillip shook his head, and King Hubert turned to Samson.

"Isn't he?" he asked.

Samson shook his head, too.

"No!" His father stomped away. "You can't do this to me! Give up the throne, the kingdom, for some . . .

some nobody?" His voice quavered, and he threw up his arms. "By Harry, I won't have it! You're a prince, and you're going to marry a princess!"

His crown toppled from his head, and Phillip darted forward, catching it.

"Now, Father, you're living in the past," said Phillip. "This is the fourteenth century. Nowadays—"

"Nowadays, I'm still the king," King Hubert said, cutting off Phillip. "And I command you to come to your senses!"

Because that was how sense worked. Phillip walked away. His father hadn't changed at all, and he was still concerned only with what he wanted, not what was best for everyone. If King Hubert could be selfish, so could Phillip.

"And marry the girl I love?" he asked, and remounted Samson.

Even though he knew he was lying to anger his father, his words gave him pause.

Wait—did he *love* Briar Rose? Surely love had to be harder won or more furiously fought for, but the word had come so easily. He had thought it so naturally and said it so freely.

No, that was a foolish thought.

"Exactly!" His father stomped and drew him out

of his thoughts, and Phillip beamed down at him. For a king, he was easy to rile up.

"Goodbye, Father," Phillip said, dropping the act.

"Goodbye, Father," said King Hubert. "Marry the girl you . . . No, no! No, no. Phillip! Stop! Come back!"

"Worry about that if you won't worry about Maleficent," Phillip said as he rode away, out the gate and toward the woods. He would have to intercept Johanna and find Briar Rose's cottage, but now he had time. If his father wasn't concerned about the sword and shield, that was his own fault. Phillip would deal with Maleficent, but he wasn't marrying the princess.

18
The Pricking of My Thumbs

NOT EVEN five minutes later, a good ways down the road Johanna should have been arriving by, Phillip began to regret splitting up from her. There were plenty of people traveling down the path, none of them Johanna. Now all he could think about was whether Eris and the others had caught up to her. Phillip sighed.

"With this many people coming to Ald Tor, she might have gotten slowed down." Phillip rubbed his face and tried to figure out what to do.

He didn't regret not talking more honestly with his father; it was unthinkable that the kings weren't more worried, even if they believed that the curse had been avoided. Did they truly think Maleficent would lie down and die if the curse failed?

"Let's go to Briar Rose and convince her and her aunts to get out of there," he told Samson. "Johanna should have gotten to the castle by then. Not that Father will listen to her, either."

Samson snorted.

"Fine, yes—I may also just want to see her again," said Phillip, flicking Samson's neck. He was grateful that horses didn't know what blushing meant. "Talking to her in real life is more fun than overhearing her life in dreams. She's smart. She already knows what's happening. Maybe she'll have an idea about what to do."

Also, he should probably update her about how he had threatened his father with marrying her. He wondered if, like him, she wouldn't find it the worst idea in the world, but he figured that was a conversation they could save for after they figured out how to handle Maleficent.

"Worst part of this all is that Johanna was right," said Phillip. "Maleficent's not just threatening Princess Aurora and Ald Tor. Everyone is in danger. We have the sword and shield, which is something, so we need to make a plan."

If only he could talk to Princess Aurora. She was the missing piece in all this. He should have stayed back at the castle and warned her when she arrived, but he had let his emotions get the better of him.

Phillip urged Samson toward the woods. The sun fell quickly, and long shadows stretched across the trees. Nestled in the valley of the forest was a thatch-roofed cottage with a creaking waterwheel. The roots of a large old tree made up the front of the building. Phillip whistled as he neared so as not to frighten Briar Rose or her aunts. Small footprints led from the well-trodden forest path over a small bridge. Phillip dismounted near the door.

How had no one ever stumbled upon the cottage? The more he learned about Briar Rose's circumstances, the stranger they seemed. It was all the more reason to help her escape.

He adjusted his hat and shared a knowing look with Samson, who gave him an encouraging nod. Phillip jokingly grasped his hands together for luck and then knocked on the door. No lights flickered inside.

"Come in," a woman called out.

He opened the door into darkness. Something heavy slammed into his head, and a gag was stuffed into his mouth. More things grabbed his legs and snatched up his arms. Rope was thrown around his shoulders, and Phillip struck out, sending something flying. Chatter filled his ears, and he struggled against the hold whoever these people were had on him. It wasn't magic, so it couldn't be Poena and Phrike. He spat out the gag.

Reaching back, he flung whoever it was off his back with his one free arm. It was one of Maleficent's goons! While growing up, Phillip had often seen paintings and heard descriptions of the small creatures in makeshift armor. Their horns and claws and fangs now nipped at Phillip's skin as sharply as their small swords, and another gagged him again. More ropes were knotted around his arms and chest. Two of the creatures clung to his legs like shackles. A raven's caw flooded his veins with ice.

Phillip fought against the restraints, but it was no use. From the shadows stalked a familiar figure.

Maleficent.

The stories did little justice to her. Her hair was bundled up beneath a black headdress shaped like two horns, the sharp peak of it highlighted by her arched black brows. Large round eyes of glittering black stared unblinkingly at him in the dark, and her heart-shaped lips were painted a vivid red. Her enchanted creatures yanked him upright like a puppet, and she smiled, lifting an unlit candle. As she neared him, it flared. The flame burned unnaturally cold.

"Well!" She grinned and leaned in close to his face to study him. "This is a pleasant surprise."

Her skin was a pale, pale green that glowed in the dim light and stood out starkly against her black-and-purple robes. Her creatures tittered about her feet.

Relief cut through Phillip's terror as he frantically looked around the cottage: at least Briar Rose wasn't there, and it didn't look as if there had been a struggle before he arrived. Briar Rose and her aunts must have left before the trap was set. They had to be gone.

But where was Briar Rose? Could she have been an illusion of Maleficent's magic? A trick to lead him there?

Phillip pushed the thought away. Briar Rose couldn't be a ruse. She was real. She had to be. She was real, and she had escaped.

"I set my trap for a peasant, and lo!" she said, striking her staff against the floor. "I catch a prince."

Phillip wasn't sure what she meant by intending to catch a peasant, but he did not plan on being around long enough to find out.

Maleficent laughed, and like a lightning strike, her mood shifted.

"Away with him," said Maleficent, gesturing to her minions. "But gently, my pets. Gently."

They prodded and dragged Phillip toward the door, and he kicked his fallen hat out of the way, hoping that if anyone showed up later—Briar Rose, Johanna, Eris— they would figure out what had happened or at least know that he had been there. He struggled against the bonds, but it was no use. The raven landed on Phillip's head and dug its talons into his scalp. Maleficent followed them.

"I have plans for our royal guest," she said.

Outside, more of Maleficent's enchanted creatures had taken control of Samson's reins, and Phillip tried to slip free of his restraints once more. One of the goons hit him hard in the back of the head.

"Gently," Maleficent repeated. "I had thought my dear princess had found some boy, common as dirt, to woo her, but your face I remember. Curious. True love often draws its victims together, but I assumed my curse would prevent a chance meeting."

My dear princess? True love?

Before Phillip could think on that, a flickering dot appeared above Samson's head. It grew as it neared them. Suddenly, Eris alighted on the bridge. Fury and grief writhed in Phillip's gut. He braced himself.

He could not let Eris see him cry.

"Mistress," Eris said, not even glancing at Phillip. She dropped to her knees in the mud before Maleficent. "I see you found your gifts."

Maleficent arched one brow. "Well, dear, that depends. I see only one gift here, and I am the one who acquired him. That is not to mention that I very clearly recall banishing you from my sight for eternity for your failures in the first war."

"Yes, and I dared not disobey and come to you

without something to make up for my failures. Prince Phillip has been with us these last two weeks, the silly boy, and your second gift is here." Eris rose and went to Samson, then pulled from his bag the pack hiding the Sword of Truth. She could not grasp it, and let it fall to the forest floor. "Poena and Phrike have the third and final gift—the Shield of Virtue. They are on their way now."

Phillip inhaled, a new worry overtaking him. They must have gotten Johanna, but she had to be all right. She had to be.

"Are these gifts or bribes, my erstwhile student?" Maleficent waved away Eris's answer. "It matters not. You convinced him to deliver them to me himself. How deliciously cruel and fortuitous."

"We would never demand forgiveness or attempt to elicit it with bribes, and we will leave again if you desire it. You need only say the word," said Eris, and finally she looked at him. As Maleficent investigated the Sword of Truth, Eris shook her head at Phillip and let her expression fall. There wasn't regret in her eyes, only disappointment. "You taught me well, mistress, and I know you never give second chances when failed or betrayed."

She swallowed the final word as if it pained her, and Phillip shook with anger. So she thought he had betrayed her? Had she really expected him to flee and save himself, leaving everyone else to die? That was worse somehow, making him feel small and foolish. She had taken the things he wanted the most—a mentor, a future, the trust of an adult—and twisted them into a mockery.

Eris turned away and bowed to Maleficent.

"Oh, Eris. You do surprise me," Maleficent said, and took Eris's chin between her thumb and forefinger. She tilted back Eris's head. "A touch overcomplicated, I think, but subtlety has never been your strength, and why should it be? Chaos suits you."

"He is yours, and he is heartbroken." Eris stared up at Maleficent, blinking fast as if Maleficent were the sun herself. "You always taught me that hopelessness tastes better when the hope was real."

"So I did." Maleficent rolled her eyes to Phillip and then turned her head. Her hand slid from Eris's chin. "But did you think this would return you to my good graces?"

"I . . ." Eris drew in a shuddering breath. "I did it for you with no hope of my own, as did the others."

"I do love how easily you lie," said Maleficent. "Are they truly on their way, my pet?"

Maleficent cast her raven into the sky and sank into

the shadows to await the other fairies, leaving Eris and Phillip alone.

Eris approached Phillip, her blue eyes skimming his injuries. Softly, she said, "How rude of you to take my offer and spit it in my face."

Phillip rubbed his cheek against his shoulder and worked his gag away.

"I couldn't let everyone die! You said you believed in me," he hissed.

"I believed you were smarter than this, but I was clearly wrong," she said. "I tried. Whatever happens now is on you."

"Why?" Phillip asked. "Why do you need to help her?"

"I told you. I love my teacher." She glanced over his shoulder at the shadows where Maleficent lurked. Eris drew herself up. "We failed her during the last war, and I will not make that mistake again."

Phillip tried to ram his head into hers, and one of the creatures snatched him back.

Finally, she met his gaze, disappointment etched into every wrinkle of her shocked expression.

"I should have known you would let me down." She shook her head, laughed to herself, and refastened his gag. "It's the only thing you're good at."

Phillip stewed, his feelings alternating between fury and grief every few minutes. Then a loud caw interrupted his thoughts as Maleficent's raven returned from the woods. Shortly after, a light appeared. It was Poena, with fire in one hand and a bound and gagged Johanna in the other. She dragged Johanna by the arm. On Johanna's back was the cloth-wrapped Shield of Virtue. She closed her eyes when she saw that Phillip was captured as well. Phrike flew through the gloaming behind them.

Maleficent glided forward.

"Mistress!" Phrike called out, landing and sweeping into a low bow.

Poena curtsied, extinguishing the flame but keeping hold of Johanna. "Mistress."

"I would not have believed the three of you capable of working together, and yet here you all stand, successful and still alive," said Maleficent. "Perhaps you have learned from past mistakes."

"Anything for you," said Phrike. She glared at Johanna. "Drop it here."

Johanna narrowed her eyes and leaned back, letting the shield slip from her back. It hit the ground with an echoing thunk, and Maleficent's raven landed on its edge. The raven cawed and hopped off, smoke curling up from its feet. Maleficent tapped her fingers against her staff.

"Yes, yes," she muttered. "This will do."

She twirled her wrists, and magic gathered around the sword and shield as a stormy cloud. Power crackled in the air. Phillip's hair stood on end.

"Go!" said Maleficent, and the sword and shield vanished. The cloud of magic slowly dissipated.

Phillip slumped.

"I must deal with the sword and shield and ensure that no one else will be able to track or retrieve them," Maleficent said. She waved her creatures off, and they scurried in the woods down some path Phillip couldn't see. "Bring him to me, alive, once you are finished, but do with her what you please."

Slowly, Maleficent walked away from the cottage. The candle in her hand went out, darkness pressing in on her from all sides, and she faded into the night like a shadow. One final call from her raven marked her departure.

"Perfect!" Eris clapped her hands and rounded on Phillip. "Let's have some fun, shall we?"

A vine whipped out from the forest and curled around his throat, then dragged him to stand next to

Johanna and Samson. Samson's lead was tied to the bridge, and Phillip let his foot catch it. He tripped, landing hard on his face. Phrike laughed.

"He's finally groveling," said Poena, tossing her flame from hand to hand. "I prefer it."

Phillip crawled to his knees. Samson's lead pressed against his back, and Phillip's fingers were too thick and ungainly to work quickly. Johanna shuffled until she was standing next to him, her legs blocking what he was doing, and he leaned against her. It was the only obvious move, and he could have cried knowing that she had recognized his feint. He couldn't think about what would happen to them soon or what was going on at the castle with Princess Aurora. He could only focus on the here and now.

If he didn't, he would fall to pieces.

"Why do we have to give him to Maleficent?" asked Phrike. "It's not fair. We did all the work!"

"Please," said Eris, rolling her eyes. "Tell the Mistress of Evil that and see what happens."

Phillip tore with his nails at the rope tying Samson to the bridge. If he could get Samson free, maybe that would be enough of a distraction for them to escape.

"There is so much we could do," Poena said, a flame twining between her fingers. "He did waste precious weeks of our lives."

"In fairness, that was our plan," said Eris.

Poena huffed. "When have we ever been fair?"

Phrike made a cutting motion with her fingers, and her shadow tore up from the ground. It grabbed Johanna by the collar and dragged her toward them.

"You're in for a treat," Phrike said. "I've had plenty of time to think up the most *poetic* suffering for you."

Phillip finally managed to undo the rope. He flicked Samson's ankle and the horse took off, sprinting through the four of them. Poena and Eris darted off to one side, and Phrike yanked Johanna the other way. Phrike shrieked and dropped her.

"She bit me!" yelled Phrike, holding up her bleeding hand. "The little gnat bit me!"

"And I'd do it again," shouted Johanna. "Phillip—"

"Run!" he screamed. "Go."

Johanna nodded, her face set, and grabbed Samson's saddle with her bound hands. She threw a leg up and took off in one fluid motion. Magic flared in the valley, but there were far too many trees for Poena's fire or Eris's vines to have a clear angle by which to grab Johanna or Samson. Phrike wrapped her shaking hand in the skirts of her orange gown while Poena turned her magic on the cottage, sending it up in flames. Eris marched over to Phillip.

"Go get her by any means necessary," said Eris to the others. "Take her to the mountain if you must. I will take our prince there."

The other two vanished in the blink of an eye, and Eris pulled Phillip by his ear to his feet.

"You ungrateful little bug!" She pinched harder. "I risked everything for you, and you threw it back at me as if it meant nothing. Nothing!"

Her magic, an ice-cold wind, tore through his thin hose and tunic, chilling him to the bone. She snapped the fingers of her other hand, and there was a shift, as if the whole world save for Phillip had twisted on its axis. Magic gripped his spine and yanked, and he doubled over with a gasp. Eris let him crumple to the ground.

Floor. There was a stone floor. Phillip choked on his gag and forced himself to look around.

"Welcome," said Eris, brushing the dirt from her gown. "I'm sure you'll appreciate my mistress's hospitality."

They were in an entry hall of dark stone. The floor was hot, nearly scalding his bare hands. The castle was old and ruined, and the natural world had started breaking through the cracks of the stones. Moss and roots curled around splintered walls, and Eris led Phillip to the other end of the hall, where a broken staircase led up to an alcove meant for a throne. The listing, shattered columns rocked as they walked past them. The wind tore through holes in the wall and ceiling.

Phillip stared up at the pale green sky, the same shade as Maleficent's skin, and swallowed.

"Oh," Eris said with a breathy sigh. "Isn't Maleficent exquisite? I couldn't even move them two inches, but she got them all the way here."

The Sword of Truth and the Shield of Virtue sat at the foot of the throne. Two of her enchanted creatures stood guard over them, and one stopped scratching its back with a knife to glare at Phillip. Eris shooed the two away, shoved Phillip toward the arms, and loosened the ropes around him enough for him to pick up the blanket-wrapped bundles. He shifted and tried to find the sword's hilt.

"It's no use," she said. "I'm not allowed to kill you, but my mistress said nothing about maiming you."

A cold breeze curled around his wrists, and Phillip shook his head. He gestured toward his mouth.

"Oh, no," she said. "You had your chance, and I don't care to hear what noble nonsense you'll spout in your defense. To think I—"

She cut herself off, raised a hand, and shook her head.

"No, you're not worth it." She motioned for him to walk ahead of her. "The stairs on the left."

It was a spiraling staircase that led up so high clouds blocked the arrow slits and crept through the cracks between the stones. Phillip's legs ached with the stress of climbing, but the sword and shield weighed nothing despite the awkward way he had been forced to carry them. He knew he was in the old fortress atop the Forbidden Mountain, though he had no idea of how to get home from there. A bitter panic clogged his throat.

"Set them in here," said Eris once they reached the top of the tower.

The tower room was small and cramped, stuffed to the ceiling with magical staffs, crumbling tomes, and a display case overfilled with what looked like small fairy statues. Phillip stumbled inside. A cold hand gripped the back of his neck.

"Drop them." Eris squeezed, and he placed the shield on the ground. He let the sword fall in such a way that the cloth around it began to unravel. "Good boy."

It wasn't hopeless yet. Johanna was still out there, his father and King Stefan were still out there, and the gift of Princess Aurora's cursed sleep would save her from death. Phillip had to figure out how to escape.

Eris removed the gag covering his mouth.

"I can hear you plotting and fuming," she said.

His retort was lost in a blast of heated air that tasted like metal and oil. With a pop, Poena and Phrike returned. Poena landed hard atop a display case of wands and drifted down on her wings. Phrike appeared on her knees before Eris and Phillip. Eris's fingers tightened.

"Johanna?" she asked

Phrike shook her head. "She's hiding somewhere within King Stefan's castle. Couldn't find her among the others."

"Are you angry?" Poena asked, gliding to them. "She is hardly anything worth worrying over. We acquired the sword and shield. Everything is going according to plan, and I am tired of following your orders."

"How? You never execute them correctly," said Eris, cracking the bones of each finger one by one. "I'm not angry. I'm counting to ten so that I don't strangle you, because I'm thrilled by your mediocrity and utter lack of care. Loose threads can fray. What do we not want?"

"Fraying," mumbled Phrike and Poena in unison.

"Fraying." Eris grabbed Phillip by the tunic and shoved him toward the stairs. "Go do your jobs and find her while I show His Highness to his room."

"There's no need to chase Johanna," Phillip blurted out. His mind was spinning too fast for him to think, but he could stall for Johanna. Maybe he could keep all three of them there. "Why bother chasing after her when you've got the prince right here?"

Poena started to elaborate, and Eris hissed at her.

"Go," she said. "He's trying to distract you."

The other two vanished in a flurry of dust and rustling pages.

"Get moving," she said, shoving him back toward the stairs, "and please stop trying to pull one over on me. I wasn't born last century, you know."

"Actually, I didn't," he said, walking slowly and committing to memory the details of the path they took. "I don't know anything about you."

"Don't be ridiculous. You know I'm smarter than you, you know I'm beautiful, and you know my name." She laughed and prodded him between the shoulder blades. "Even if you can't spell it backward."

He held back a groan, remembering the thieves. *Sire.* Of course.

"Yes, if this has taught me anything, it's that I should have been more paranoid," he muttered. "Do the others know you let me run?"

"You really do want me to cut out your tongue." Eris directed him through a crooked wooden door down a narrow hallway. They traveled deeper into the mountain. "I thought you were more ambitious, but you did refuse our first offer of magic. I should have known."

"My condolences to your ego," said Phillip. "It must be quite fragile."

"Yes," she drawled. "Of the two of us, I'm the insecure one."

The dungeons were deep in the bowels of the castle. Phillip could barely keep track of the twists and turns in the falling structure, scuffing the corners with his boots whenever he could. The farther they went, the emptier he felt. Hopelessness was more potent after glimpsing a good end.

"Well, have fun," said Eris, opening a thick door with a wave of her wand. "I would say it's been a pleasure, but it's mostly been tedious."

The ropes holding Phillip took on a life of their own and dragged him to the stone bench in the corner. Chains rose like snakes and snapped around his wrists. Another set of shackles clamped around his ankles. Phillip collapsed onto the bench as the ropes slithered back to Eris. They curled around her outstretched arm and went still.

"Why befriend me?" he asked softly. "Did you think I would let Maleficent destroy my home to train with you?"

"You didn't care for your father, betrothed, or kingdom, so I thought you might. I'd never had a student before, but I saw something in you that pulled at my heartstrings. You were so uncertain. So afraid." She tilted her head from side to side, curls rustling against her round shoulders. "There were so many options open to you, and you turned your nose up at all of them because you didn't like your responsibilities. I could have poured water in the dirt and told you lapping it up like a dog would give you a way to escape your father, and you would have done it and barked. But I didn't. I gave you a chance to embrace the life you wanted. I will not make that mistake again."

Phillip's stomach rolled and protested, and his eyes burned. He hadn't known. He had been right there the whole time, clay in her hands. He had been so desperate that he had handed the life of everyone he loved over to Maleficent. For what? The life he wanted?

He was a prince whether he liked it or not. What life wasn't within his grasp?

No life, now.

"Don't wallow. It's unbecoming," said Eris, her eyes rolling up. She brushed Phillip's tear away with her hand and flicked the tip of his nose. "You're just some boy lucky enough to be born a prince in a wealthy kingdom, you know. There's nothing special about you."

Phillip swallowed, fighting to keep from crying more and feeding into her love of his suffering. "You haven't won yet. Aurora's not dead, and her true love is still out there."

"Oh, Phillip," Eris said, and clucked at him. "No matter. My mistress's plan for that is underway, but I'll forgive you for not being able to read the board. Enjoy your stay, Your Highness. While you wait, consider how you were always a player and how you removed yourself from the game. None of this would have been possible if you had paid attention to your kingdom. You would have almost certainly known about the Sword of Truth. Isn't that funny?"

She laughed her way out the door and locked it behind her.

"A prince not having power!" she said. "Poor little

boy has to grow up to become a king and marry a beautiful girl. How tragic." Her voice echoed until the terrible cackling was all he could hear.

And the worst of it all was that Phillip knew she was right: he had dug this grave for his kingdom and himself.

19
Fairly Hopeless

PHILLIP FLUNG himself at the door, ignoring the tightness of his chains, and collapsed to the floor. The chains were taut and heavy, slowly dragging him to the wall. Hopelessness tightened around him like the shackles.

He had to get out and fix this.

He ran his fingers over the chains, a frantic energy trembling through him. The shackles were solid pieces of metal with no place for a key or for them to be uncuffed. He stumbled to a war ax wedged into one of the fallen stones and looped the chains over the blade, then dragged them against it. Magic sparked where the blade bit into the chains, and the scent of damp autumn leaves filled Phillip's nose. His stomach rolled.

"Come back here!" he shouted. "Come back and I'll really spit in your face, you traitor!"

He picked up the chains and checked the links that had struck the blade. They were whole and unblemished.

Phillip would have bet anything that the shackles could only be removed with magic. He sank to his knees.

He couldn't give up. He couldn't let this dread and worry drown him.

The castle suddenly shook violently. Dust rattled out from between the stones and rained down on Phillip. The commotion hit a crescendo, and Phillip buried his face in his hands. Shouts echoed through the crumbling walls, and howls filled the frigid air. Slowly, the shaking eased.

A door creaked outside Phillip's cell. He wiped his dust-covered face and lifted his head. A horned shadow fell across the floor, and Phillip followed it to the face in the barred window of his door. Maleficent smiled.

She unlocked the door to his cell and opened it silently, her gaze sweeping from his chains to his face with an unnerving slowness, as if she had all the time in the world to look.

As if her plan was already well past the point of no return.

Her raven fluttered in ahead of her, alighted on the handle of the ax, and bowed low. Maleficent glided toward Phillip with a put-upon frown.

"Oh, come now, Prince Phillip. Why so melancholy?" asked Maleficent. The clack of her raven's claws was like laughter. "A wondrous future lies before you."

She motioned to him and then drew her arms against her chest, clutching her staff to her and leaning against it. The dark silk of her robes hung like furled bat wings about her shoulders. Phillip drew back from her.

"You . . . the destined hero of a charming fairy tale come true," she said, and savored every word.

Confusion broke through Phillip's panic. He wasn't destined to do anything, and he wasn't part of any fairy tale. It was Princess Aurora, cursed and awaiting her true love, at the heart of everything.

Oh.

Maleficent had assumed he was the princess's true love. It was laughable! She didn't know the details of her own curse, and now her plan was already falling apart. He wasn't the destined true love; he was just Phillip. He grinned, opening his mouth to hold that fact over her, but before he could speak, she laughed.

Maleficent swirled a hand over the green gem atop her staff. The air tightened around them, charged by the summoning of her magic. She was the green skies that heralded twisters and monstrous storms, the clench in Phillip's chest that was his instinct to flee. Danger had arrived.

"Behold . . . King Stefan's castle," said Maleficent,

tilting the staff toward him. The crackling magic within the gem twisted like smoke and cleared from the center. An image appeared, the white castle towers stained indigo by night. An odd stillness had settled over every window and rampart. The picture narrowed, as if they were staring through the eyes of a bird drifting toward the tower's window. "And in yonder topmost tower, dreaming of her true love, the princess Aurora."

The image wavered and changed. On a bed of blue linens, with its curtains drawn open beneath the flickering stars, rested a young woman, her face peaceful and her fingers loosely clutching a rose against her chest. The high arches of her cheeks were sharpened by the slackness of sleep. Her hair, so familiar, was twisted through the band of a golden crown.

Even though he had never seen her sleeping . . . even though he couldn't hear her voice . . . even though his memories were of bare feet dancing on overgrown grass and curled hair rustling in a forest breeze, Phillip knew.

"But see the gracious whim of fate," said Maleficent. She laughed as though this was the best joke of all. "Why, 'tis the selfsame peasant maid who won the heart of our noble prince but yesterday."

Briar Rose—who had been raised by three mysterious aunts who lived oddly close to King Stefan's castle yet had never been found, and who had never been allowed to leave her home due to a mysterious danger—was Princess Aurora.

His betrothed.

The girl who had been tied to him since childhood.

The girl he had been dreaming of just as long.

He had been too caught up in his life for too long and hadn't figured it out. He really should have. It seemed obvious to him now.

If she was sleeping now, Briar Rose's first introduction to the world must have been pricking her finger on a spindle and succumbing to the curse. He had known something was coming, but not for her. She was supposed to be safe.

But why was Maleficent showing *him* this? He was only Princess Aurora's betrothed, and Maleficent didn't know about the dreams. She must have known about their meeting the day before, but that didn't make them true loves.

The image changed again, focusing on Briar Rose's—no, *Princess Aurora's*, but that name didn't fit yet; it had never been hers—face, and Phillip clenched his teeth to keep from speaking. He had always assumed that meeting Aurora would be terrible and insufferable and that he would hate her on sight, but it seemed like he would be marrying the peasant girl he told his father about after all if they got out of this. Unfortunately, it would be with none of the satisfaction of annoying his father.

Humor usually calmed him down, but the thought only chilled him.

Briar Rose's face grew clearer as Maleficent spoke. "She is indeed most wondrous fair: gold of sunshine in her hair; lips that shame the red, red rose . . . in ageless sleep she finds repose." If Maleficent was confessing her ultimate plan, she owed it to Briar Rose to mention more than her pretty face. She wasn't some princess who existed only to be beautiful and cursed. Briar Rose had a life before all this!

Maleficent chuckled, as if she could read his thoughts, and Phillip winced. He had let his concern show. He would have to be more careful if he wanted to know what Maleficent had planned.

The image swirled again, and Maleficent's own face appeared before him. "The years roll by, but a hundred years to a steadfast heart are but a day. And now the gates of a dungeon part . . . and our prince is free to go his way."

Phillip leaned in closer to the image, uncertain of what he was seeing.

This new picture was of Phillip, old and slouched, with the Shield of Virtue on his arm and a weary Samson carrying him through the gates of Maleficent's castle. A hundred years older he was supposed to be in this future of Maleficent's. Alive and hale enough to get on a horse.

Phillip looked away, unable to witness more. Maleficent's plan—to leave Briar Rose in an accursed sleep for one hundred years until everyone she loved was dead or old and then send him to wake her with true love's kiss—made no sense. In one hundred years, unless she used magic to keep him alive, he would likely be long dead, and Samson would, too. But most ridiculous, most bizarre—because how had Maleficent gotten her own curse wrong?—was the idea that Phillip was the princess's true love.

Maleficent was blowing it out of proportion. Phillip wouldn't deny that he had feelings for Briar Rose, feelings that were far softer than he might have expected ever to have for her or anyone else, but he wasn't in love with her. Sure, she was clever and kind and as competitive as anyone he had ever met, and he liked the way she always kept him on his toes, and . . .

Phillip turned away from Maleficent's crystal, not wanting her to see the thoughts he was sure were rippling across his face.

Maleficent had cursed Princess Aurora. One of the fairy godmothers had decreed that Aurora would be awakened by true love's kiss. They had left before anyone asked about who that true love was, and now Maleficent was certain enough to hang her entire plan on the fact that it was Phillip. She was only playing into the fairy tale of it. It didn't mean anything.

But was this what Maleficent had meant at the cottage when she mentioned true love drawing its victims together and her curse? That couldn't be the reason for the dream wood and the thorn wall.

Even if Briar Rose and he had been dreaming of each other for ages, even if he was dying to speak with her again if just for a moment, and even if Maleficent believed it to be true, there was no way Briar Rose could love him.

"Off he rides on his noble steed—a valiant figure, straight and tall!—to wake his love with love's first kiss and prove that true love conquers all."

Phillip forced himself to look at the final image, but there was none. Maleficent leaned in close. Phillip lunged at her, his chains yanking him back.

"Come, my pet. Let us leave our noble prince with these happy thoughts," said Maleficent, holding out her fingers for her raven. "A most gratifying day."

Phillip tried to follow her, but the chains held and the door shut with a final, horrible click.

Maleficent laughed again. "For the first time in sixteen years, I shall sleep well!"

He couldn't breathe. It didn't matter if Maleficent was wrong and he wasn't Briar Rose's true love. He couldn't leave her alone to suffer the curse.

Phillip's mind whirled with Maleficent's plan. She would go to war against the kings and humanity while Briar Rose slept and Phillip languished in chains, breaking the hearts of King Hubert and King Stefan.

And her entire plan hinged on Phillip's not being able to escape while Briar Rose slept.

Oh.

A cursed sleep was still sleep.

Alone but comforted and more desperate to visit the wood than he had ever been in his life, Phillip curled up in his cell and tried to rest.

When Phillip opened his eyes, he was not in the dungeon but in the old forest of his dreams. Dappled with shadows and peppered in fallen leaves, Phillip sat up. His arms didn't ache, and the wounds from his fight with Maleficent's minions were gone. He took a deep breath and reveled in the bright scent of fresh grass and old trees.

Maleficent's curse shouldn't even have gotten to Briar Rose. There had been no spindles in the cottage, and the fairies pretending to be her aunts had almost certainly not allowed them near her. She had been safe and sound in the cottage until dusk, so even if the curse was destined to come true, how had it happened?

Surely her aunts hadn't dragged her to the castle at sunset and dumped everything on her at once?

"I might have pricked my finger to escape that," he muttered. "All right, Phillip. You messed everything up. You need to get up, face it all, and fix it."

Briar Rose would be here. She had to be. They would have however long they needed to figure a way out of Maleficent's web, since she was cursed and he was captured.

Or she would be so furious at him and his mistakes that dreaming would become far worse than his real life for the first time.

Phillip pulled himself up on a tree. The forest seemed different, lighter and brighter despite the canopy being as thick as ever. The leaves felt more real between his fingers, and the thick bark didn't crumble away with age. Phillip walked between the trees, letting his fingers trail across each one, and frowned as he passed a large rock covered in moss. That was where he had sat before the thorn wall became a hedge maze, which meant the wall should have been close.

But the thorns, wall, and hedge maze were gone entirely for the first time.

"Briar Rose?" he shouted.

"Phillip?" Her voice was softer than he had ever heard it, raspy with sleep, but he couldn't tell where it was coming from. She was nowhere in sight. "Oh, good. I had hoped this would happen."

"Hoped?" He spun around and shoved his way through a thicket. "Where are you?"

"I honestly don't know," she said. "I have a better question, though: Where are you in the waking world?"

He sighed and followed the sound of her voice. "Maleficent's castle."

"That does make my plan less useful," said Briar Rose. "How did you get there?"

"Maleficent." He hesitated, uncertain as to how much she knew. "Well, she was waiting for me at your cottage, because you're . . . well, I'm supposed to be—"

"Because I'm Princess Aurora and she thinks you're my true love? You don't have to dance around it, *Prince* Phillip. Learning who I was, who I was betrothed to, and who I was cursed by were all part of my birthday surprise," Briar Rose said with a laugh. "Imagine my surprise, Prince Phillip, when I was told that I was betrothed to a prince, whose name escapes me, and now imagine my horror because of how sad I was, Prince Phillip, to be betrothed unknowingly to this prince. Oh, I also—surprise—have a true love who is supposed to wake me from this curse. Imagine that, Your Highness."

He winced and followed her voice around an outcropping of rocks.

"Sorry. We had only just met and I didn't want to add 'betrothed prince' to the list of things about me that might complicate . . ." His voice trailed off as he caught sight of her.

Briar Rose *looked* like Princess Aurora now. The crown he had seen her wear in Maleficent's image had carried over to the dream, and carefully curled strands of golden hair held it in place. The blue skirt of her gown was spread out around her, the silk like water spilling across the grass, and a there was tension in her shoulders that hadn't been there in the forest. It was as if she was scared to breathe and mess up the artwork that had been made of her. She blinked up at him with tired eyes.

That expression, the one of exasperation and affection when she saw him, was the same as when they had met in the woods and far more beautiful than any silk or jewels.

"I feel sleepy, even here," said Briar Rose with a yawn. "What's happening in the real world?"

"I'm sorry," he said. "I don't know much. Maleficent found me when I went to the cottage in the glen to see you."

Briar Rose groaned. "My aunts made me leave. They broke the news about who I am and then dragged me to the castle. And then, after I had learned of the curse and had cried over news of my upcoming marriage to Prince Phillip, I thought of you. How many nobles are there in Artwyne and Ald Tor named Phillip? How many who might be targeted by a trio of evil fairies, do you think?"

She gestured from herself to him, and he winced.

"Yeah, sorry about that," he said. "I liked that you didn't know I was a prince, and I wasn't thrilled about the betrothal. I was hoping it would solve itself."

She snorted. "Well, glad that worked out how you wanted."

"Considering this solved is very optimistic of you." Phillip ignored the flutter in his chest—she hadn't asked to break the betrothal yet—and sat down next to her. "I am sorry about leaving it all out."

"It makes things make more sense," said Briar Rose. "I can't really blame you for wanting to keep some things private when our lives have apparently been public knowledge since birth. You know, for years I asked what happened to my parents, and my aunts just said that I had to be raised by them. Then suddenly I was a princess and betrothed and cursed. I felt so bad for hating it, but I did."

"You're the one whose world got turned upside down, and you're the only one among us cursed," he said.

"Exactly!" She stretched out her legs, her bare toes peeking out from beneath her gown. The golden cloth slippers discarded a few steps away made him smile. "I shouldn't feel bad at all, because my aunts never prepared me for emotional upheaval—only how to organize seating arrangements for court dinners and how to play the harp."

"You can play the harp?"

"Phillip, please," she drawled. "We're betrothed. You should know me better by now."

He flushed, cringing at how swiftly his cheeks heated, and tugged at his shirt. She grabbed his hand.

"Relax." She squeezed his hand. "I won't hold you to the marriage if you don't want it."

"That's kind of you," he said, his heart sinking at

the idea that she wanted out of their marriage. Phillip swallowed. He couldn't assume things about her again. He had to be reasonable. "Earlier, to avoid the betrothal to Princess Aurora, I told my father I was marrying this peasant girl I met in the woods today."

"Oh, another marriage I was unaware of." She glared up at him, but he could see the quirk of her lips. "I don't recall you proposing."

Embarrassment flooded through Phillip, but he took a deep breath and pressed on to try to determine how she felt about him. "Simply telling my father that I was falling for a mysterious peasant girl wouldn't get me out of my betrothal, so I had to exaggerate."

She stared up at him, face utterly unreadable, and said, "Maleficent told you that you were my true love."

Phillip swallowed. "She did."

Briar Rose kept staring, as if she was waiting for something, but Phillip had no idea what it could possibly be. Panic and humiliation burned through him.

"Well, I only told my father that I planned to marry a peasant because I knew it would infuriate him," said Phillip quickly. He watched Briar Rose's expression carefully, but she gave nothing away. "When I got to Ald Tor, our fathers were drinking and singing and playing games." He sucked on his teeth and shrugged.

"And worse than them not preparing for your return or Maleficent's, they had planned our whole lives. My father had a castle built for us to live in with plenty of room for a lot of children. The way they talked about us made me angry."

"Great. I wanted another reason to be furious," she mumbled, and dropped her cheek onto his shoulder. He willed his cheeks to not turn pink at the touch. "Marrying for spite is better than marrying because our parents demand it."

That gave him hope, but he wasn't sure what to do with it.

"Agreed." Phillip tucked his nose against her hair and said, "I have never liked you more."

"You've never liked me."

"Exactly. My opinion of you is eternally increasing," Phillip said, a silly grin spreading across his face.

"I have some larger concerns about the nature of gifts and fate, but admittedly, our parents are extremely concerning." She sighed. "But you know what I'm the most concerned about? The curse that wasn't even my fault has taken over both of our lives."

"And Maleficent's, honestly," said Phillip. "She's planning to drag this out for over a century."

Briar Rose stared up at him, blinking slowly, and he

brushed a strand of hair from her cheek, unable to help himself.

"What?" Phillip asked.

"Maleficent's plan is so confusing," Briar Rose said. "She's so intent on upsetting me. It's not like my parents will be around to see me heartbroken in one hundred years."

"But how did the curse even happen?" he asked, and removed his arm from around her waist. "I know there was no stopping it, but where did you even find a spindle?"

"Oh, I pricked my finger on purpose."

Phillip opened his mouth, shock stealing his voice, and she laughed.

"Maleficent found me, in the castle, and she did something to me with magic. It made me go into this strange room with a spinning wheel. I could have fought it, I think. I felt like I could have, but you told me curses always come true, so I didn't fight her," said Briar Rose as if it were the easiest thing in the world. "There was no point: if curses always come true, I had to let it happen. Better it be on my own terms than on hers, and I knew that I would fall into a cursed sleep. I was hopeful that meant I would wake up here and be able to speak to or at least hear you eventually. This way, we can come up with a plan. She thinks she's winning. Maybe she'll under-estimate us."

"She definitely thinks she's winning," Phillip said. "She delivered a lovely soliloquy about how she's going to let you sleep for one hundred years before allowing me to leave and try to save you."

"Very optimistic about your life span," Briar Rose said. She laughed and squeezed his hand again. "Well, what are we going to do?"

"Do?" Phillip asked. "You're in a cursed sleep, and I'm locked in Maleficent's dungeon."

"And? So we just let her win? I only just got to leave the woods." Briar Rose leapt to her feet and clapped her hands, then pointed to him. She began to pace. "All those years when I could have been with my family, all those years when I could have been learning about my curse and what to do, and all those years when I could have been getting to know you in the real world, I was instead stuck in a wood, learning how to rule a king-dom with a heavily redacted history so that I wouldn't discover anything about Maleficent and get suspicious. I know every possible way to greet someone of every rank, but I didn't know who I was until today!"

Her tone was the one that meant she was so angry she couldn't think about anything else, and Phillip loved matching it to her expression. He had always known she was a pacer.

"How is it fair that my parents cut me off from everything and everyone for my own good and then expected me to be the perfect, willing daughter?" She spun to him, hands out, and nearly bowed over from the force of her words.

"It's not fair," said Phillip, slipping from his seat and keeping pace with her. She had been alone and would be for so long that he couldn't let her be alone now. "But to them you're their child, not a person."

It was the only way he had ever been able to rationalize his father's opinions of him. Phillip would always be his father's son first, and his father would always think of him like that. He wasn't a person with his own hopes and dreams, strengths and challenges. He was King Hubert's son.

"They're not thinking of you as Briar Rose, the young woman who is their daughter," Phillip continued. "They're thinking of you as Princess Aurora, the daughter they gave up, and everything they did has to be for the best, because if it's not, what was it for?"

"So they made a mistake!" She gripped his wrist and dragged him with her. "Even if their intentions were good, why would they think I wouldn't be me now?"

Phillip followed her gladly. "Because they want their daughter."

"Not me." She halted, dropping his hand, and stopped him from following her. "If I could, I'd rip myself from this dream and abandon my parents in a wood for years without a word and only a lifetime of lies to see how they like it. Do you know how much *this* hurts? Knowing that if I do get to meet them, I will never be able to make them understand that protecting me like they did was a disservice? I needed protection, but I also needed them!"

She swept the tears from her face and shook her head. Phillip hated the anger and pain in her voice, but he had overheard so much of her life that he knew she deserved to be angry in that moment.

"That's all I needed," she whispered. "Family. Friends. Other people who knew me. I needed the truth! They took my name from me. They took my life from me. They took me."

She flexed her fingers and drew three steadying breaths.

"You want to let them sweat for a year or two?" Phillip asked, moving closer. "I can exist in the dungeon for a while. I don't mind."

Briar Rose shook her head and then bit her lip. "It's tempting."

"Say the word, and I'll do it. I'll sit and do nothing until you give me the thumbs-up," he said, grasping her shoulders.

She fiddled with the button at his collar. "You do love doing nothing."

"Well, I never said I would do nothing *solely* for you." He reached up, untangled the crown from her hair, and tossed it aside. "However, doing nothing does have its perks: Maleficent or Eris will have to feed me, hopefully, and I can sneak some information out of them so we can actually plan. Unless your fairy godmothers had a plan for when you were cursed?"

"If they have a plan, they didn't share it with me," she said. "It would help if I could hear the things happening in the real world like I could before. Otherwise, I'm useless."

"Hardly. Between us, you're the smart one. Once we know more and I figure out how to escape, we can come up with a more solid plan. You've never been useless, and you're not starting now. That's my job."

He kissed the top of her head and then panicked, afraid that it was too much. He made a move to pull away, but she held tight to him.

"You were never useless, either," she whispered, a pretty blush dotting her cheeks and making Phillip's heart skip. "Even if your father thinks that of you, you were always there for me."

A breeze rippled over the wood. The trees were blurring, as if a fog was creeping through them. He blinked, and it didn't get better.

"Oh, it looks like you're waking up," she said quickly. "Learn what you can, I'll think about ways we can get out of this, and we will save ourselves. But if my aunts, the fairies, come to you, trust them. I doubt they'll leave us both to die."

"Whatever you want," he said, and suddenly it felt as if he were underwater. He looked down at her, and his vision became even hazier. "I will always be there for you. Once I'm out of that cell, I will go find your true love and help you."

"Your voice is getting soft, like it does when you wake up, so this is the end for now." She kissed his cheek, and the dream wood waned to black. "And, Phillip? Before you go off looking for my true love, why don't you kiss me?"

20
No Rose Without Thorns

*P*HILLIP AWOKE alone, the dungeon ceiling crumbling above him and the broken stone bench stabbing into his back. By the barely there crease of his sleeve across his arm, he figured he hadn't been asleep long. The ghost of Briar Rose's touch still lingered on his hand, and he rubbed his fingers together. If Maleficent wanted Phillip alive for one hundred years, someone would have to visit again. He could figure out how to escape.

And Briar Rose was right: they could get out of this if they tried.

But why did she have to ask him to kiss her? She had a true love who was probably disgustingly chivalrous and shining, and Phillip couldn't entertain the idea that it could be him. He knew better than to expect things, and Briar Rose's meeting her true love right after he realized he liked her was just the sort of disappointment the world enjoyed throwing at him. There was so much going on—for both of them—that there wasn't time to deal with the fallout that would cause. Better to assume it wasn't him.

It wasn't him. If he thought that often enough, then when it wasn't, he wouldn't be upset.

Hopefully.

Except Briar Rose knew she had a true love. She knew there was someone out there who would perfectly complement her, and she didn't seem eager for Phillip to find that person. She had told Phillip to kiss her first.

She didn't think Phillip could wake her, did she?

Phillip rolled into a seated position and tugged at his hair. Her request could only mean that she liked him well enough to choose him over her true love or believed that he could be that true love, and the thought made him feel as if every rib in his chest were curling around his heart. He wanted to be that person.

He wasn't sure he could be.

But none of it mattered if he couldn't get out of there.

His shackles had no lock, but the walls were crumbling. He could use that. And the three fairy godmothers were still out there.

"Flora, Fauna, and Merryweather, I don't know if

you can hear me," he whispered in case Briar Rose was listening to him from the dream world, "but—"

"Shhh!" said someone outside his door.

Phillip stilled. That wasn't Maleficent.

"But how are we going to help?" asked someone else.

The shusher shushed again, and a third person sighed.

"Can't you feel it?" the third person asked. "The Sword of Truth and the Shield of Virtue are nearby, and while I don't know why, I'm not looking this particular gift in the mouth."

"Horse, dear."

"What horse?"

Phillip knew those voices. He had grown up hearing them in dreams. Laughing, he dropped his face into his hands. How often had he heard Briar Rose's aunts bickering over her?

Three small specks like glints of light drifted through the barred window in the door. Magic preceded them, scenting the air with apples and reminding him of spring. He lifted his head as they enlarged their fairy forms, and the three of them got to work immediately. Each wore a different color, though it looked as if the Forbidden Mountain had sapped the sheen from them. The tallest took his bound wrists in hand.

"Shhh!" she said. "No time to explain."

The fairy had had more than fifteen years to explain, but he let that slide. As she freed his wrists, the one in green used her magic to burn through the shackles on his ankles, and the one in blue slowly destroyed the lock on the door. Their powers were flashier than Eris's, sparkling like stars in the dim cell. The chains fell away, and he stepped forward to fully free himself. He had to get to Briar Rose as quickly as possible.

"Wait, Prince Phillip," said the one in dull red. She gestured for him to come back. "The road to true love may be barred by still many more dangers, which you alone will have to face. So arm thyself with this enchanted Shield of Virtue."

She waved her wand, and there was a tinkle of bells. The Shield of Virtue appeared on his arm with a flicker of magic. Phillip pulled back, surprised, and then groaned. Eris had said summoning that and the Sword of Truth required purely good intent, practically confessing her alliance with Maleficent. He had been too caught up in his own problems to notice.

The fairy carried on without explanation. "And this mighty Sword of Truth."

The sword appeared, as sharp and ready as it had

been when he last carried it, and the hilt was even warm against his hand. He tested its weight to ensure Eris hadn't done anything to it.

"For these weapons of righteousness will triumph over evil," she said. Before he could ask how, she said, "Now, come. We must hurry."

The fairies ushered him out of the cell. Outside, Maleficent's raven glided around the spiral staircase, cawing angrily when it saw them. It fluttered up, and the fairies raised their wands but did nothing. It squawked and flapped its way up the northern stairs, and Phillip led the fairies south. When they were halfway up the stairs, the clatter of hooves and claws against stone echoed down. A wave of Maleficent's enchanted creatures raced down the stairs to them, the raven in the lead. Phillip pivoted.

"Down, down, down," he mumbled. "I don't know another way up."

There was a large window, empty and looming over a broken wall, and he darted for it. The fairies twisted into their small forms that were little more than specks of light. He reached the window first. A steep drop from the mountain was the only view he could make out. The first of the creatures neared.

He slashed the sword through the air. It knocked the club of a creature aside, throwing both to the floor. More tumbled over each other, spear tips and broken knives flying through the air after the fairies, and he blocked as many as he could. He couldn't even feel the weight of the shield on his arm as he raised it to take the hit of a mace. The fairies cleared the window without getting hit, and Phillip leapt out. They would've told him if the drop was sheer.

He landed on the falling edge of an old rampart and jumped to a nearby crumbling wall, then slipped from it and slid down a pile of shattered rocks. A horse squealed in fear, and Phillip rolled to his feet in a courtyard.

"Samson!" he breathed. A chain held Samson to a heavy rock on the other side of the courtyard. "How did you get here, boy?"

"Maleficent must have captured him," said the green fairy. "I'm saddened that we're meeting in such dire circumstances, but it is good to meet you, Phillip. I am Fauna. The others are Flora and Merryweather." She gestured to the fairies in red and blue.

"My friend, a knight—she escaped when Maleficent captured me, and went to warn people with Samson," he said, and rounded on the fairies. "Have you seen her? Can you summon her like you did the arms?"

Fauna wrung her hands together. "Oh, dear. No. Summoning people is much more difficult, and the old magic that lives in this mountain refrains us from attempting it."

Fear froze his hands, and Phillip took a deep breath to calm himself before heading into the courtyard.

"Phillip!" cried one of the fairies. "Watch out!"

Samson squealed again, and Phillip threw up his shield arm to cover as much of himself as he could. Rocks plummeted from the wall above, and magic shot toward them. With the toll of a small bell, the rocks became bubbles and burst. Phillip lowered his shield.

He sprinted toward Samson. He had to figure out what had happened to Johanna and make sure she was all right. If she had come after him or gotten captured, that meant his father might not yet know what was going on. More help might not be on its way.

Bowstrings snapped in unison, thrumming in Phillip's ears, and he spun with the shield raised. Flora glowed a soft pink and slashed her wand through the air. The arrows sprouted and bloomed. Flowers fell limp against the shield.

"Maybe save your magic for Maleficent," he murmured. He felt so conflicted: they were helping, but if this was what they were capable of, why hadn't they trained

Briar Rose or him or anyone to fight for themselves? Why all the subterfuge? It was infuriating and confusing. "Those kinds of arrows wouldn't have pierced this shield."

Flora bristled. A scream rang out over the courtyard. Johanna's voice and the clash of steel against stone reached him, and Phillip darted to where it was coming from. In a small ruined garden over a wall of the courtyard, Johanna, with her sword drawn and a trail of downed goons in her wake, had her gaze fixed on Eris, Phrike, and Poena. The fairies, on the other side of the garden, looked furious, with smoke pouring from Poena's sneer and the wind whipping violently around Eris. Johanna must have fought her way into the Forbidden Mountain. Phillip whistled.

"Not everything going to plan?" he shouted, and raised the Sword of Truth.

Phrike screeched, "You little—"

Johanna used the distraction to charge. She split the trio, separating Phrike from the others. Phrike threw herself back, the tip of Johanna's blade tearing across her side, and vanished in a ripple of shadows. She reemerged against a wall and grasped at the gash in her arm. Eris laughed, but Poena raised her hand.

A ribbon of white-hot fire unfurled from her wand, twisted around Johanna's sword, and melted through the blade. Johanna yelped, and Phillip started to jump over the wall to join her. Flora held him back.

"We need to go," she said. "Now."

"I am not leaving Johanna to deal with them on her own," said Phillip. It was impossible for Johanna to take on all three of the fairies, no matter how skilled she was. Johanna might have known how they fought, but they were still powerful magical beings with decades of practice. Phillip had nearly killed her on accident without even trying. He'd had to . . .

"You can't kill her!" Phillip laughed and leaned out over the garden. "None of you can hurt her! Curses, gifts, and deals—you can't break a promise, remember? You cannot harm Johanna."

Eris's smile fell, and she rolled her eyes to stare at him.

"Destroy her weapons all you want, but you cannot hurt her," he said.

Eris raised a hand to him. "What about you?"

A frigid wind struck his back, and Phillip would have tumbled headfirst into the garden had the three good fairies not grabbed him. They were far stronger than he would have guessed. With an insulted huff, Merryweather darted in front of Phillip and jabbed her wand toward Eris. What looked like a soap bubble grew and grew and grew until it completely covered the whole garden in a shimmering dome. Eris scowled and gestured with her wand. The bubble stretched toward Phillip but didn't pop. He didn't even feel the chill of her magic.

Eris threw up her arms, but whatever she yelled was trapped in the bubble with her.

"We can't leave Johanna in there," Phillip said, trying not to sound ungrateful.

"If they truly promised not to hurt her, she'll be right as rain," said Flora, frowning down at Eris. "But we really must go now."

In the bubble, Johanna waved a hand at him and faced the fairies. She opened her arms wide to the fairies and said something Phillip couldn't hear. Eris threw another burst of magic at the bubble and hollered when it didn't break. Phillip turned away.

"All right," he said. "I guess it's more like they're trapped in there with Johanna."

"How do you know Eris?" Flora asked as Merryweather muttered, "I should have known she would stick her nose into this."

Phillip sprinted to Samson to avoid answering.

Merryweather freed Samson of his chains, and Phillip swung himself astride. The fairies flew with them right above his shoulders.

"Whatever you do, don't stop," Phillip said to Samson, taking the reins in his shield hand. "Just get us out of here."

The enchanted creatures huddled atop the door of the castle, and the raven cawed from the ramparts. Slowly, the creatures overturned great cauldrons of hot oil. Flora shielded them with a rainbow that made the oil slide uselessly to their sides and fizzle on the ground.

The gate of the castle grew nearer and nearer, and the portcullis began to fall. Phillip urged Samson to go faster, and the grating crashed to the ground the moment they cleared it. Outside, the drawbridge began to rise, and the fairies swept over the edge. Phillip gripped the reins tightly.

"Watch out, Phillip!" Fauna said.

Samson leapt, magic keeping them aloft for a moment, and landed hard on the opposite side. The rock crumbled under his hooves, and he pulled himself onto solid ground. They raced down the mountainside, with bright light chasing them. Phillip glanced back.

Maleficent had climbed to the tallest of her towers.

"Hurry!" said Flora. "Hurry, Phillip."

Clouds of green swirled in the sky above Maleficent, and she lifted her staff. Thunder crashed and lightning struck the arch of stone above the mountain path. The rock shattered and fell. Phillip knocked the debris away with the shield.

Lightning tore through the rock path before them. They fell down the side of the mountain. Samson jumped from one ledge to another, scrambling for a hold. Phillip's bones ached with the landing. Samson cleared the final chasm with a wild neigh.

Phillip took a deep breath as they left the jagged land of the Forbidden Mountain and King Stefan's castle came into view on the horizon. They had escaped—for now.

Storm clouds dark as night reached out across the sky and encircled the white towers. They gathered in a deepening fog, casting the whole countryside in shadow. Lightning split the world.

Phillip risked another look back, and Maleficent—a laughing, horned shade against the green sky—stood at the center of the clouds.

Samson whimpered. Phillip pulled up on the reins, turning around. An endless forest of thorns as long as Phillip's legs sprouted through the ground, cracking the earth like an egg. They writhed and twisted, and a great tangle of them covered the road. Samson stopped just in time, rearing away from the pikelike thorns. Phillip urged him on slowly.

"Like the thorn wall in the dreams," said Phillip, cutting through a thorny vine and ignoring the dread in his gut. "But somehow worse."

Phillip tore through the thorns with the sword. He would not be stopped by them—not ever again.

"Why did you think Maleficent's curse wouldn't happen?" he asked the fairies, hacking at the thorns. "Curses always come to pass."

The fairies flitted above him, and Flora sniffed.

"Maleficent's power was greatly reduced after she was banished," she said. "Given that Merryweather's gift altered the curse and we would be assisting, we were hopeful that it wasn't set in stone."

"While it's true that curses always come true, like our gifts, the details of how they come true can be manipulated to be more beneficial," Fauna added. She hovered over Phillip's shoulder. "We were not aware you studied curses and fairy magic, Your Highness."

"I didn't," he said as Samson continued to charge ahead.

Phillip slashed the thorns out of their way with his sword, and he and Samson bounded over an outcropping toward the stone road. The thorns had grown the thickest there, trying to block access to the castle completely. It was exactly like the thorns from the dream, which had grown through everything in their path.

Phillip urged Samson onto the bridge over the river and glanced at the fairies "Where is everyone? Are they safe?"

"Asleep, to be awakened when Princess Aurora wakes," said Flora. "They are perfectly safe."

"Asleep?" asked Phillip, incredulous. "How is that safe? They're about to be in the middle of a battlefield. They can't get to safety if they're asleep, and now we need to worry about protecting them and keeping the fight contained."

"It will all work itself out," Flora said, and tensed at the sight of the thorns twisting up through the road ahead of them.

Phillip snapped his head to her. "Will it? Briar Rose won't thank you for placing her life above everyone else's."

"Well . . ." She paused. "What do you mean 'Briar Rose'?"

"*No!*"

Maleficent's scream echoed across the land, cutting

off his answer, and the sky grew painfully bright. "It cannot be!"

A twisting knot of purple-and-gold magic tore overhead, slammed into the stone bridge before Phillip, and splashed across the stones like liquid fire. Samson reared, and Phillip struggled to comfort him. Maleficent must have discovered that he had stolen the sword and shield. She appeared, wreathed in green flames and black smoke.

"Now shall you deal with me, O Prince," she said, raising her staff, "and all the powers of hell!"

Phillip held tight to Samson. The fire burned brighter and more violently, and smoke covered the bridge. Maleficent's form twisted, bones and magic crackling like a fire, and the ghastly burn of brimstone filled Phillip's nose. She stretched all the way to the clouds circling above, and from the clouds emerged the toothy maw of a great dragon. Her terrible wings unfurled across the sky and blocked out what little sun was left. Green flames spilled from her cackling mouth.

Fear froze Phillip. He couldn't do this. He wasn't a hero; he was the one who had gotten them into this mess in the first place. This was a display of power so awesome the mere sight of it nearly stopped his heart. How could he defeat her? He wasn't . . .

Her tail flicked, knocking against a castle tower, and the stones wobbled as if they might fall. The image of Briar Rose, cursed and asleep, came to him, and Phillip shuddered. She had been cut off from the world for so long, and she would be stuck sleeping in that tower forever if he didn't win. He couldn't let that happen. He would do anything to ensure she got to see the world.

Phillip urged Samson on despite the terror trembling through him and the rattle of Maleficent's footfalls in his bones, and he peered up at the tower through the thorns.

Why don't you kiss me?

Briar Rose's question played in his head over and over again.

Maybe she thought he was her true love because *this* feeling—the heady mix of joy and terror and unyielding drive to keep going until she was free to live the life she'd always wanted—could only be love.

Phillip loved her.

He loved her, and he had to do this. No one else could.

If Briar Rose, who knew him better than anyone, loved him enough to think he could be her true love, then he wasn't as cowardly or as bad as he thought. She believed in him, and for once, he believed in himself, too.

"Just you and me, boy," he muttered to Samson, and pressed the horse to run. "We can do this."

Samson took off, galloping across the stones toward Maleficent's feet, and she reared back, smoke spilling from her nostrils. Phillip raised the shield to block her spout of flames, and the force of them knocked him from Samson. He landed hard on his back, the heat of her power scorching his clothes. His shield arm, though, was fine. It wasn't even warm.

Phillip leapt to his feet, and Maleficent spat more flames across the bridge, forcing him away from her. The stones melted beneath his feet.

He had to get to her underbelly, where the interlocking black scales faded to an almost translucent purple. All creatures had a heart, and all hearts could break. He only had to find hers.

He rose, his eyes locked with the dragon's, and stood at the edge of the crumbling bridge. She buffeted him with fire again, forcing him back. The shield stayed cold and steady on his arm. Samson squealed behind him.

The thorns were at Phillip's back, and he dove into them. His years in the dream wood had broken his fear of them. A prick from a thorn, or a spindle, was nothing in the face of what needed to be done. Phillip waited behind a thick vine.

Maleficent tucked her face into the thorns, fire burning any that got too near her. She stretched out her neck more, her jaw right above the ground, and Phillip lunged, bringing the Sword of Truth down atop her snout. Her face slammed into the dirt. The scales beneath the blade bent but didn't break. She snatched her face away from him.

Phillip thrusted for her eyes, and she twisted, snapping out at him. Her fangs ripped through the air where he had been, and he swung for her eyes again. She reared up onto her hind legs and out of his reach. Phillip darted back into the thorns, fear racing in his chest.

Maleficent burned through them, spewing flames across the land. The thorns went up in an acrid black smoke that choked his lungs. Phillip cut and shoved his way through the thorns. He skidded into a steep cliff, the stone rising high before him and the flames creeping closer behind.

"Up!" cried one of the fairies. "Up this way!"

Gripping the sword with his shield hand, he began to climb with his other. Maleficent's footsteps thundered behind him, and the forest of thorns shattered beneath her form. The scorching heat of her drew nearer and nearer.

"The fire's spreading!" he shouted at Flora, struggling to scale the cliff. "Will people wake up if they're in danger?"

The fairy twisted her hands together and didn't answer. Phillip groaned, climbing as quickly as he could. He had to finish this now.

He yanked himself to the top of the cliff, and the shield jerked his arm around. Maleficent's teeth clacked together where his arm had been. He struck out with the sword. It whistled through the air and grazed her jaw. She snapped at him again. He dodged and swung. The fire burned higher beneath them.

Maleficent climbed up the cliff, curling her body over the rocks and forcing him back yet again. The sword was barely longer than her teeth, and he couldn't land a hit. Her scales weren't even scratched.

The familiar grip of futility took him, and he barely jumped out of the way of her jaws.

The cliff edge crumbled under his foot. He swung his arms for balance, throwing the suddenly heavy shield forward. It righted him but slipped down his arm. Maleficent spat another bout of flames at him.

The shield took the brunt of them, but the force of her magic toppled Phillip and ripped the shield from his arm. It tumbled over the cliff and down into the inferno. Maleficent's laughter cut through Phillip like a knife. He swallowed and raised the sword.

If he couldn't beat her, maybe he could distract her long enough for the fairies to get everyone else to safety. He opened his mouth to shout, and a bright warm magic washed over him. The three good fairies flitted down to him and hovered over his shoulder.

"Now, Sword of Truth, fly swift and sure," said Flora, "that evil die and good endure!"

Fly?

They wanted him to throw his only weapon!

Phillip tightened his grip on the sword. Swords weren't made to be thrown, magic or not. And what did the fairies know about fighting? He could wait. He could lure Maleficent forward and wait for the cliff to crumble. He could hit her heart then.

But Briar Rose's voice echoed in his head.

Trust them, she had said.

Maleficent lunged for Phillip. He took a breath, adjusted his grip, and flung the last weapon he had at Maleficent's monstrous form.

2 1

True Love's Kiss

THE SWORD flew true. It struck Maleficent in the chest, and blood spilled down her amethyst underbelly. She howled and recoiled. Phillip braced himself, glaring up at the slivers of her eyes. Her head bobbed back.

Phillip's terror sharpened the world to that single moment, and he leapt over her gnashing jaws. The cliff crumbled beneath them, and Phillip threw himself backward. His fingers tore through rock, barely catching the edge. He clung as tightly as he could, panic holding his hands in place despite the pain. Maleficent crashed to the ground.

Oily black smoke clogged the air, and her screams died. Phillip crawled onto the top of what was left of the cliff. The smoke lingered in his throat and stopped his shout. He wiped his face and peered over the edge. All that was left of Maleficent was a midnight smear pinned to the earth by the Sword of Truth.

Phillip almost laughed. It was done.

The slow clack of hooves against stone came up the cliff behind Phillip, and he smiled at Samson's unharmed form. The courser snorted softly, and Phillip gripped his reins. The fairies lingered over Phillip's shoulder.

"You all right, Samson?" Phillip asked, focusing on the horse so he wouldn't have to think about everything that had happened and what he still had to do. "Endless carrots. Infinite carrots. As many as you can eat without dying."

Samson nickered and laid his head against Phillip's shoulder, letting Phillip pull a few scorched pieces of wood from his mane. There was so much left to do despite the exhaustion tugging at his bones, and Phillip sat up until he could see the spires of the castle in the distance. He had to wake Briar Rose first and tell her what had happened.

And find out for sure if he was her true love. The very idea of her not waking turned his stomach. Or maybe it was the smoke. Definitely the smoke.

"Your Highness," said Flora, flickering in the corner of his sight, "Princess Aurora and the others are waiting."

"Johanna," he said. "Is there a way to retrieve her?"

Merryweather nodded sharply and flicked her wand,

creating a cloudy image between them so like the one Maleficent had summoned that Phillip shivered.

"Now, let's see . . ." she said, moving her wand like a spyglass and adjusting what the image was showing. "Your squire will need her horse as well. With Maleficent gone and the old magic binding her to the Forbidden Mountain gone with her, this should be much easier."

There was a burst of warm air that reminded him of spring and a whistle like a bird. Down the cliff on the road to the castle, Johanna and Taliesin appeared in an explosion of soap bubbles. Johanna, exhausted and soaked with sweat but beaming, threw her arms around Taliesin's neck, and Samson cantered over to bump Taliesin's flank. Phillip met Johanna in the middle.

"How'd it go?" he asked, wrapping her in a hug.

"What's going on?" she asked, but returned the embrace. "Where's Maleficent?"

"Gone," said Phillip. He stepped back and wiped some ash from her face. "She's dead. For good. I think?"

He glanced back at Merryweather, and she nodded.

Johanna gently punched his arm a few times, and he grinned.

"Time is of the essence, Your Highness," said Flora, fluttering over to his shoulder. "The other fairies are still trapped, yes?"

"Poena's out cold, and Phrike's spent the last while flying around and crying because of that cut on her arm," Johanna said, and shook her head. "Eris either is invisible and hiding or got out. She panicked when I downed Poena."

"Good girl!" Merryweather applauded quietly. "Two fairies taken down and one scared off is nothing to sneeze at, you know."

Phillip smiled and knocked his shoulder against Johanna's. "Worth a knighthood at the very least."

Johanna blushed, and Phillip patted Taliesin's snout.

"Come on, Sir Johanna." Phillip helped her onto Taliesin and then mounted Samson. "Everyone in the area is asleep until Princess Aurora is awakened. Get to the healing house and prepare to help once everyone is awake. I'll get the princess."

"Asleep?" she asked.

Phillip nodded. "You'll see."

They traveled in silence, staring at the distant towers of the castle. The forest of thorns was gone, but there was still an unsettling prickle on the back of Phillip's neck. The only sounds were the flutter of the fairies' wings and the stomp of Samson's hooves. Phillip flinched as they passed the first people.

"I see," mumbled Johanna, her mouth falling open.

People had slumped over where they stood. Some swayed and others had slipped all the way to the paving stones. A child slept alone in the corner of the gate, and a woman was half submerged in the center fountain. Phillip maneuvered Samson through the crowd like he would navigate a wood.

"We did not wish for Princess Aurora to awaken alone," said one of the fairies. "Not that we had anything but the utmost confidence in His Highness quickly rescuing her, but it was a precaution. No one should be hurt or even notice they fell asleep."

Johanna touched one person's shoulder, and they snored. She jerked back.

"Right," she said. "I'll go make sure the healing house is ready in case anyone wakes up and panics."

"Please do," said Phillip, reaching across Samson and tugging Johanna close. He gripped her collar. "Do not start writing a book about this."

She grinned and batted his hand away. "An ode it is!"

"Better than your eulogy," he muttered, and she laughed all the way to the healing house.

Phillip jogged into the courtyard, where the groves of people were thinner, and glanced around for the tower entrance. The sooner he could speak with Briar Rose, the better. He wanted to know that she was well. He wanted to tell her everything.

He wanted her, awake, before him so that they could speak without the threat of everything hanging over them.

He just wanted *her*.

But what if she didn't wake up? They were getting along well now, and he wanted to be her true love, but knowing someone and wanting them wasn't love. True love was supposed to be all-encompassing and legendary, and while Phillip knew how he felt, true love still seemed too much like a fairy tale to involve him. Briar Rose *had* asked him to kiss her, though.

All that was left to do was honor her request, and hope.

The fairies led the way through the castle. Phillip chased after them, furious he hadn't paid more attention when visiting. Higher and higher they spiraled, but Phillip's exhaustion fell away as he felt himself getting closer to Briar Rose.

He sprinted up the final steps and into her resting place. The sight of her still took his breath away. The life had been sapped from her, blanching her skin to a bluish white and leaving her lips a pale pink. Briar

Rose had always been vibrant, in life and in dreams, and this stillness made his hands shake. Phillip had always longed to see her, but now, all he wanted was to hear her voice.

The fairies hovered near the door, watching. He knelt at Briar Rose's side, nerves fluttering through him. He braced a hand on his knee to keep from shaking.

Her chest rose with a slow breath, and he sighed. He was far more afraid of what came next than he had been of fighting Maleficent. What would he do if he kissed her and she didn't wake? Would he be forced to go off and find her real true love? Could his heart suffer such a task?

Phillip leaned close to her. He touched her hand, half hoping the cursed sleep had lifted when Maleficent died, but Briar Rose didn't move. Phillip bowed over her head and hesitated a hairbreadth from her lips.

Phillip pulled away, his heart racing, and shook his head. He didn't want it not to work.

But Briar Rose had asked him to do this. He had to try for her.

Gently, Phillip pressed his mouth to hers and then moved away. He stayed on his knees at her side, one hand gripping hers. Her chest rose and fell with steady breaths, but the rest of her stayed as still as the grave.

Dread and disappointment began to creep over him, and Phillip slipped his hand from hers.

It hadn't worked.

Phillip gritted his teeth and tried to hide his grief from the three good fairies looming at the door. He had known it. He wasn't—

Briar Rose blinked up at him, her violet eyes dark in the dim light. His heart condensed, and every thought in his mind quieted.

"I know you defeated Maleficent," she whispered, "so why do you look so terrified?"

"I woke you up," said Phillip, still in disbelief. "Me."

"You," she said. "Is it really so terrible?"

"It's just . . ." He swallowed. Shook his head. Swallowed again. "You really love me?"

Briar Rose laughed softly and beckoned him down to her. "You literally just woke me with True Love's Kiss. Is the evidence not enough? Yes, I love you."

Phillip couldn't stop a painfully wide grin from taking over his expression, and he was sure he would never stop smiling.

Phillip gestured to himself. "Me?"

Him!

"You're lucky you're pretty," Briar Rose said, and tossed the rose in her hands aside.

Briar Rose grabbed his collar and tugged him down to her in an embrace. She smelled like spring in the dream wood, fresh leaves and cool water. He tucked his face into the curve of her neck and inhaled. Her fingers combed through the sweaty tangled ends of his hair.

"I heard everything while I was in the dream wood," she said.

One of the fairies cleared her throat, and Phillip glanced at them. Briar Rose stilled.

"Aunt Flora?" she asked.

"What dreams do you mean, dear?" asked Flora.

Merryweather cleared her throat again. "And what did you hear?"

"Oh, well, everything Phillip did," said Briar Rose, blushing. "I suppose I kept a secret from you all as well— Phillip and I have always dreamed of each other."

"There's this old forest," Phillip added. "And there was this thorn wall that was separating us. We could never talk, until one day we could. But these last weeks the forest became this maze and then it . . ."

He looked at Briar Rose, and she raised her eyebrows.

"It vanished the last dream we had, but neither of us knew why it was there or why we were even dreaming of the other."

"Oh!" Fauna clutched her chest, tears in her eyes.

"It looks like Merryweather's gift had more impact than we thought," Flora said and smiled. "True love is its own kind of magic, and true love always finds a way to bring people together, even when curses seek to keep them apart. The curse was always within you, my dear, at first as the thorn wall and then as the maze that separated you. But I would guess that this last dream was the first one you shared after falling in love?"

"We only found our way out of the maze after we stopped fighting," said Phillip.

Briar Rose nodded. "And we could only talk to each other once the curse was almost here."

"True love," said Merryweather, beaming at both of them in turn. "Striving to bring you together before the curse took hold."

"So magic believed in us?" Phillip turned back to Briar Rose and grinned.

"I believed in us," she said. "And you. You did so well. I told you that you would."

"Did you?" he mumbled. "I missed your humility."

"I will not apologize for being right."

"I would never ask that of you," he said, and laughed. *True love.*

"I'm going to kiss you again unless you wouldn't

like that," she said softly, running her thumb along the hollow of his throat. "I think you owe me a proper first kiss."

There were no thoughts left in his head, so Phillip said, "I would hate to be in debt to you."

Her lips slid over his as easily as he usually slipped into dreams. The blood rushed in his veins, and the bottom of the world fell away, leaving nothing but the warmth of her fingers against his throat and the flutter of her lashes against his cheek. She gripped him tighter. His tongue—

A throat cleared behind them.

Briar Rose pulled away first and peered over his shoulder. Phillip had forgotten about the fairies, but he couldn't find it in him to be embarrassed. He felt buoyant. There was no opinion that could ever drag him down again.

He was unbelievably happy for the first time in years.

"I thought he was supposed to kiss me," said Briar Rose, putting on a confused tone, and he hid a laugh in her shoulder. "What's wrong?"

"You are truly lovely," he muttered, and kissed her cheek.

"You'll be the death of us, girl," said Flora. "You

are both expected downstairs. There is still a party to attend, your parents to meet, and a story to tell."

"They can wait. I had to," said Briar Rose, and she narrowed her eyes at the spluttering fairy over Phillip's shoulder. "I just awoke from a curse on top of finding out who I was today. Perhaps you should go warn them we'll be there in a moment?"

The fairies whispered behind them, and Phillip struggled not to mind or worry about what they were saying.

Phillip helped her sit up, keeping one hand on her arm.

"Happy birthday, by the way," he said, enjoying the decadence of being able to see her expressions and play with her hair. Growing up knowing he was betrothed to Princess Aurora, he had never allowed himself to bask in affection. He spent a few minutes summarizing his flight from the Forbidden Mountain and the fight with Maleficent. Briar Rose gasped at all the right parts, mostly to mock his serious tone. He kissed her brow once he was done. "Also, I think our wedding is happening downstairs."

She made a face. "We're not getting married tonight, right?"

"Absolutely not, and I cannot wait to see their faces when they find out." He kissed her quickly and held out his hands. "Do you feel up to disappointing your parents for the first time? It's a momentous occasion. I remember mine fondly."

She laughed and took his hand, rising from the bed. "How do I look?"

"So disappointing," he said, brushing her hair over her shoulders and twisting a strand around his finger.

"Well, you would know," she said, but there was no sharpness behind the words. She stood on tiptoe and kissed his cheek. She whispered, "We defeated Maleficent. If anyone is actually disappointed, it's their loss."

Phillip laughed, and she tugged him closer.

"Phillip," she said, holding both of his hands in hers, "I know you spent years struggling against your—our, I guess—betrothal and hating the idea of obeying even though you were prepared to go through with it. If you want to leave now, I wouldn't blame you."

He wasn't sure love could flourish with only a few words, but this was the most beloved he had ever felt. Briar Rose was watching him through slightly narrowed eyes, clearly concerned but offering him the thing he had wanted the most. She knew exactly what the Phillip of a month earlier would have chosen: to leave. Yet she was letting him decide even when she thought his answer would hurt her.

But he wasn't that Phillip anymore.

"I don't want to go." He glanced at the fairies and dropped his voice. "I don't want to get married now, and I don't want to follow our parents' plan for us. I don't even want to stay in Ald Tor or Artwyne. I want to travel and figure out who I am outside my father's shadow, and I want to do all that with you . . . if you would like that as well."

Briar Rose nodded, her nose scrunched up from smiling. "I want to go everywhere."

Joy like he'd never before known flooded his veins, and Phillip knew that this was true love—wanting to face the world with someone who knew all your best and worst parts, helping them achieve their dreams, and basking in their successes. Trust. Bravery. Love.

Together, they could do anything.

The fairies fluttered about them as they descended. Voices rose up the stairwell as they moved down. It was obvious that everyone was awake, and there didn't seem to be any panic. All Phillip could hear were happy shouts and distant bursts of song. It sounded like a grand party downstairs. Once they reached the main floor, the fairies flew off to alert the heralds.

"Do you think they noticed that they fell asleep?" he asked Briar Rose. She watched the dancing and shook her head.

"I don't think I would have noticed if I hadn't been expecting it and hadn't woken up in a different place," she said. "I won't tell them if you don't."

He grinned and kissed her hand. "I'll bet you everything in my purse they don't mention Maleficent for a whole hour."

"Deal."

The fanfare of trumpets echoed through the castle. Phillip tucked her hand into the crook of his arm, slowly walking down the main staircase. King Stefan and Queen Leah sat on their thrones at the end of the hall, and Phillip's father lounged near them. The queen's eyes widened when she spotted them, her sad smile making his heart ache. Briar Rose stiffened, and he brushed his thumb over her hand. King Stefan's smile, though, was all joy.

"It's Aurora!" he said, stepping hesitantly toward them. "She's here!"

"You're not very good at disappointing people," whispered Phillip. He grinned at her and squeezed her hand against his side. "Still time to back out, but if we leave, we'll miss my father's floundering."

She laughed under her breath, staring ahead and clearly trying not to look at all the people around them. "He won't be that bad, will he?"

Phillip snorted. "You're lucky we're not betting on it."

"And—and—and Phillip!" cried King Hubert.

Briar Rose's shoulders shook against his for a moment, and he bowed his head to hide his own laugh.

A few steps from the platform, they came to a stop. He bowed, and Briar Rose curtsied, still clutching his arm. Phillip straightened and felt Briar Rose stiffen again, her gaze rising to her parents. Then she seemed to shrug off her hesitation and squeezed his arm. He moved to let her go.

Briar Rose ran to her mother. Phillip took a step back, looking at his nearing father from the corner of his eye.

"What does this mean, boy?" King Hubert asked Phillip.

Before Phillip had time to come up with a quip, Briar Rose swooped in and kissed King Hubert on the cheek. He went quiet.

Phillip took that chance to sweep Briar Rose away. He pulled her into his arms, ignoring his father's babbling. Briar Rose and he fell easily into the same steps as in their dance in the wood, and the people around them watched. Phillip couldn't find it within him to care. He simply pulled her closer and smiled. Let his father be confused. Let everyone stare.

No opinions on this mattered save for Briar Rose's and his.

There was a tickle in his throat, and what felt like a spring breeze rustled through his hair. Briar Rose groaned.

"They're so competitive," she muttered as her dress shifted from blue to pink.

The people around them began murmuring.

"Competitive," said Phillip, laughing when it switched back to blue. "Yes, I'm beginning to understand that. Do you want them to stop?" He eyed the good fairies off to the side.

"No, they wouldn't be themselves if they weren't like this, and I do love them," she said, and kicked up her heels so the dress swished just so as it changed to pale pink again. She tilted her face up to him. "What now?"

Phillip twirled her once more, and the people watching them faded away with the troubles of the past day. "We live happily ever after, of course."

Epilogue

"*THEIR HAPPINESS was as if they were floating upon the downy clouds of dawn, and they danced amongst the morning.*"

"Absolutely not," said Phillip, tossing aside the flower crown he had been weaving, and burying his face in his hands. "It's only been two years. How can you not remember exactly what happened in a way that is to my liking?"

Johanna snapped her book shut—he never should have gifted it to her—and grinned. "I knew you would hate it. That's why I wrote it like that."

Sir Johanna of Artwyne had been the first to put the story of Maleficent's defeat to paper. Much to Phillip's chagrin, it was mostly accurate. It did feature far more than simply his mistakes, fortunately, and plenty of the stories of the people who had been caught in Maleficent's work decades earlier and recently. Johanna had found old stories, between Maleficent's first defeat and return, of towns sieged by strange, unquenchable wildfires down south and roads where shadows danced and stalked all who traveled along them. A dozen farms out east had been deluged with storms, and children told scary stories of the lady in the dress like lightning. Before they had tricked Phillip, Maleficent's fairies had been busy sowing chaos.

There was far more to the story than an evil fairy, a curse, and a princess. Johanna was still uncovering all of it, and that included hunting down Eris.

Phillip had taken a far more relaxed approach to the two years after defeating Maleficent.

"That's fair enough and all, but you never threw me over your shoulder when helping me learn magic," he said.

Johanna arched a brow at him and said, "Prove it."

Phillip snorted. It was easier to joke about Maleficent and his time with the fairies now. Briar Rose's birthday had made everyone nervous the past year despite their certainty that the evil fairy was gone, so this year, her parents had indulged her. The party was only close friends and family, though Kings Hubert and Stefan were loud enough for a whole crowd and had gathered in the sun-warmed grass of King Stefan's gardens beneath a canopy of climbing roses cultivating by Briar Rose. Most of the guests were caught up in their own conversations, so Phillip didn't mind the ribbing.

"I think it's a lovely ode," said Briar Rose, and the barely contained laughter warbled in her voice. "Better you get thrown a few times than some stranger writes about how noble and shining and handsome and wonderful you are and then everyone expects you to be like one of those perfect knights of old."

"Yes, I would hate to be described as handsome," he muttered, and leaned back in the grass.

Briar Rose laughed, loud and unrestrained. Sunlight caught the curls of her hair and the lines of her throat, and it took everything within Phillip to keep from smiling.

"You wound me," said Phillip, and he clutched his chest. "Where is a cursed sleep when you need one?"

She laughed again, and Phillip kissed Briar Rose's cheek. She squeezed his hand.

Johanna watched with a wry smile. Her interest in romance was still strictly academic.

"I left out how you ruined my dubbing ceremony a whole year in advance," she said loudly, glancing toward his father.

Phillip groaned. His father loved telling that story.

"Amis themself in my castle!" King Hubert shouted,

slapping the blanketed ground. "Nearly ripped the whole wall down when they took the Shield of Virtue!"

It *had* been a sight: Johanna attired in her best, her black hair woven with gold and her hands stained in flowing designs. Phillip's father was presenting her with the sword she would carry from then on when the scent of linseed oil and the rattling footfalls of Amis's armor had filled the hall. They had declared their intentions against the thief Phillip—the politest thing he had ever been called, though a solid blow to his pride—and retaken the shield. They had left without another word, only inclining their head to Johanna.

"You had the most memorable ceremony in centuries!" said Phillip. "And they acknowledged you, Johanna the Honorable."

He jabbed his finger at her to emphasize the words, and Johanna hid her smile.

"Of Artwyne!" King Hubert applauded. "Our Johanna chosen by Amis!"

Phillip laughed. His father's boisterous attitude was mostly easier to handle now. They'd "had it out," as his father put it now, yelling at each other in turns in the weeks after Maleficent's defeat. Phillip had still been furious about everything, even if he liked his father's newfound pride in him, and his father hadn't been able to figure out why Phillip was upset that his father was proud of him. There had been several awkward fights before Phillip had brought up Eris, and then King Hubert had understood how much he had hurt his son. He had spent a whole week just talking with Phillip after that. That was the first time he saw his father cry.

Their relationship wasn't perfect now, but it was fine. Nice, even.

"And now we're all busy living happily ever after and dancing at dawn," said Briar Rose, "though 'happily ever after' does seem very vague."

"I'm sorry." Phillip stole her cup of barley water. "Are you not happy, birthday girl?"

Her parents and King Hubert perked up at that, pretending not to listen closely. Getting over Phillip and Briar Rose's calling off their wedding had been one of the steps toward reconciliation. Queen Leah had seen the sense in it first, once she realized how unprepared Briar Rose was for the life she'd been thrust into. King Hubert's conflating of Phillip with his ideal heir was the same issue at the heart of the betrothal: they thought of their children as extensions of themselves. Briar Rose's parents had come around first, eager to build a relationship with her. They were being as gentle as Briar Rose usually was with injured baby animals.

Epilogue

In the past two years, there had been heavy discussions, teary family meals, and a lot of talks Phillip had heard about from Briar Rose. She had gotten used to most parts of her new life—though not doing her own darning had taken far longer to learn than holding court and bookkeeping—but large crowds still unnerved her. Queen Leah had spent weeks trying to decide if the picnic would be appreciated.

"I am devastated," Briar Rose said, and sniffed, tilting her head to stare down her nose at him in a perfect copy of her mother. "Only this party and Johanna's gift of our story have kept me from dying of a broken heart."

"I'll be taking my gift back, then," Phillip said, and held out his hand.

Briar Rose tightened her grip on the crate next to her. "I didn't say you should do that."

The crate of flower bulbs he'd had imported from the far north was more a promise than a gift. They hadn't traveled outside of Ald Tor and Artwyne yet. Briar Rose had wanted to see the kingdom that was her home, and there had been a lot to do to ensure both kingdoms were safe after Maleficent's fall. They had spent the better part of the years getting to even ground with their parents and figuring out what their roles in this new world were. Briar Rose finally seemed used to life outside the

cottage in the glen. Though he knew she was still desperate to see the world.

"So fickle," he said, and tapped her nose. "That was
only part of the gift, anyway."

And he hoped to make the rest happen soon.

"Part of?" She glanced around them. "Is the rest a
secret?"

"Maybe."

The party was winding down. King Stefan was
laughing at something Queen Leah said, and Phillip's
father slapped him on the back. Johanna beamed, and
Phillip's father toasted her. Knighthood suited her far
better than it had ever suited Phillip.

"Want to get out of here?" Phillip whispered to Briar
Rose, pointing at the queen, who was refilling Johanna's
cup, and King Hubert, who was downing his. "That is a
game of skumps in the making, and I may love my father
now, but I know better than to play drinking games
with him."

Briar Rose laughed and nodded. They slipped from
their seats with no one but the fairies noticing. Flora
gave Briar Rose a little wave. Phillip hoped the others
would understand the pair's need to escape from the
crowd and noise, and he would take the blame if they did
mind. Phillip carried the crate of flower bulbs and nodded

toward the edge of the garden. Their horses perked up as they neared.

"Your father's much improved," she said. "Still loud, though."

"Oh, I don't think any amount of long talks will quiet him down," said Phillip. "He apologized. Never heard of him doing that before."

It had been the most awkward moment of Phillip's life. But King Hubert was proud of Phillip and would say so to anyone within hearing range, even if he didn't quite agree with Phillip's turn into statecraft over knighthood. Politics was far more like a game of chess than the war games King Hubert preferred.

And Phillip had gotten quite good at chess of late.

"Hello, Bear." Briar Rose stroked her palfrey's side and offered her an apple slice smeared with plum jam. She kissed her horse's temple. "Happy birthday!"

Phillip and Queen Leah had spent weeks finding the perfect horse for Briar Rose's birthday the past year, and Briar Rose had taken one look at the warm brown palfrey munching on every piece of food in sight and named her in a heartbeat. They hadn't really been apart since.

"It's not *her* birthday, you know," he said, and let Samson fish a small apple from his pocket.

Briar Rose glanced at him. "I don't know her birthday, so the best I can do is celebrate the day we met."

It was exceptionally easy to love her.

"I want to find the perfect place to plant these," said Briar Rose, eyeing a distant corner of the garden. "Do you think Johanna would like any if I manage to grow a few?"

Johanna would accept it with a smile and come to him in a panic because she didn't know how to keep anything except him and Taliesin alive.

"She hasn't got a green thumb. Too much ink," he said. "They fit you far better anyway—sleeping until spring, when they come alive again."

Briar Rose smiled. "Did she write a poem?"

"It's in the works, but act surprised if it's your next birthday gift."

She laughed and nodded. They made their way toward the plot slowly, Samson and Bear ambling behind them. It was difficult to believe that only two years earlier their futures had been precarious and they had never even spoken to each other. If not for the dream wood, he wasn't sure what would have happened. They hadn't dreamed of it since the curse ended.

Briar Rose circled the little nook of the garden she liked, tied up the long skirts of her gown to keep them from getting too dirty, and knelt in the grass. A squirrel crept forward and sniffed at her crate of bulbs.

"No digging these up," said Briar Rose. "I'll give you all the food you want, but you can't go rooting around in the garden, understood?"

The squirrel chattered in a way that might have been agreement and dashed off to the others watching from the tree. She shooed them away with a grin and got to work, testing out the earth with her hands. Phillip settled next to her and passed her each bulb as she went. She hummed as she worked.

There was something intimate about silence, something cozy and safe in knowing so much about another person that there wasn't any conversation that could improve the moment. To know she was comfortable enough to be Briar Rose and not Princess Aurora around him was so dear to him his heart ached.

"I love you," he said softly.

They had been together and apart in equal measure the past two years, and Phillip didn't want to be apart from her more than necessary from then on out. He picked up the final bulb, cupping it gently in his palms, and watched her press the dirt over the bulbs as if she were tucking them into bed. They had grown together, and he couldn't wait to keep growing with her. Phillip offered her the final bulb.

"I love you, too." She brushed off her hands and turned to him. "What's wrong?"

"Absolutely nothing," said Phillip, his heart in his throat. He knew she loved him better than he knew anything at all, but still the words would barely come. "How do you feel about long engagements?"

She planted the final bulb, her only tell the pink blooming high on her cheeks. "An odd question since we're technically still engaged."

"But that is our parents' doing, not ours." He folded his shaking hands in his lap and focused on a spot just over her shoulder. "Now that you've had a chance to settle into Ald Tor and you've been to Artwyne, how would you feel about visiting some other kingdoms, like the one that's home to those flowers?"

She grinned and nodded, leaning into him until she could catch his gaze. "I would love to do that, but what does traveling have to do with engagements?"

"An engagement means our parents won't mind us being gone for a while."

"Phillip." She pressed her forehead to his. "Is this theoretical engagement solely for their sake?"

He swallowed, nerves writhing in his chest. "No. It's

just, you know, they're so loud, and I thought . . . so I already planned it all regardless of if they agree to it or not, and we leave at night if they don't. Johanna's in on the trip, as are some of the other knights. I don't really care what they say, but you've been building your relationship with them, so I didn't want to shatter it by just taking off with you, because I know you'll go. Not that you have to. We can still go no matter what their response or your answer is. I just—"

Briar Rose kissed him, stopping his rambling and nerves, and he followed her when she pulled away. She pressed a finger to his lips.

"I would give you an answer if you asked me a question," she said.

Phillip grinned, relief bubbling out of him as laughter. "Will you marry me?"

"I would love to marry you when we return from this grand adventure of yours."

She kissed him again and tasted as sweet as the words sounded.

"Our parents are going to shriek so loudly they'll wake up Maleficent from death," she said when they parted. "We have to wait to tell them."

Phillip shrugged. "We'll keep you away from spindles on our wedding day, then."

"That would make a good story." Briar Rose leaned back and dragged him down with her until they were both staring up at the sky through a veil of leaves. "Can we make Johanna our official historian?"

"Only if you want the history books in iambic pentameter." Phillip brought her hand to his mouth and kissed her knuckles. "How would you tell our story?"

Briar Rose laughed. "Curses and dragons and fights are all well and good, but our story started far earlier than that. It all began with a dream I had as a child. . . ."